HALO

Fallen Angel Series #1

ELLA FRANK
BROOKE BLAINE

Copyright © 2019 by Brooke Blaine & Ella Frank

www.brookeblaine.com

www.ellafrank.com

Edited by Arran McNicol

Cover Design © By Hang Le

Cover Photography by Rafagcatala

Cover Model Victor A

No part of this book may be reproduced in any form or by any electronic or mechanical means, including information storage and retrieval systems, without written permission from the author, except for the use of brief quotations in a book review.

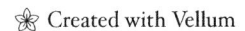

❦ Created with Vellum

Also by Ella Frank

The Exquisite Series
Exquisite

Entice

Edible

The Temptation Series
Try

Take

Trust

Tease

Tate

True

Confessions Series
Confessions: Robbie

Confessions: Julien

Confessions: Priest

Confessions: The Princess, The Prick & The Priest

Sunset Cove Series
Finley

Devil's Kiss

Masters Among Monsters Series
Alasdair

Isadora

Thanos

Standalones

Blind Obsession

Veiled Innocence

PresLocke Series
Co-Authored with Brooke Blaine

ACED

LOCKED

WEDLOCKED

Co-Authored with Brooke Blaine

Sex Addict

Shiver

Wrapped Up in You

All I Want for Christmas…Is My Sister's Boyfriend

Also by Brooke Blaine

South Haven Series
A Little Bit Like Love
A Little Bit Like Desire

The Unforgettable Duet
Forget Me Not
Remember Me When

L.A. Liaisons Series
Licked
Hooker
P.I.T.A.

Romantic Suspense
Flash Point

PresLocke Series
Co-Authored with *Ella Frank*
Aced
Locked
Wedlocked

Standalone Novels
Co-Authored with *Ella Frank*
Sex Addict
Shiver
Wrapped Up in You

All I Want for Christmas…Is My Sister's Boyfriend

ONE

Viper

EARLY MORNINGS. THERE was nothing I hated more. Yet here I was at the ass crack of dawn at Electric Sound Studio in NoHo waiting to meet the latest wannabe Trent Knox replacement. It was the third time this week Killian had dragged our asses out of bed and told us to get over to the studio, and this shit was wearing thin.

It'd been nearly seven and a half months since our illustrious lead singer had walked out during a recording session, and about seven and a half months since I'd decided I hated his fucking guts. Trent Knox had deserted TBD—and his bandmates—at the worst possible time. We'd just come off a worldwide tour that had been a gigantic success and were heading back to the recording studio, when he decided he needed to go and "find himself." Meanwhile, the rest of us had been left holding our dicks in our hands.

Yeah, did I mention I hated his guts?

"Viper?" Killian, TBD's bassist and my longtime friend, cut into my not-so-pleasant thoughts and had my attention returning to the reason I was up before noon. "You ready?"

I barely resisted the urge to roll my eyes. *Ready?* Considering I'd never expected to be in this position in the first fucking place, that would be a hard *no*. But I couldn't say that to Killian after everything we'd been through, and if he wanted to try and find someone to replace Trent, who was I to stop him?

"I guess" was my less-than-enthusiastic response.

A snort from across the room had my eyes landing on Slade, our drummer, who was sprawled on the red velvet couch twirling his drumsticks through his fingers. "Yeah, you sound real excited over there."

"Eat me."

"You'd like that, wouldn't you?" Slade retorted, to which I shot the finger.

"The last three weren't *that* bad," Killian said, trying to make the most of the shit situation we were all in.

"'Weren't that bad' isn't gonna work for me, Kill," I said. "As much as I hate to admit it, Trent was dynamite on the stage—"

"Fucker," Slade grumbled, to which I nodded. Trent *was* a fucker, and I'd made sure to let everyone who asked me about him leaving know it.

But I was getting off track, something that happened a lot whenever I thought about the way my dream had come to a grinding halt because of one goddamn person. I walked over to Killian and said, "Whoever walks through that door needs to be able to match Trent. You know that and so do I. I'm not about to settle for less." If anything, I wanted more. I wanted better if it existed. So we could shove it up Trent's ass.

"You're right." Killian looked at Slade, and then to his watch. "Where's Jagger?"

"Dude, I don't know. Out getting his shoes shined? Picking up his dry cleaning? Take your pick. You know if you need him somewhere, he needs more warning than two hours to be presentable for the public." Slade's comment drew a chuckle from me but had Killian shaking his head.

Since our rise to fame, our keyboardist, Jagger, had developed quite an affinity for the finer things in life. Finer clothes, finer cars, and, as he would say, fine-ass women.

Whereas the only thing I liked finer these days was my alcohol. Right now I'd settle for a shot of whatever was on hand to get me through the next couple of hours of hearing some aspiring singer do covers of our hits.

"Text his ass and see where he's at, would you?" Killian glanced at his phone, checking a message, and then added, "Halo should be here any minute now."

Wait up... "The guy's name is *Halo*? What kind of a fucking name is that?"

Killian aimed a pointed glare my way. "Okay, *Viper*."

"You know what I mean. Halo doesn't exactly make me think TBD. This ain't no church choir."

"Thanks for clearing that up for me. But right now, I wouldn't care if he was a priest. As long as he can sing. You wanna sit here for another seven months?"

Letting out a sigh, I took up a spot by one of the windows. I crossed my arms and resigned myself to the fact there was no way I was getting out of this unless I quit—and *I* was not a quitter. But before this morning of monotony began, one thing needed to happen.

"You think I could get a drink sometime this century?"

"It's nine in the morning," Killian pointed out.

"It's noon somewhere. And if you want me to sit through hours of some amateur chewing up and spitting out our songs, I need something to dull the pain. Okay?"

Killian held his palms up. "Whatever gets you through it." Then he pulled open the door and called out for four whiskeys. Before he got an answer, Killian raised a hand and waved to someone down the hall, and it didn't take a genius to know that *Halo* had obviously turned up.

"Hey there," Killian said, while I braced myself for another torturous audition. "I see you found the place okay?"

The response was muffled but had Killian grinning, and when he looked inside the door to me, I could see the message in his eyes loud and clear—*play nice*. Killian should've known better, though. We'd been friends for nearly thirty years now, and one thing about me he knew damn well was that when I played, I certainly wasn't *nice*.

TWO

Halo

AM I REALLY DOING THIS? I thought, not for the first or even tenth time, as I stepped inside the front doors of Electric Sound Studio. I'd been pinching myself since I'd gotten the call from Killian Michaels himself, telling me he'd seen my audition tape, and could I come in for a face-to-face with him and the rest of TBD?

Uh, meet one of the biggest rock bands in the world? To audition as their *lead singer*? It was surreal.

But as I signed in with the receptionist and she pointed down the hall to studio 1B, the initial excitement I'd felt when Killian called twelve hours earlier started to morph into full-on anxiety. What the hell had I been thinking when I sent that video in? Then again, someone had to step into Trent Knox's shoes. Why couldn't that be me?

My steps faltered, and I almost dropped my guitar case as I turned the corner and stared down the long corridor. The walls were lined with what looked like rich black velvet, chandeliers shimmered overhead every few feet, and at the end of the hall, behind the door with "1B" etched in silver, would be the guys of TBD. A band I'd listened to for a decade, through all my formative years, and now here I stood, on the brink of something that could change my life.

But I couldn't make myself move. If I turned around and walked out the door now, they wouldn't have a chance to reject me, and then I could live the rest of my life without the soul-crushing anguish that snub would bring.

Or…I could man the hell up, walk into that room, and show them exactly why I was the perfect guy for the job. Life was about risks, right? If I didn't try, I wouldn't fail, but I'd also never get anywhere, and I wasn't content playing covers at mostly empty dive bars for the rest of my life. Not when I knew what I was capable of.

With my decision made, I took a step forward just as the door to studio 1B opened and Killian Michaels appeared in the doorway, yelling out for four whiskeys. When he saw me, his eyes lit up and he waved me over.

"Hey there," he said, smiling my way, and I almost looked behind me to make sure there wasn't someone else he was calling out to. "I see you found the place okay?"

I forced my feet to keep moving as I nodded. "Yeah, hi."

"Hi." Killian glanced over his shoulder, back into the studio, and then faced me again as I came to a stop in front of him. He stood tall, about the same height as me, with a shock of dark hair that was longer on top and styled back in a way that screamed indifference, though it had probably taken him a half hour to perfect. It was so strange to see him standing there in regular jeans and a hoodie instead of the rocked-out persona he used onstage.

"I'm Killian," he said, holding his hand out like everyone in the free world didn't know who he was.

"Halo." I switched the guitar to my other hand and gave him a firm handshake.

One of Killian's eyebrows rose. "That your real name?"

"Is Killian yours?" It came out before I could stop it, but instead of being offended, Killian laughed and clapped me on the shoulder.

"I like a smartass. Come meet the guys."

He led me inside, and immediately my senses were overwhelmed. The first thing I noticed were the thick crimson curtains that were artfully draped from floor to ceiling and took up an entire wall. The second thing that caught my attention was the massive chandelier in the middle of the room that made the ones in the hallway look like ants. *Good God, this is how the other half lives.*

"Hey, hey," came a voice behind me, and with his hand still on my shoulder, Killian turned us around to where Jagger, the keyboardist for TBD, strolled inside. Dressed to the nines in a long-sleeved black collared shirt and matching slacks only a few shades darker than his skin, Jagger was the impeccably put-together charmer of the band, which was evident as he came to stand in front of us.

"You're late," Killian said.

Jagger ignored him and gave me a winning smile. "You must be Halo."

"And you're Jagger," I said. As I shook his hand, it was hard to miss the gold Audemars Piguet on his wrist, or the diamonds winking from the rings on his fingers.

"I didn't miss the show, did I?"

"No, he just got here," Killian said, shooting him a look that made me think Jagger's late arrival wasn't unusual.

"Then I'm not late." Jagger winked and then went to where the other two members of TBD were sprawled across the velvet couches in front of a row of windows.

Shit. They're right there.

As Killian brought me front and center, he nodded toward the man covered from neck to toe in colorful tattoos. "Halo, meet Slade."

With a piercing stare and his head shaved except for the two-inch-thick section at the top that he sometimes mohawked out, the drummer of TBD may look intimidating, but he wasn't the bad-boy member of the band. No, that honor went to the man on the opposite couch.

"And this is Viper," Killian said, and as I looked at the lead guitarist, my first thought was that this guy didn't look at all pleased to see me. With an ankle thrown over his knee, and casually stroking his lip with his forefinger, his body language may have read relaxed, but his dark eyes said something completely different. They were narrowed, assessing, and even if I didn't know from my years following the band that he was the toughest critic of the group, I still would've been wary based on that look. There was a reason he'd earned the name Viper, after all. Observant, but quick to strike—that was what all the stories about him claimed over the years.

My heart began to pound a bit harder, and I prayed they couldn't hear it.

"Guys, this is Halo. I watched the video he sent in last night—really good stuff." Killian faced me again and said, "Show us what you got."

"Okay," I said, but my voice came out raspy.

The door to the studio opened again, and a woman entered with a tray of four glasses half-filled with amber liquid. She passed one to each of the band members, and when Killian took his, he offered it to me.

"Need some liquid courage?" he asked.

I wasn't one to down hard liquor first thing in the morning, but I wasn't sure I'd get through this audition without it, so I gratefully took the glass and swallowed it in one go. It was a smooth burn going down, nothing like the cheap stuff I was used to. But of course it wasn't. This was the big time, with fuckin' chandeliers and velvet in studios instead of ripped egg crates covering a room the size of a closet.

With all four pairs of eyes on me, I bent down to unlatch my guitar case, which I managed to do on the first try—amazing, considering my hands had begun to shake.

Just breathe. Don't think about the rock gods sitting six feet away. They're just another dive bar crowd half listening.

I strapped on my guitar and tuned up, and when I was ready, I ran my fingers through my hair, blew out a breath, and faced the four men who held my fate in the palms of their hands.

"Was there something in particular of yours you'd like me to play?" I asked.

Killian shook his head. "Anything you like."

"Right." I plucked quietly at the strings as I debated whether to just go for it with one of TBD's biggest hits, and after a few seconds of deliberation, I figured, fuck it—go big or go home—and began to play the opening notes of "More than Enough."

I closed my eyes, humming along with the intro, and then...I began to sing.

THREE

Viper

FUUUCK. ME.

YEAH, that was the thought that ran through my head when Killian stepped aside and *Halo* had entered the studio around ten minutes ago. And it was still running through my head now, as I sat by myself on one of the couches facing the guy who was singing a song Killian and I had written two years ago, like we'd written it specifically for him.

Served me right, I supposed. If I'd bothered to look at the video attachment in the email Killian had sent to us all last night, I wouldn't have been trying to mask the reaction I was having to the guy—and yeah, I was having one hell of a reaction.

I'd been trying to work out why any hopeful rocker would call himself Halo since Killian had mentioned his name. But when he walked through the door and I'd gotten my first look at him, that had been cleared up for me real quick.

The guy was a fucking showstopper. He had hair the color of sunshine or spun gold—a shade poets would write about or some shit—and it waved in a sexy tangle of loose curls that hit the collar of his jacket. And that face of his, *Jesus*. It was perfect. Almost otherworldly. And with eyes a light shade of green, like sea glass... he was almost too damn beautiful to look at.

I shifted on the couch and wished like hell Killian had asked for the entire bottle of whiskey, because suddenly I wasn't drinking to dull the pain of someone singing our songs. I was drinking to try and take my mind off how hot this guy was. Especially when you added in his voice—and what a voice he had.

He delivered the words in a husky, deep way that you felt down your spine and in your soul, and as he strummed on his guitar, he closed those gorgeous eyes of his and lost himself in my song—I mean, *our* song.

Shit, this was not good. Of course the first guy who showed any potential had to be someone who made my dick hard, and when I glanced Killian's way and saw him watching me for my reaction, I hoped to hell he was only looking at my face.

Halo came to the end of the song, and color me shocked, he was the first guy who'd managed to get through the entire thing without screwing it up.

When the room plunged into silence, Halo opened his eyes and blinked, and when they widened slightly, I almost laughed. Had the guy forgotten where he was? Well, if that were the case, he sure as shit was remembering now.

"Wow." Killian was the first on his feet, as he slow-clapped and looked our way. "I told you he was good, didn't I?"

"Good?" Jagger said, and then chuckled. "That was awesome, man."

Out of the corner of my eye, I saw Slade nodding in agreement, but not offering much more than that, and finally Killian looked to me.

"Well?"

My eyes shifted from Killian to Halo, who was looking at me, waiting for my reaction. And while I wasn't one to blow smoke up anyone's ass, I was also man enough to admit when I was impressed. "Not bad."

Killian's lips twitched. He knew me well enough to know that that was high fucking praise from me—but the one next to him looked less convinced.

"I can play another if you like?" Halo offered, but Killian shook his head.

"Just give me a second, would you?"

"Okay," Halo said as Killian crossed to stop in front of me, and as he drew near, I couldn't help my eyes from drifting back to Halo, who had stepped back a bit to give us some privacy and was now showing great interest in the sound booth behind him.

With his back to Halo, Killian looked over at Jagger and Slade, who both gave a nod of approval, and then his eyes were back on me.

"You want to ask him some questions?" That was Killian's way of asking if I liked Halo enough to give a shit if he was available to come back and *really* try out with us. As in, run through a full set and see if he meshed. But the only kind of meshing I had in mind didn't require instruments, my bandmates, and, well...clothes. Somehow I didn't think that was what Killian meant.

Again, there were so many reasons this was a bad idea.

My eyes must've relayed at least that much of my thoughts, because the second I opened my mouth to suggest Halo wasn't the right fit, Killian lowered his voice and said, "He's fucking amazing, V. What's your issue?"

Deciding it best not to voice what my particular *issue* was, I glanced down at my lap, and Killian's eyes followed. When he saw just how amazing I thought this guy had been, Killian's lips quirked up at the side.

"I'd say that's a positive response. Wouldn't you?"

I ground my teeth together and shook my head. "I don't think so."

"Come on, V. He's the first guy we've seen where you haven't fallen asleep halfway through."

That was true, but I wasn't sure this was any better.

"If he can do this to you, imagine what he could do to an arena full of screaming fans."

Okay, Killian had a point, and fuck him for that. But did I

really want to subject myself to this kind of torture day in and day out? I'd been there and done that, and look how that turned out.

I narrowed my eyes, but before I could say anything else, Killian straightened and said to Halo, "Right. Why don't you come take a seat and we can shoot the shit a little?"

Goddamn Killian. Well, at least he couldn't say I hadn't warned him.

FOUR

Halo

HOLY SHIT. I'D just performed for TBD, and I hadn't forgotten the lyrics, passed out, vomited all over myself, or pulled any other equally embarrassing stunt. Instead, I'd closed my eyes and let myself fall into the song, blocking out my audience completely. It wasn't until I'd opened them again and saw the stunned reactions from three of them that I felt the weight leave my shoulders. Who knew what they'd decide, but for myself, I knew I'd killed it—even if they didn't think I was the right fit, I couldn't have done any better.

I put my guitar away and then lowered myself into the chair Killian had pulled around to face the couches. I hadn't thought about the audition featuring an inquisition, but that was exactly what happened as Jagger, Killian, and Slade lobbed question after question my way.

"How'd you get into music?"

"Why do you think you'd be a good fit for TBD?"

"How old are you?"

I had a moment of panic at that one. I didn't think I looked young, but I still got carded everywhere I went, so admitting I was only twenty-three—a full decade younger than them—made me wonder if that'd be a deal-breaker.

But no one reacted to that info, and the questions rolled on. With each one that passed, I began to slowly relax, especially when they veered into the ridiculous:

"All right, I've got one." Slade leaned forward, his elbows on his knees, his expression dead serious. "It's the end of the world and only one superhero can save you. Who do you choose?"

Jagger snorted. "Seriously?"

"What the hell does that have to do with whether he's right for the band?" Viper said.

Slade put his hand up, blocking out the other guys' protests, and then motioned for me to go ahead.

"I guess I'd say...maybe Thor? His dad's a literal god, so he might be my best chance." In truth, I didn't know much about anyone in the superhero world, so I wasn't sure if that was a good choice or not. "What about you?"

"Iron Man," Slade said.

"Well, I'd pick Wonder Woman," Jagger said. "If it's the end of the world, I wouldn't mind goin' out with a bang."

Beside him, Killian groaned and gave him a shove. "Ugh. That was fuckin' painful."

Jagger's head fell back as he laughed, and I couldn't stop my own chuckle. Was I really sitting here, joking around and laughing with TBD? I just knew any minute now I'd wake up in my shithole apartment, eat some ramen, and head out for a gig. I even pinched myself to be sure.

"Favorite song of ours?" Slade asked.

I had a few favorites, but I was going to play my hand wisely. It hadn't escaped my notice that Viper stayed silent throughout almost all the questions, though his keen eyes didn't miss a thing. I wished I knew what was going through the guy's mind, because I had a feeling if I didn't make it to the next round or whatever came after, it would be because Viper put his foot down.

"'Dark Light,'" I said, and out of the corner of my eye, I saw Viper smirk. "Dark Light" was one of Viper's, a song he'd written for the *Daybreak* album. Yeah, I'd chosen it on purpose, hoping to sway him—so sue me.

"Was there something you wanted to add, V?" Killian asked, looking pointedly at his bandmate. Viper's smirk dropped, and he stared Killian down for a long minute before craning his head in my direction.

My throat went dry as I waited for him to speak. He took his time, running his hand over the dark scruff on his jaw, and as I tried not to fidget under his intense gaze, I finally got a good look at him.

Bad boy. Player. Heartbreaker. All words I'd heard about Viper, and I could understand why. The warm, bronzed skin, jet-black hair that was long enough he could tuck it behind his ears or let it fall down in his face, and strong jaw line tied together the rebellious look of someone who drove the men and women who followed the band crazy. Rumor had it he had a preference for the former, but that was none of my business.

Viper stretched his arm out along the back of the couch, those obsidian eyes of his focused directly on me. "Okay, *Halo*." He said my name like a challenge. "If you could change something, anything, about the band, what would it be?"

Shiiit. He'd successfully put me on the spot, asking a question there was no good answer to. It was like in job interviews where they asked what your weaknesses were. The last thing you wanted to do was cop to being less than perfect and fucking up a shot at a job, and that was exactly what was happening here. What would I change about TBD?

Okay, there were two ways to look at this. I could be honest, or I could play it safe. The safe answer was that there was nothing I'd change about them, blah blah blah, but the honest answer...

"You need me as your frontman," I blurted out before I could change my mind. A couple of eyebrows shot up, but I kept my focus on Viper, waiting to see his reaction. But like he knew what I wanted and wouldn't give me the satisfaction, his face remained impassive.

Was that good impassive? Bad impassive? Or you've-gotta-be-kidding-me impassive? I couldn't tell. But then Viper said four words that seemed to seal my fate:

"We'll be in touch."

My stomach dropped. *"We'll be in touch"*? Shit. Shit shit shit. I had just bombed that answer. I'd just bombed, and now they were all looking at me like I needed to get the hell out of the room and—

"I'll walk you out," Killian said, getting to his feet.

I quickly packed up my guitar as a sinking sense of dread came over me. *Keep it together until you get outside.*

"It was great meeting you guys. Thanks for the opportunity." I walked to each of them and shook their hands. Slade and Jagger nodded at me in return, but when I reached Viper, he held on to my hand longer, his grip firm and his gaze traveling down over me before he let go.

As I backed away, I wondered what Viper saw when he looked at me the way he had. Did he see some young guy trying too hard? Or had he been even the slightest bit impressed at all?

Guess I'd soon find out.

FIVE

Viper

"YO, V. PIZZA OR MEXICAN?" Killian called out from his kitchen, as I fell down into one of the leather couches in his sprawling Tribeca penthouse later that afternoon. We'd just gotten home from a long-ass day over at MGA, our record label, where we'd sat in one meeting after another with our manager, Brian.

Ever since Trent walked, MGA had been putting the pressure on for us to find a new frontman stat, because there was no way in hell a record company was going to "continue funneling money into a sinking ship"—their words, not mine.

I mean, we'd brought them enough money to last a goddamn lifetime. You'd think it would at least buy us some time to figure our shit out. However, they saw things differently. *Assholes.* We'd been given a deadline, which we were fast approaching, and that was one of the reasons Killian had been pulling us from our beds at ungodly hours this week to watch these auditions.

We'd been searching for months now, and all of them had gone nowhere fucking fast. But today's...today's had been a different story altogether, and was the reason we'd ended up spending most of the day in meetings across town—something none of us enjoyed.

"Pizza," I said, then rattled off my usual topping of sausage, onions, mushrooms, and extra cheese.

Killian grabbed his cell off his kickass guitar-shaped coffee table. "As if I didn't know that. Don't you get sick of ordering the same thing every single time?"

"I like what I like. That ain't gonna change anytime soon." What could I say, I was a creature of habit.

Killian chuckled as he called the number and placed our order. Once he was done, he took a seat in his favored club chair that sat facing the bank of wall-to-ceiling windows, and then looked my way.

"Speaking of things you like..." Killian eyed me as he propped his ankle on his knee. "What'd you really think about Halo today? He was good, huh?"

Uh, that was one way to describe him. Probably not the way I would. But I doubted Killian wanted to know I couldn't stop thinking about the way Halo might look stripped naked in my bed.

"Yeah," I said, giving my standard noncommittal response. "Like I said, he's not bad."

"Not bad, my ass. That guy is fucking brilliant. Admit it. He's almost as good as—"

"If you say Trent, I just might kick you in the balls."

Killian laughed, and I decided I just might kick him anyway. "Why? Because there might be someone out there who can actually match him or—"

"Because his name makes me want to commit violent acts."

Killian sobered in an instant. "I swear, one of these days you're gonna have to stop talking shit about him every time you open your mouth."

"Yeah? Well, one of these days I might stop hating him. There's hope for us all."

Killian let out a sigh and ran a hand through his hair, and I knew it was too much to hope for that all conversation would be over, and the TV be turned on. And not a minute later, Killian was right back on topic. "So...Halo. Did you finally look at the video I sent you last night?"

Had I looked at it? That would be an affirmative. As soon as Halo had left, and the guys had gone outside for a smoke, I'd been quick to open that email and the attachment. Quick to get another look at that face—because what a fucking face.

"Yeah, I looked."

"*Aaaand?*"

"And what do you want me to say, Kill? He's good. Really fucking good. You've got ears, but—" I drew up short, and when Killian just sat there giving me his *what* look, I thought, *To hell with this*. "He makes my dick hard, okay? I can't stand on a stage with that guy. Did you see him? He's too damn pretty for his own good."

"Which is exactly why he'd be perfect for TBD."

Killian had lost his mind. "Are you deaf? I just told you that—"

"I know exactly what you told me. I *saw* it too. But I'm not worried. He's straight. Didn't you hear the lyrics in the second song he wrote?"

Lyrics? I was too busy focusing on the way his mouth moved. Not what was coming out of it.

Killian grinned. "He was singing about his broken heart—about how *she* broke his heart. But good to know you didn't notice. You think he's sexy. And you think he's sexy singing *our* songs. I haven't seen you act that way since—"

My glare had Killian biting off *his* name, and then he scooted forward to the edge of his seat. "Chemistry, V. It's all about chemistry on that stage. You know that better than anyone, and you need to have it with our frontman."

"Chemistry? If I have any more chemistry with him, I just might explode all over him."

Killian snorted. "Maybe keep that to yourself when we call him back in, yeah? Don't want to scare off the newbie."

"So we're really going to do this? Invite a guy into the fold who looks as pure as a fucking angel?"

"Hey, people find the idea of corrupting someone just as hot as they do taming the bad boy. Women and men are gonna love it. His face and our words coming out his mouth. We can play with that. Plus, Halo's voice is killer, and his guitar playing was off the chain. He didn't fuck up once today, even though he had to be nervous. And I know that impressed you."

Damn Killian. The asshole knew my weakness well, and the fact that Halo *hadn't* messed up our music had been his one-way ticket to the next round. "I can't decide if you're hiring him as our frontman, or trying to convince me to sleep with him. Either way, I guess I'm in."

"I'm going to pretend you don't mean that in any way other than—*in* with the plan."

I grinned at Killian, a wolf's grin that made no promises. He was smart enough to know what he'd be inviting if he brought Halo back for more—but that wasn't my problem. I'd been up front about my concerns, and if Killian was willing to risk it for some good old-fashioned chemistry, then who the fuck was I to stop it?

SIX

Halo

I'D BEEN HOME LESS than two minutes when the pounding on my door started. After leaving the audition, I hadn't wanted to go home, so I'd wandered to Central Park and commandeered a bench for hours, people-watching, freezing my ass off, and occasionally playing my guitar. Trying to keep my mind off the way the audition had ended.

The pounding started up again, and I sighed and kicked off my shoes before going to answer it. I knew who was on the other side, and the last thing I wanted to do was answer a million questions. Why had I decided to play the role of cocky bastard for that last one? It cost me my shot, and all I wanted to do now was crawl into bed and pretend today had never happened. Well, maybe just the ending. Meeting the band had been amazing, and maybe once my frustration at myself wore off, I'd be able to think back on it in a positive way.

"Halo!" Imogen yelled. "I know you're in there. Open up!"

No doubt my sister had been looking through her peephole to see when I'd gotten in, which was how she'd made it up here so fast. Perks of living in the same building as your sibling—not.

I barely had the door open before Imogen said, "Finally. How'd it go? Tell me everything. Did they love—" But when she got a good look at my face, her smile dropped. "Oh no. What happened?"

Without a word, I left the door open and headed into the kitchen—or what passed for a kitchen in my tiny apartment, anyway. There was enough room for a small sink, two burners, and a mini fridge, which was fine considering I didn't cook *ever*. I grabbed a beer out of the fridge, and as I popped the tab, Imogen's green eyes widened.

"You've been gone for hours. And...you're drinking? Oh, Halo..." She followed me to the couch, and when I collapsed onto the worn cushions, she took the seat beside me, not giving me an inch. "You're killing me here. Did you lose your voice or something?"

I almost wished I had. Would've been easy to keep my mouth shut.

Flipping the tab back and forth until it broke off between my fingers, I kept my eyes on the cold can instead of having to see the disappointment that would fill Imogen's eyes when I told her what happened. "I fucked up."

"Impossible."

"Nothing's impossible, trust me."

"You're the best singer, performer, musician I know, and that's totally not me being biased, so I think maybe you're being too hard on yourself."

"It wasn't the audition that was the problem. I killed it." I thought back to the look Viper had given me as he asked the final question, the one that had put the nail in my coffin. "Let's just say sometimes I should think before I speak."

"Oh, Halo, you didn't."

"Yuup." I swallowed several gulps of beer and then lay back, resting my arm over my eyes.

"Hey, maybe it wasn't that bad. What did you say?"

"They asked what I'd change about the band."

"Oh shit."

"Yeah. And telling them I should be their frontman didn't exactly get a good reaction."

"Wait. What?" Imogen pulled my arm away from my face. "Is that all?"

"What do you mean is that all? They practically shoved me out the door after that."

Imogen stared at me for a long moment before busting out laughing.

I sat up, glaring. "What the hell's so funny?"

"You." She wiped her eyes and shook her head at me. "Did they tell you to have a nice life?"

"They said they'd be in touch."

"They'd *be in touch*? You dumbass. That's a *good* thing." As I lifted the beer to my lips, she swiped the can from me and set it on the ground beside her. "Listen, we need a come-to-Jesus here, okay? Look at me."

I rolled my eyes but tilted my head in her direction.

"I'm just gonna be blunt here. I get you're hard on yourself. That's why you're as good as you are, because you push hard and you don't take no for an answer. *That's* why you told them they need you as their singer. Hello, you were honest. You know you'll make them better. And you know what? They don't want some pussyfooting wallflower on stage with them—they want the confident badass who flat-out tells them he's the best."

I blinked at Imogen. With her long red hair draped around her shoulders in waves, and with her emerald eyes flashing, she looked the epitome of the feisty redhead you always heard about, and at this moment, she sounded like one too. I didn't even get a chance to respond before she was firing off another question.

"So which one got in your head? Was it Slade? You know he only looks scary, right? I've heard he's actually a nice guy."

I thought back to the meeting, and how all the guys had, at one point or another, laughed and cut up with each other...all but one.

"There," Imogen said. "I see it all over your face. Who?"

"Viper was...interesting."

"Interesting? You mean freakin' hot."

"I wasn't really looking."

"Yeah, but you can admit when you know another guy's good-looking. And Viper? He's, like, outrageously hot."

"I get it. You think he's hot. Maybe he also gets off on giving others a hard time, because that guy didn't smile once."

"Well, if you believe *Entertainment Daily*, he gets off *often*." Imogen winked at me, and when I gave her a shove, she laughed.

My cell vibrated in my pocket, and as I pulled it out and saw the number on the screen, I broke into a cold sweat. "Shit."

"Who is it?"

I looked up at her. "Killian."

"What?" she shrieked. "Answer the damn phone!"

"But—"

"*Answer. The. Phone.*"

Oh God. Here it was. The *thanks but no, thanks* line I'd been dreading all day. I brought the phone to my ear and closed my eyes like I could block out what he was about to say.

"Hello?"

"Halo, it's Killian."

"Hi," I said, and licked my lips, ready to throw out an apology. "Listen, I'm—"

"Available tomorrow at eleven?"

My eyes flew open. "What?"

"We all think you're great, and we'd like to see where this thing can go."

The blood rushing in my ears almost drowned out his words, and I needed to make sure I'd heard him right, because it sounded like he'd said—

"You want me?"

Killian chuckled. "You sound surprised."

"Uh, yeah." Imogen was bouncing on the couch, her hands over her mouth to stop from squealing.

"Don't be. You fuckin' rocked it, man. We can't wait to hear what else you can do."

Holy shit, this was happening. I hadn't screwed things up after all, which meant they hadn't been offended by my answer, and Viper hadn't blackballed me.

I'll be damned...

"So eleven tomorrow, yeah?" Killian said. "We'll be rehearsing at my place. Got a pen?"

I mimicked writing in the air to Imogen, and she jumped up and ran off to grab a pen. When she came back with a paper towel and a marker, I wrote down the address Killian rattled off and told him I'd be there at eleven sharp. It didn't occur to me until I ended the call that I had Killian Michaels's address in my lap. Not only that, but I'd just been invited to join the band on a trial basis.

My mouth moved, but I couldn't find the words. Imogen let out the scream she'd been holding back, grabbing hold of me and shaking me in excitement.

"Oh my God, Halo," she said, a huge grin on her face. "So you're in?"

Dazed, I gripped the back of my neck, a smile slowly creeping across my lips. "I'm in."

SEVEN

Halo

THE NEXT MORNING, I stepped off the elevator of Killian's building and onto the penthouse floor, my guitar in hand and a backpack slung over my shoulder. It felt strangely like the first day of school, all anticipation and excitement and nerves battling it out, especially in such a swanky setting. As I looked up and down the hall, I noticed there was only one door on this floor, which meant Killian's place took up the whole thing.

I blew out a breath as I knocked on the door, determined to walk in there as an equal. There was a reason I'd been asked back, and I needed to show these guys that they'd made the right choice.

The door swung open and Killian cocked a grin at me, resting his arm against the doorjamb.

"Hey, man. You ready for this?"

Something about the way Killian said it made me think he knew I thought I was in over my head but wasn't about to show it, so I answered honestly.

"Is anyone ever ready for it?"

He laughed and moved off the door. "Fuck no. Just gotta wing it."

"Fake it till you make it," I said, stepping inside as he shut the door behind me.

"Exactly. See, you're more prepared than we were when we started out." He led us into a huge open room with red walls and exposed beams that seemed to be a combination of living areas, the kitchen and dining room, and an entertainment area. None of the other guys seemed to be around, and as Killian rounded the oversized granite island in front of the refrigerator, he said, "So what's your poison? I've got coffee, tea, sodas, and a full bar."

"Water's good for now."

He handed me a bottle from the fridge and pointed out where everything was. "I'll give you a tour later, but this is where we rehearse, so make yourself at home."

I looked around, curious as to where, because I didn't see any instruments, and a drum kit wasn't something you wanted to lug around all the time.

Like he could see what I was thinking, Killian laughed and shook his head. "Not literally in here. We soundproofed a room through there." He pointed out a towering wooden door to our left, and after pouring coffee into a tumbler, he nodded for me to follow him.

I've got this. No need to be starstruck. They're just normal guys... normal guys who've sold millions of records and live in penthouse apartments. No big deal.

As I stepped inside the rehearsal space, I saw the others tuning their instruments, snickers ringing out as Jagger said something that made them roll their eyes. Compared to the rest of the penthouse, the room was surprisingly simple. Carpeted floors, wood walls, and framed black fabric-wrapped panels on the walls to absorb the sound. Nothing fancy, just their instruments and a couple of leather couches and chairs against a wall.

Slade saw me first and lifted his drumsticks in greeting, and then Jagger's and Viper's heads turned my way.

You're the fucking frontman, I told myself, straightening, and then I nodded at the guys. "Hey."

"Halo, my man," Jagger said, grinning and holding out his fist. I set down my guitar case and then bumped his fist with mine. A few feet away, Viper stood watching us, his arms crossed over his guitar.

"Viper," I said in greeting.

He inclined his head ever so slightly. "Angel."

"It's Halo."

Viper smirked. "Same thing."

Okaaay, so obviously Viper hadn't warmed up much to the idea of having me onboard since yesterday, but he hadn't told me to fuck off either, so I figured he'd come around. Eventually.

"So let's get started," Killian said, rubbing his hands together. Excitement sparked the air around him, and I wondered how long it'd been since they'd come together in this space to rehearse. Had any others who'd auditioned before me been invited here? Was I the first? And more importantly, would I be the last?

I set my guitar case and backpack off to the side, swallowed some water, and took my place behind the main mic stand. I wasn't sure if I'd be playing a guitar like Trent had on occasion, or if they wanted me just to sing, but I'd brought my own in case.

"We're gonna start with the *Daybreak* album, since that's the most recent," Killian said, stacking a few sheets of paper that contained lyrics on the stand in front of me. When I opened my mouth to protest that I didn't need them, he held his hand up. "I know you said you're familiar with the songs, but even we forget the lyrics sometimes."

Right. Good point. It would be worse forgetting a line in front of these guys than having to look at the words in front of me.

"Thanks," I said, as Killian moved to my left and strapped on his bass guitar.

"'Crossroads,'" he called out to us. I glanced down to make sure that was the lyric page on top as Slade counted us down to the intro. When he launched into a heavy beat, a thrill shot through me, goosebumps popping up all over my skin. If I'd thought yesterday's audition had been surreal, it had nothing on what was happening at that moment, when the others began to play. Their sounds blended together so perfectly that for a moment, I was frozen in awe, completely blanking out on the fact that I had a role to play.

Killian held his hand up when I missed my cue and the music stopped. Then he raised an eyebrow at me. "Everything okay?"

"Shit, sorry," I said, but I was unable to stop the huge grin from taking over my face. "That was just so fucking cool. You're just"—*damn mind-blowing*—"amazing." I tried to tamp down my excitement and glanced over my shoulder at the other guys. "Sorry. Can we do that again?"

Behind me, Killian chuckled, and then Slade counted down and kicked off the song again.

This time, I was ready even as I tried to take in every second of what was happening. I shook out my arms as the music swelled, and then I grabbed the mic and began to sing.

It was fucking magic.

I'd been in a couple of bands before, but holy shit. The way it all came together when you had musicians at the top of their game was leaps and bounds over anything I'd experienced before. And though my voice was naturally a bit deeper than Trent's, I still matched him note for note.

The first song went off without a hitch, and they went straight into the next song off the album. Never one to stand still for long, I ripped the mic off the stand and prowled the room, getting a feel for my surroundings and my place in this band. As I faced them again, all four guys playing masterfully, I could barely believe this was my life. Would *be* my life for years to come, because after having this taste of what being part of TBD was like, there was no way I was giving it up. And since this was another test to see how I fit in, I wasn't going to dick around.

Part of any successful band was stage presence. It didn't matter how good you sounded on an album. If you sucked ass in front of thousands, if you didn't give the crowd something to watch, then they wouldn't stick around for the next tour. So with that thought in mind, I sauntered over to Viper, and when he saw me coming for him, his dark eyes flared.

Not missing a note, he stared back as I moved closer, his wickedly fast fingers flying up and down the neck of his Fender Telecaster. There was a reason he was known as one of the greatest living guitar players—dude was a legend. And, according to Imogen, every person on the planet thought he was "bad-boy gorgeous" or whatever, which, now that I was face to face with the guy, I supposed could be true. With a penetrating gaze and stubble along his strong jaw and lining his smug mouth, I could see the appeal.

Wait, what? Uh, no. I could see the appeal for my sister or anyone else. Not for me. I wasn't checking out another guy's lips. I was just focused on winning over the one person I knew could potentially stand in my way of making this situation permanent.

EIGHT

Viper

UNFUCKINGBELIEVABLE. AFTER YEARS on tour with Trent as our frontman, and being surrounded by some of the most talented musicians in the world, not much shocked me these days. Rarely was I rendered mute by someone's ability to hold a stadium captive, and I was even less impressed by someone trying to sing the words I'd poured my heart and fucking soul into.

But from the moment Halo opened his mouth and sang his way through the first song to right now, he'd held my attention in a way that I knew was going to be a big goddamn problem.

As I played the intro to the second song off *Daybreak*, a simple six-note arpeggio I repeated and modulated with the pedal by my foot, Halo pulled the mic off the stand and turned in my direction.

With those light eyes of his, he sized me up as though trying to decide whether he should stay where he was or come closer, and when the rest of the band joined in and the beat began to really throb, it seemed to act as the shove he needed.

Halo walked in my direction with more swagger in his little finger than most people had in their entire body, which was a good damn thing considering the song he was singing. As he came to a stop in front of me, his fingers tightened around the mic as he sang the first verse, and I couldn't help but wonder what was running through his head as his eyes swept down my body to where I was plucking the strings of my guitar.

This close, I could smell the fresh scent of whatever soap he'd used this morning as he sidled in closer, and I allowed myself a moment to really look at the guy since he'd walked into the studio.

In well-worn jeans, a black T-shirt, and Converse, Halo wasn't dressed to impress—more likely dressed for comfort. But with a leather strap wrapped around his right wrist, that tangle of messy waves on his head, and a full mouth singing a song I'd written about unrequited lust, I was pretty fucking glad I had a guitar covering the lower half of my body.

I'd known this was going to happen. From the second he'd walked into the audition to last night, when I'd told Killian this was a bad idea. The frontman always played off the lead guitarist, and our band was certainly no different. Chemistry, that was what Killian said he wanted. So, let's see what the angel had up his sleeve.

As Halo sang toward the first chorus, and Slade sped up on the drums, I flicked my eyes over to Killian, whose gaze was locked on the two of us; he was probably wondering what the fuck I was gonna do next—but hey, that was his problem, not mine.

Instead, I returned my attention to Halo, singing the background vocals to go along with his. I was just in time to catch his eyes dropping to my mouth, and fuck if that did anything to squash the arousal licking through my veins from having him so close, and when he seemed to realize where he was looking and his eyes flew up to clash with mine, I couldn't stop the smirk that crossed my lips.

Arching an eyebrow, I all but dared him to come closer, and as we came up to the next round of the chorus, he lowered his arm, leaned in, and shared the mic with me, putting his lips in dangerously close proximity to mine.

The guy had balls, I had to give him that, and as the beat of the drums pulsed around the room, driving us toward the second verse, Halo wrapped his hand around my mic stand and angled his face toward me, as we sang the final line of the chorus in complete sync with one another.

As the words cut off and the music took over before the second verse, Halo released the mic stand and took a step back. His eyes were still fastened to mine as though he couldn't believe what he'd just done, but then an arrogant smile curved his lips and it was obvious he was pretty fucking pleased with himself—and so he should be.

I'd once been asked in an interview what three things I found sexiest in a person, and at the time it had been easy enough to rattle them off, since I'd been sitting next to Trent.

Confidence.
Talent.
Sexual self-awareness.

And as Halo moved back to the center of the room and slid the end of his mic back into the stand slowly, like a caress, I found my answer hadn't changed one fucking bit. Because the confidence Halo was now throwing off as he shut his eyes and began to sing the next verse made me think for the first time that there might be something better out there than Trent Knox, and he might be standing here in Killian's rehearsal studio.

As the song wound down, the energy in the room practically vibrated as Halo's voice faded into the silence, and when it was over, Jagger was the first to speak up.

"Are you fucking kidding me right now?"

Halo opened his eyes and glanced in my direction, even though Jagger had been the one to practically bust a nut over his performance.

"That was incredible. Fucking incredible. Right, guys?"

Halo swallowed and then turned to the lip of the stage, where the drum kit was set up, to bend down and pick up his bottle of water. I knew I was supposed to be concentrating on the music and his voice, and how damn good he'd just sung our songs. But with the way the denim was now stretched across his ass, my attention had shifted gears.

"Seriously. Kickass job, man," Slade said as he twirled the stick in his left hand up and down four of his fingers. "You nailed it. Even got all up in Viper's space and held your own."

I was about a second away from offering to let Halo hold something else of mine if he wanted to, but luckily for him, Killian got in first.

"I have to admit, I knew you were good, but this right here was on a whole other level of good." Killian looked in my direction. "V?"

I took in the excitement etched into the faces of my friends and bandmates, something none of us had felt for months, and I had to give credit to Halo for not only singing the shit out of our songs, but also reminding us why the hell we were here in the first place.

"Yeah, you did all right," I said.

A flush crept up Halo's neck, and it wasn't lost on me or my dick that my words were the ones that had caused that reaction. Not Slade's. Not Jagger's. Not Killian's. Halo had been wanting my approval today, and I wondered if he realized what that kind of ego stroking did to a man like me. I was thinking not, otherwise there'd be no way on God's green earth that he would still be holding my stare.

"Right," Killian said, effectively pulling my gaze, which was his intention, judging by the *quit it* look in his eyes. I shrugged it off. "How 'bout we go through the rest of the set and see how they feel?"

Halo set the water back down by his feet and ran a hand through his hair. "Sounds good to me. Is there anything you'd like me to change? Do differently?"

"Not a thing."

"Okay." Halo glanced down to the papers in front of him on the stand, then he looked over his shoulder to Slade and said, "Ready when you are," like he'd been doing this his entire fucking life. And as Slade held his sticks above his head and banged them together, I found I couldn't take my eyes off the man behind the mic.

Confidence. Halo had it in spades. And hell if that didn't make him even more tempting.

NINE

Halo

SIX HOURS AND a successful first rehearsal later, and I was riding a high like I'd never felt. It'd been so natural fronting the band, like I'd been born to do it, and there was no way I was going to be able to get rid of the wide grin on my face anytime soon.

"Great job today, Halo," Jagger said, as we packed up to leave. He slipped on a fine overcoat as I zipped up my backpack and shrugged it up my shoulder.

"Thanks, man. That was..." I shook my head. I didn't have the words, but luckily he knew exactly how I was feeling and clapped me on the back.

"You did great. Glad to have you with us."

"I'm happy to be here." God, that was an understatement. Fucking ecstatic was more like it.

I headed out of the rehearsal room with my guitar case and said my goodbyes to Killian and Viper, who were in deep conversation with each other. We had another rehearsal scheduled for the same time tomorrow, and after the way things had gone today, I was starting to visualize many more in my future.

Stepping onto the elevator, I hit the button for the ground floor, and as the doors began to close, I heard someone call out, "Hold the door."

I shot my hand out, forcing the elevator doors apart, and then Viper stepped inside. His presence in any room was tremendous, an air of dominance radiating off the guy, and it was especially potent in such a small area. I could barely believe I'd gone head-to-head with him in rehearsal. When I performed, it was like I could push the envelope, like the music took over and made me do things outside my comfort zone.

Viper pulled out a pack of cigarettes from the inside pocket of his burgundy leather motorcycle jacket and tucked one over his ear. "Want one?"

"No, thanks. I don't smoke."

He smirked and slipped the pack back inside his jacket. "Course not."

"What's that supposed to mean?"

"Nothin', *Angel*. You a virgin, too?"

I ignored his swipe at me. "You keep calling me Angel. Why?"

"Look at you." Viper swept his gaze over me leisurely, taking his time. Under his perusal, I felt the need to move, unable to stand still. When his eyes came back up to my face, he said, "Still wondering which way you'll fall. Are you as pure as you look, or are you a dark angel in disguise?"

The elevator doors opened, but I stood rooted to the spot until Viper swept his hand forward. "After you."

I tightened my fingers around the guitar case's handle, the feel of it slippery in my palm, and walked out and through the exit. The blustery wind whipped my hair across my face, the cold instantly stinging my exposed skin. January in New York was never any fun, but at least the heavy snowfall had held off so far. I started in the direction of the closest subway entrance as a cab stopped in front of Killian's building. As Viper opened the door to get inside, he looked over his shoulder at me.

"Hey, Angel. You hungry?"

I moved the hair off my face to make sure it had indeed been Viper asking and not some figment of my imagination.

He raised his brows. "Well?"

With perfect timing, my stomach growled. "Yeah, I could eat."

Viper nodded for me to join him, and as I started forward, the cab driver came around the back to put my guitar case in the trunk.

Surprised was the word I'd use as I joined Viper in the back seat and he rattled off an address nearby. I wasn't sure why he'd invited me, since he didn't seem to be the most social guy, but maybe this would be a good opportunity to get to know him. I'd certainly heard a lot about him, but who knew what was true and what was gossip?

"Chinese okay?" Viper asked. My stomach rumbled again in response, and he chuckled. "I'll take that as a yes."

We didn't say much during the short drive, and when the cab pulled up in front of a nondescript brick building, Viper handed the driver a few bills and we grabbed my case from the back.

"It looks like a hole in the wall, but the food is unfuckingreal," Viper said, seeing my confused expression as we headed downstairs to what looked like a basement. A small sign on the door with the words "Li's Kitchen" was the only tipoff that it wasn't a residence. As he pushed open the door, the warmth from inside was a welcome relief, but the decor left a lot to the imagination. With faded red walls that peeled in some spots, it looked like it hadn't been updated since they'd opened, which had to be decades ago.

Is this some kind of joke?

But to my surprise, as Viper led us to a table in the corner, I saw the restaurant was packed. Not only that, but the stares that followed him came from not only the women, but some of the men as well. Jaws dropped, teeth bit down on bottom lips, and audible gasps could be heard. Did Viper even notice the reaction people had to him, or was he so used to it by now that it was white noise?

My answer came when we passed a group of women and one of them reached out to touch him. He caught her hand, brought it to his lips, and then placed a kiss on the back of it. She sucked in a breath, and when he winked at her and walked off, the whole table burst into shrieks.

As we took our seats, Viper choosing the one that kept his back to the rest of the room, I could only shake my head. "Jesus, my sister was right."

"Right about what?"

"Everyone's, like...in love with you." I'd never seen anything like it, and even with his back to them, people still stared. Would they come over and hit on him later? Leave him napkins with their numbers written on them?

"They don't love me," Viper said, throwing his arm over the back of the chair. "They just wanna fuck me."

My eyes went wide. He wasn't one to mince words, was he?

"Don't worry, I'm not gonna abandon you here," he said, his lips tilting up. "They're not my type."

What is your type? I almost asked, but that wasn't any of my business. Instead, I shrugged, wanting him to know I wasn't about to judge. "You do you."

Before Viper could respond, a thin older man joined us and set down a bottle of something called Baijui, two small glasses, and two iced waters.

"Thanks, Li," Viper said, and then small-talked with the man I presumed was the owner, if his name was any indication. After Li left, Viper poured us both some of the Baijui.

"You come here a lot?" I asked.

Viper raised his glass as I did the same, and then swallowed a mouthful of the white spirit. Fuck me, that was strong. My insides burned as the liquor made its way down.

"Good, right?" Viper grinned. "And yeah, whenever I'm in the neighborhood. Doesn't look like much, but it's the best authentic Chinese in the city. If they cleaned shit up in here, some newspaper would be all over it, and then the tourists would take over. Fuck that."

Made sense. Tourists ruined all the good spots. I skimmed the menu, my eyes catching on the dim sum options and refusing to look elsewhere.

Viper didn't bother looking at the menu, pouring us another round of Baijui instead.

"Let me guess: you get the same thing every time you come here," I said.

"Bingo."

"Surprising. I thought a guy like you would say variety is the spice of life," I joked.

Viper's eyebrow arched. "A guy like me?"

Okay, that didn't come out like I meant it. "Just that you seem like someone who enjoys life's pleasures. You know, not getting bogged down by the same old thing."

"Oh, I do enjoy life's pleasures, Angel. You've got that part right."

Jesus, it was like everything out of the guy's mouth sounded sexual. I didn't even know what to say to that, so I took another swallow of the liquor, and this time, it didn't scorch my insides. Much.

"Careful there," Viper said. "That stuff packs a punch."

"You don't think I can hold my liquor?"

"I hope not. I'd like to see what a drunk Angel looks like."

I suddenly felt too warm in my jacket and shrugged out of it. The alcohol must've hit already—that or embarrassment from the way Viper seemed to enjoy teasing the shit out of me. As I looked around the room, all eyes were still on the man in front of me, and I leaned across the table. "Everyone's still staring at you. Does this happen every time you go out?"

"Yes."

I shook my head. "I don't know if I'd ever leave my house if I were you."

"You're gonna have to get used to it if you want to be our frontman. It'll only be worse for you."

Worse? Worse than everyone in the room watching your every move? I hadn't really thought about that side of being in a band, but since I wasn't technically *in* the band, it didn't seem like something I'd need to worry about.

That train of thought was interrupted when Li came back to get our orders. He asked for Viper's even though he apparently ordered the same almond chicken combo every time, and once he was gone, Viper rubbed his chin.

"So how'd it feel today?" he asked.

I thought about how to describe the way every second of today's rehearsal had felt like a dream, but it all sounded so cheesy and not something I wanted to admit. So I went with "Perfect."

"I'm glad to hear it. Because we'd like you to join us."

The chatter in the room seemed to go silent, the whole world disappearing as I focused in on Viper's words and tried to make sense of them. Join them? I was already joining them for another rehearsal tomorrow, so did he mean—

Oh fuck. Surely he didn't mean...for good?

"Uh..." My throat seized, and I reached for my water, chugging half the contents before I could speak again. "Join you where, exactly?"

Viper snorted, shaking his head. "Join the band. On a permanent basis."

I opened my mouth, shut it, opened it again, and all that came out was: "Holy shit. Holy *shit.*" They wanted me as part of TBD after one rehearsal? Was he pulling my chain, or was this for real? "You're not bullshitting me right now?"

Viper lifted the glass to his lips. "Not bullshitting you. What do you say?"

"Uh, fuck yes," I blurted, practically jumping out of my chair as Viper chuckled at my reaction.

"You'll need to fill out a bunch of boring-as-shit paperwork in the next few days, but the job's yours if you want it."

If I want *it?* Twist my fucking arm. I dropped my head in my hands, hiding the way I was smiling so hard my cheeks ached. I was in the band. *I* was the lead singer of TB-fucking-D.

"Cheers," Viper said, and when I lifted my head, I saw him holding up his glass.

I raised mine to his and downed the rest of the liquor, and all I could think was how completely life-changing this year was already starting out.

TEN

Viper

WHEN I VOLUNTEERED to be the one to break the news to Halo that we wanted him on a permanent basis, it had been for purely selfish reasons. What better way to get the guy in a one-on-one situation where I could get a better gauge on him than taking him out to dinner and delivering the best fucking news he'd received in his life?

But as I sat across from him at the decades-old table and watched the pure elation spread across his face, the last thing I felt was selfish. Halo looked as though he wanted to jump up on the table and scream out his good fortune to anyone who wanted to listen, and judging by the curious eyes that had been glued to us since our arrival, that would be every single person in the place.

These days, I rarely noticed the prying eyes, the intrusive stares that came along with the kind of fame TBD had acquired. It was something I'd became accustomed to and learned how to deal with as we'd clawed our way to the top of the charts through hard work, sweat, and perseverance. But experiencing it all over again through Halo's eyes tonight was a stark reminder of just how green this guy was—how green *we* had been. The difference was that we'd all had a minute to come to terms with it. Years. Halo? He was going to get a week.

TBD had a charity gig coming up in Savannah. It was a smaller event than we usually played, but it'd been booked for over a year now—before Trent had decided to fuck off. That was one of the reasons the record company had been riding our asses so hard over the last couple of months, and Killian and I thought it was the perfect opportunity to see how Halo was going to handle the stage, handle us, and, more importantly, handle a crowd.

If he was anything like he'd been this afternoon, he'd have them eating out of his hand.

"Your orders," Li said as he stopped alongside our table and placed my almond chicken in front of me, a small steamer basket in front of Halo, and a basket of white rice between us. When he added another bottle of Baijui, I immediately reached for it, and after thanking him, I gestured to Halo's glass.

"Another?"

Halo picked up his glass and held it out. "You really are trying to get me drunk, aren't you?"

"Nah. We're celebrating." When his glass was full, I refilled mine and then picked up my chopsticks. "It's a momentous occasion. You got the job with TBD, and I no longer have to listen to people butcher my songs until my ears fucking bleed. That right there is reason enough to drink up."

Halo grinned as he took the lid off his meal, and when he put it on the table beside the basket, I leaned over to peer inside.

"What's that again?"

Halo raised his eyes to mine. "The Pork Siu Mai."

I rolled my eyes as I sat back in my seat. "And that tells me exactly nothing. What's *in* it?"

Halo chuckled as he spooned some rice onto his plate. "Ground pork and shrimp. Why?"

Damn, that sounded really good. But who knew how it'd taste? At least I knew my almond chicken wasn't money wasted. "No reason."

Halo picked up his chopsticks and grabbed the dumpling closest to him as I shoveled some rice and chicken into my mouth.

When he swallowed his food and made this sexy groan in the back of his throat, my hand paused where it was holding my second helping.

"I take it it's good?" I said, and waited for Halo's eyes to focus on me.

"Huh?"

I pointed to his food with my chopsticks. "Your food. You just groaned like someone sucked your dick. I'm guessing you're enjoying what you just put in your mouth."

Halo's lips parted. I'd shocked him, which, admittedly, I'd been trying to do. But then his eyes narrowed a fraction as though he realized what I was up to, and he nodded.

"You were right. Their food is really good. Bet you wish you'd been a little more adventurous now, don't you?"

I licked over my bottom lip and wondered what he'd do if he realized exactly *how* adventurous I wanted to get with him. But, not wanting to run off the frontman the same night we'd offered him the job, I settled for something a little less...in your face.

I reached over with my chopsticks and plucked the half-eaten dumpling from his basket. Halo's eyes widened as I popped it in my mouth and chewed—and fuck if he wasn't right. That was some good shit, and when I was done, I flashed him a grin.

"You don't mind sharing, do you?"

I could see the guy's mind working overtime, as he probably tried to decide if I meant that in any way other than his meal.

Halo let out a snort of laughter. "Sure, why not. What's mine is yours."

With the Baijui coursing through my veins, and the adrenaline still pumping from the first successful day of rehearsing that we'd had in months, nothing could've stopped what left my mouth then. I was in a mood, and while the alcohol and the good day were half the reason for it, it was the hot fucker sitting across from me that had me feeling overly...stimulated.

"You know, you should really be more specific with what you're offering, Angel. I doubt we're thinkin' the same thing right now."

Halo seemed to ponder that for a moment before he reached for his glass and quickly swallowed a gulp of his drink. Then he began piling some rice onto his chopsticks again. "So is this your thing?"

I watched him closely as he brought the utensils to his lips, fucking obsessing over the way they closed around them and then slid down off the sticks drawing the food into his mouth. "My thing?"

"Yeah," Halo said, nodding. "The player? The bad boy? Come on, you know the reputation you have. You flirt with everyone?"

Well, would you look at that. The alcohol was making the angel bold now, wasn't it? "The lucky ones."

Halo let out a bark of laughter. "Fucking hell."

"What?"

"I don't think I've ever met anyone as—"

"Hot as me before? It's okay, I get that a lot." I aimed a wink Halo's way as I chewed a mouthful of my dinner, and he shook his head.

"I was going to say arrogant."

I shrugged, unaffected. I'd been called a whole lot worse over the years, that was for sure. "Hey, you gotta work with what you got. It's not my fault people see me and think of sex."

Halo coughed a little, and then looked around us. "Are you for real?"

I sat back and crossed my legs at the ankles under the table, and when my foot bumped up against Halo's leg, he startled a little, making me chuckle. "Yeah. You're thinking about sex right now. Aren't you?"

"Only because you keep talking about it."

"That's because I'm thinking about it too." That drew Halo up quick fucking smart, and I decided to keep right on going while the angel was feeling chatty. "Speaking of sex..."

"*You* were speaking of sex. I was trying to eat my dinner."

"Potato, *potah-to*. But to answer your original question on whether I flirt with everyone, then yeah, I guess. It's easy to make someone feel good by paying a little attention to them. But do I fuck 'em all? Hmm...the media likes to think so. That doesn't mean it's true, though, does it?"

Halo contemplated me in silence, as though trying to decide what the real answer to that was. But when he said nothing else, I glanced around Li's at the eyes still on us and said, "For example. At least half the people in this restaurant are wondering who you are to me right now. Are you my friend? Are you my latest fuck? And considering my 'reputation,' what conclusion do you think they're coming up with?"

The color drained from Halo's face in an instant.

"Exactly. Just because they think it, doesn't mean it's true...does it?"

Halo's back stiffened, and I chuckled as I pointed to the bottle of alcohol, but this time he shook his head—probably smart.

"So," I said, running my eyes over his suddenly rigid posture, "since we both know you aren't sleeping with me. You got some girlfriend at home waiting for you?" When Halo just looked at me blankly, I said, "You dating anyone?"

"Why? Is that not allowed?"

"It's allowed. But the fans, they can get pretty intense. Just trying to work out if we're gonna have to keep an eye out for any crazy jealous shit."

Halo's mouth parted as though he were going to say something, but then he snapped it shut and ran a hand through his hair. "I didn't think about that."

"You think people are looking at me right now? Wait until you hit the stage with that face and voice. Shit, people are going to be throwing themselves at your feet."

A flush, much like the one that had crept up his neck in rehearsal earlier today, flooded Halo's cheeks, and I couldn't stop the rumble of laughter that left my throat.

"Oh yeah, Angel. With that innocent face of yours and the songs you're going to sing, you're gonna have your choice of the women *and* the men."

That finally seemed to get a reaction out of Halo. His lips quirked at the sides. "Worried I'm going to horn in on your territory? Don't be—I'll leave the men to you."

"I see." I rubbed my thumb and forefinger over the stubble on my chin. "And that doesn't bother you?"

When Halo's eyes filled with confusion, I elaborated.

"That Kill and I aren't into the ladies."

Halo's nose screwed up and he shook his head. "No. As long as you don't care that I am."

I did, but not for the reasons he thought. "Doesn't bother me. In this business, you see everything. Men who like men. Men who like women. Men who like both...I'm just making sure you're cool."

"I'm cool. Doesn't bother me at all."

And because I couldn't fucking help myself, and the liquor—yeah, I'd blame that too—I added, "Good. So you've never looked at a guy before like that? Not even once?"

When Halo shook his head, I thought back to earlier and the way he'd been eyeing me during the first few songs, and the devil that I'd managed to keep at bay most of the night decided to come out and play. "You sure about that?"

"Yeah, I think I'd remember checking out a guy." Halo chuckled, and I shifted in my chair to lean forward and put my arms on the table.

When I had closed the distance between us, I lowered my voice so only he would hear and said, "So you've never looked at a man's mouth? His lips? And thought, what if...?"

Halo's eyes locked on mine, and as we sat there in Li's run-down restaurant, his light eyes darkened. "Have you ever looked at a woman and thought...what if?"

"Yes," I answered immediately. "Fucked her, too. It's the reason I know I prefer cock."

When Halo's eyes widened to the size of saucers, a low laugh escaped my lips.

"Relax, Angel. I'm just screwing with you. Or *not*, in this case." I shifted back to my side and reached into my back pocket for my wallet, and when Halo didn't say anything, I gestured to the table with a tilt of my head. "You done?"

Halo glanced down at his empty basket and nodded. "Oh, yeah."

I pulled several bills free and threw them on the table as Halo reached for his wallet. "I got it tonight."

"No. You don't have to—"

"Don't worry. I don't expect a kiss or anything before you leave."

As I got to my feet, Halo did also, throwing his napkin on the table. "You're a real shit, you know that?"

"So people tell me. It's part of my charm."

As I headed toward the door with Halo following, I was more aware than I had been in years of the eyes on me, and I hadn't been lying when I said some would be speculating over who Halo was. Little did they know they were all looking at the new lead singer of TBD, but they would soon enough.

When we got outside and Halo told me where he lived—on the opposite side of the city to me—it became apparent we wouldn't be sharing a cab ride home. As one pulled up at the curb, I shoved my hands into my pockets and said, "You take it. You've got more stuff you're lugging around. I'll get the next one."

Halo pulled the door open and slid his guitar in the back seat, and after he climbed inside, I reached out to shut the door. The wind chose that moment to howl up the street, and as it caught around my legs, it ruffled that golden hair of Halo's around the stunning face he'd angled my way.

Christ, he was beautiful. His eyes, that hair, and his generous lips as they curved into a half smile.

"Thanks for dinner. Today was fucking amazing."

The comment was innocent enough, but my cock didn't take it that way. My cock was imagining what it would be like to climb in that cab with him and end this the way I really wanted to.

I licked my lips, and when Halo's eyes automatically dropped down to them, I gripped the car door a little harder. The conversation from earlier came back in full force, and before I shut the door, I said, "Hey, Angel?"

"Yeah?"

"Now you can't say you've never looked at another man's mouth and wondered. See you tomorrow." And before Halo could say another word, I shut the door and the cab drove away.

ELEVEN

Halo

"YOU LOOK NERVOUS."

I raised my eyes to Viper's, who sat across from me in the back of the limo that was taking us from the private jet MGA had chartered for us to the venue. It was a week after I'd officially been named a member of TBD, and though rehearsals had gone well, tonight would be the true test.

Nervous? No shit. Excited? Hell yes.

"You've got this," Killian said, bumping his shoulder against mine. "They're gonna love you."

"They'd be insane not to," Jagger added. As he straightened his cuff links, he winked my way. "Just don't fuck it up."

I snorted out a laugh. Easier said than done, right? But if things had gone as well as they had the last week, I didn't have anything to worry about...other than performing my first show with the biggest rock band in the world. No biggie.

As we neared the arena, I could already see the masses of people standing around the entrance, and when they caught sight of the limo as we passed by, the screaming started.

"Oh shit." I leaned forward, my gaze on the fans waving after us until the limo rounded the back of the arena and passed through a security gate.

Okay, maybe now I was nervous.

I didn't have time to dwell on it, though. We were rushed through sound check, through introductions with the radio station that was hosting the charity event, and then to our joint dressing room. I had to admit I was relieved we were all in the same room, because the last thing I needed was to get too into my own head and freak out. It was also a weight off that there would be no meet-and-greets with fans tonight, something MGA had been insistent on until they saw how the show went, which I took to mean this was still a tryout in their eyes. But I'd show them they'd made the right choice. There hadn't been much time to prepare, but I was as ready as I was ever gonna be.

As the others joked and crowded around the catering table, I took my time getting ready. There was no way I could eat now, not with the way my stomach flipped every five seconds as I listened to the crowd file in, their excitement filtering into the room.

I ran through my warm-up as I put on a pair of black jeans and a matching T-shirt, and then I wound my leather bracelet around my wrist. I didn't want to overdo my outfit for tonight, didn't want my first outing to look like I was trying too hard. I'd already have enough attention my way, and I'd rather they focus on the music.

A shot glass of white liquor appeared in front of me, and as I glanced up at the mirror, I saw Viper behind me. Ever since the night we'd gone to dinner, I'd made sure to keep my eyes on his whenever he was around—and *not* on his lips.

"Thought you might need this," he said, and I took the glass and sniffed it.

"Is this...?"

When Viper held up a bottle of Baijui in his other hand, I chuckled. Even after downing half the bottle at Li's, I'd woken up without any kind of hangover, which made it the perfect choice for a preshow drink.

The rest of the guys gathered around, shot glasses in hand, though theirs were varying shades depending on their poison.

Killian held his shot up in my direction. "Tonight's the first night of a new chapter for TBD, one that's gonna be bigger and better than ever. I know I speak for all of us when I say we're fired up as fuck to have you, man, so let's go out there and show everyone how it's done."

Choruses of "hell yeah" rang out, and we threw back our shots just as the crowd began to chant.

God, here we go. We were doing this. *I* was doing this. I took up the rear as the guys filed out of the room, heading up to the wings, where we were outfitted with in-ear monitors.

As I cracked my neck from side to side and stretched out my limbs, trying to get rid of the nervous energy, Viper came to stand beside me. His hair was still damp from his shower and brushed back off his face, though once he started playing, it wouldn't stay that way for long.

"You good?" he asked.

I blew out a breath. "I think so."

"That's not the right answer."

"Then fuck yes I'm good."

Viper's mouth quirked up, and he nodded. "That's better." As the lights went out and the crowd began to scream, he said, "Good luck out there," and then went onto the stage with the rest of the band to take up their spots.

I stood alone in the darkness of the wings, awaiting my cue, and seconds later, Slade kicked off the opening notes of "Dark Light."

Boom. Boom boom.
Boom. Boom boom. ROCK.
Boom. Boom boom.
Boom. Boom boom. ROCK.

The thundering beat shook the arena floor, vibrating through my body and shooting adrenaline into my veins as ten thousand TBD fans began to roar.

I hadn't even hit the stage yet, but already I could feel the intense energy radiating off the crowd, and it was something completely unexpected and like nothing I'd ever experienced before. If I hadn't been confident in rehearsals, then I could've easily panicked, but I had this. Even though it wasn't my original music, I came alive on stage. I always did when I performed, and I would rock the shit out of our set.

All at once, the pounding of the drums ceased—my cue—and even though the arena remained blacked out as I walked out of the wings and hit my mark center stage, the piercing screams filled my ears.

Let's do this.

With my head down, I took a deep breath and grabbed the microphone, and then I began to sing.

This song—a huge hit for TBD—began with vocals alone. Me, the microphone, and the dark, and as my voice echoed around the arena, all I could see were lights from cameras and flashes in the dark, as the crowd vibrated with anticipation. The energy was palpable, as the words left my lips, and when I hit the final note before the band joined in, I swore the thundering in my ears couldn't get any louder—then the lights flashed up.

The drums kicked out the previous rhythm, this time harder and faster, and then Viper and Killian joined in, along with Jagger on the keyboards, and the crowd lost their minds.

Unable to hide my grin at the overwhelming reaction, I ripped the mic off the stand and strode across the stage, my eyes taking in the filled-to-capacity arena. It was huge and terrifying and fucking amazing, and I couldn't believe I was here, playing to this crowd of people, all of whom were screaming and jumping up and down to the beat Slade was pounding out.

It was hard to pinpoint when it happened exactly, but as we launched into the second song, and then the third, I sensed a change in the air. It was slow at first, my eyes catching on a few frowns here and there, people whispering to their friends. I'd been to arena shows before as a fan, and I'd never felt as though the people on stage could actually see me, but let me tell you—I could fucking see. I could see everything, and the disappointment welling in the crowd had me almost dropping to my knees.

My heart rate kicked up a notch, this time from the anxiety overriding the initial adrenaline, and as I made my way back center stage, I caught Viper's eyes. He looked as baffled as I was at the change in reaction, but he mouthed, "Keep going," so that was what I did. I kept singing, doing my best to win over the crowd, even though in their eyes I seemed to be failing miserably. But how? Why?

It was at the end of the third song when I got my answer. The shouts of "We want Trent!" and "Where's Trent?" and "Who the hell are you?" slammed into me, and they didn't let up. I saw people leave. I heard the boos—fucking boos. I'd had my share of rejection in my twenty-three years, but ten thousand people aiming all that hate your way? I wouldn't wish that on an enemy.

But the guys kept playing, and I kept singing, even though I wanted to crawl into a hole and die. I'd known taking over lead vocals for the band wouldn't be easy, but I'd never, and I mean never, imagined such a volatile reaction.

Ninety minutes passed like it'd been ninety days, and as I practically crawled off the stage, beaten down and exhausted, I wondered how everything had gone to shit so fast.

TWELVE

Viper

WHAT THE FUCK WAS THAT?

A goddamn nightmare, that was what. One where you drifted off to sleep and dreamt you were on stage, only to hear thousands of people booing your name. And who could we thank for this little nightmare turned reality shitshow? You got it—Trent fucking Knox.

As Slade somehow managed to get us through to the end of the set, and the lights finally—thank fuck—went down, I tore the strap of my Telecaster over my head and marched off stage, my anger roiling through me like a freight train.

Shit. Shit. *Shit.*

Tonight had been a damn disaster, and not because of anything any of *us* had done. No, it was a disaster because our original lead singer had bailed and left us up shit fucking creek without a paddle.

Christ, it was infuriating. Not only had Trent's abandonment caused us months of monotonous auditions, but now that we had found someone to replace his punk ass, we were getting booed off the motherfucking stage.

Are you kidding me? We'd never been booed out of anywhere, not even when we started.

Fuck. Trent. Knox.

"Viper!" Killian called out behind me, but I wasn't slowing down for anyone. I stormed off the stage, not giving two shits if anyone was following, and made my way back toward the dressing room.

The shouts and jeering calls of disappointed fans still echoed in my head—or who the hell knows, maybe the ones who'd hung around until the end were taking delight in twisting the knife in a little harder, staying behind to make sure we heard just how much they thought we sucked. Either way, as I shoved open the door to the dressing room and it crashed into the wall, I made a beeline for the bottles of liquor and uncapped the top of one, determined to drown them out by getting shit-faced drunk.

The rest of the guys filed in after me, and I could hear Jagger and Killian murmuring to one another, but didn't pay much attention. I was too busy thinking of all the ways I could express just how much I hated the man who'd left, the boy I'd grown up with, the guy I'd stupidly thought would never screw us over as hard as he had.

"Viper? You couldn't have waited back there for us?" Slade said as he shut the door behind them, and it wasn't lost on me how quiet Halo was right then, how withdrawn he looked as he moved to the corner of the room and took up a spot away from the rest of us.

"I'm sorry. I didn't realize I was supposed to fucking wait so we could do the walk of shame together."

"V..." Killian said, but the glare I sent his way stopped him.

There would be no calming me tonight. Hell, as far as I was concerned, the guys should be thanking me for not throwing my microphone stand at the ungrateful crowd. I raised the bottle to my lips, took another swig, and then eyed Halo, who still hadn't said a word.

"That was a disaster." Jagger moved to one of the couches in the room and slumped down into it, his usually put together self looking somewhat defeated as his eyes shifted around the room.

"No shit," Slade agreed, as he ran a hand over his head and gripped the back of his neck. "I've never heard anything like that."

"What, boos so loud they practically made the stage vibrate?" I said as a full-on scowl twisted my lips. "Or maybe you're talking about the way they were all calling out that fucking prick Trent's name so loudly that he probably heard it in whatever hole he crawled into."

"*Viper*," Killian shouted, and I pinned him with a stare that should've cut him at the knees.

"What?"

"You need to calm down."

"No. I need to get drunk." I upended the bottle and took another long, hard pull of the whiskey. "This is all his fuckin' fault, and you know it."

Killian balled his fists at his sides as he ground his teeth together, and when he didn't respond, I turned my attention to the one who hadn't made a peep since we'd left the stage. The one who looked as though he wanted the ground to open up and swallow him whole. And that was another reason I hoped Trent could feel our wrath wherever he was tonight—the total dejection written all over Halo's face.

God only knew what he was thinking right now. He'd already been a ball of nerves before hitting the stage, but after that epic failure he was probably wishing he'd never heard of TBD. Who was I kidding? Right now, I was wishing the same damn thing.

Taking pity on him, I crossed to where Halo stood and thrust the bottle out to him. When his eyes caught on my hand, and then flew up to mine, the confusion, disappointment, and apology in them made me temper my own foul mood for one second as I said, "Now, do you wanna get drunk with me?"

Halo grimaced but reached for the bottle, and just as he was about to bring it to his lips, the door opened up and Brian, our manager, stepped inside. Great, just what we needed.

"Guys..." Brian started, his eyes roaming around the room from Jagger and Slade, then to Killian, and finally, they settled on Halo and me. When he saw the bottle of alcohol in Halo's hand, he slowly shook his head. "That was, um, not your finest hour out there tonight."

Was he fucking serious right now? Talk about stating the obvious. "You ran all the way back here in your shiny Oxfords to tell us that, Brian? Newsflash: we already know. We were up there, remember?"

"V..." Killian said in a warning tone, knowing how close to the surface my nerves and anger were.

"Look," Brian said as he walked farther into the room. Brave of him, all things considered. "I don't want to be the bearer of bad news—"

I snorted. "Then how about you turn around and get the hell out? We don't need you to tell us how the crowd felt out there tonight. I think we got it."

"That's not what I'm here to tell you. Jesus, Viper, how about you shut your mouth for five seconds so I can talk."

"How about you go fuck yourself—"

"Viper," Slade said, pointing his sticks my way. "Dude, we're all fucking bummed right now, but you gotta rein it in. Cool it."

Halo shuffled on his feet, and when I looked in his direction, his eyes pleaded with me to simmer down, to not make it worse than it already was, and something about that look—that silent appeal—banked my fury in a way I didn't think was possible.

"Thank *you*, Slade." Brian's eyes moved to Killian, and he held up his cell. "I just got off the phone with MGA. They had someone here tonight in the crowd, and the reports they got back, not to mention the beating you guys are taking online, has not made for a happy record label."

I scoffed, but before I could say anything, Halo shoved the bottle of alcohol against my arm and shook his head—so I zipped it.

"They're not happy, guys. Actually, they're..." As Brian trailed off, Jagger sat forward on the edge of the couch.

"They're what, Brian? Spit it out."

Brian took in a deep breath, and then let it out. "They want your asses home, pronto. They're cancelling all upcoming gigs, and the final word I got from them was they don't care what you do, or how you do it, but you need to fix shit quick."

My eyes flew to Killian's, and I swear to fuck if Trent had been there, I would've strangled him. "Fix shit? What the hell does that even mean?"

"I don't know." Brian looked to Halo, and I felt something primal claw up inside me, something that made me want to protect the man beside me.

I stepped in front of Halo, blocking him from Brian's line of fire. "Then I guess you better leave us alone so we can pack our shit up and head home. Shouldn't you?"

Brian's eyes narrowed on me, but I didn't care in the slightest. I'd gone head to head with him on numerous occasions, especially over the last few months. But if he was implying Halo was the reason we'd just gotten our balls handed to us on stage, then he was way off track.

Trent was the reason for this colossal mess, and I'd be damned if Halo took any of that on his shoulders.

"Fine. I'm gone," Brian said as he opened the door. "But you guys need to take this seriously. Think about what's at stake here."

"I think we're aware of what's at stake, Brian. It is *our* careers." With a final *fuck you* look in his direction, I turned back to Halo, whose lips crooked at the side as he held his hand out for the whiskey.

I passed it back to him, and Halo said, "Thanks for that."

"What?"

"Standing up for me."

"You deserved it. We rocked the shit out of it tonight. *You* killed it. There was nothing you could've done any fucking better." I cocked my head to the side, my eyes roaming over Halo's face, and I found a part of myself relieved to see the apology from earlier had been replaced with...respect. "It's not your fault they wanted Trent. Just like it's not our fault. So fuck 'em. I'm not going to let them talk shit about you when you're doing everything you can."

As Halo grinned, I made no attempt to hide where I was looking, and if I didn't know better, I would've thought he purposefully licked his lower lip. Then he raised the bottle, took another drink, and said, "I think I just might get drunk tonight. Can I keep this?"

"It's all yours, Angel. Plenty more where that came from." And before I did something stupid, I made myself step away from him and head back to the catering table, where several unopened bottles sat. I planned to take all of them back to the hotel room with me and drink at least half of them before we had to catch our flight tomorrow. Because I hadn't been lying to Halo just to make him feel better—we *had* owned that stage tonight. We'd played better than we had in years. The problem was, we were missing one key element—and fuck Trent Knox for that.

THIRTEEN

Halo

HOURS LATER, I found myself slumped behind a baby grand piano in the empty lounge of our hotel, my head resting against the top of it as my fingers moved of their own accord over the keys.

Numb. In shock. Bewildered. My brain couldn't seem to wrap itself around what had happened tonight, and as I ran through the show again and again, I tried to pinpoint where I'd gone wrong. But my voice had been strong, the energy had been high...it was a flawless set. Which meant the problem had been...me.

The problem is me. I wasn't Trent, and tonight proved that the fans of TBD weren't going to be accepting of whoever took his place. I'd stupidly assumed that because the rest of the guys were still there, the lead singer could be interchangeable. It wasn't like the music had been revamped; I'd matched Trent note for note.

Wrong. Dead wrong.

The chorus of boos echoed in my head, and I squeezed my eyes shut like it would force out the sound. No such luck. I'd probably hear the chants and see the disappointment on the faces of those in the crowd for the rest of my life.

"Excuse me, sir?" I lifted my head, and the bartender gave me a hesitant smile. "I'm about to close things down. Can I get you anything before I go?"

I looked at the almost-empty bottle of alcohol I'd taken from the venue—the one Viper had given me—and shook my head.

"Okay. Stay as long as you'd like." She set a bottle of water on the lip of the piano and then backed away, giving me my space.

She hadn't been the only one. I hadn't seen the others since we'd arrived at the hotel, though I had a feeling they weren't much better off than me. After Viper's epic throw-down backstage, it'd been a surprisingly quiet ride to the hotel, everyone caught up in their own misery.

Viper. He'd shocked the hell out of me tonight. Of anyone, I'd have pinpointed him as the last person to come to my defense, but he'd ended up being the only one.

A rush of warmth filled my chest as I thought about the way Viper had told our manager to fuck off when Brian had insinuated they needed to take care of the problem—meaning me. It was still a strong possibility they'd tell me to get lost, and maybe it would be the smart thing to do. Drop me, beg Trent back, bam—shit fixed. But with the way Viper hated Trent, I doubted it'd be a smart idea to get the two of them back in the same room, so... what was the solution?

"There was nothing you could've done any fucking better."

Viper wasn't the kind of guy to throw out praise, but he'd done that tonight, hadn't he? Vouched for me like he thought I added something to TBD, not like I was a second-rate imitation of who everyone had wanted to see. And if Viper, the toughest critic in the band, thought I'd done well, then it had to be true.

At least, that was what I was telling myself.

Sitting up, I ran a hand over my face and then positioned my fingers over the keys. Sitting at the piano or with a guitar in my lap always felt like coming home, and even after the train wreck of the last few hours, I couldn't stop the itch in my fingers from wanting to play. I didn't have to think while I played; I just had to feel.

I poured my emotions out through music the way I always had, letting it soothe the ache and put me back together again. It was while I was mindlessly playing that I stumbled over a melody that had me pausing and going back to play it again.

My fingers moved over the keys, the rhythm flowing out my fingertips and onto the instrument in front of me as my foot tapped down on the pedal below. I hummed along then paused, repeating the riff.

Sometimes I played to release the frustration or disappointment of a rough day. Sometimes it was just me creating a bunch of nothing, notes I threw together that didn't make any sense. Other times...it was magic.

As I played the riff over and over again, I realized this was one of those times.

It was clear as day the way the song would start, where the bass and guitar would come in...then the drums. I could hear Jagger on the synthesizer, rounding out what would be a slower, sort of alternative rock track. It wasn't anything like what TBD played, but maybe that was exactly what I needed. To get their music out of my head and create something all mine. Something no one else would hear. Something no one else could reject. Something all mine.

I could deal with the slap of reality tomorrow.

FOURTEEN

Viper

BAM.

THE DOOR to Killian's presidential suite slammed shut behind me as we all filed in after one another. Well, all of us except Halo, who'd bowed out and said he needed to go and chill, and with the way he'd been clutching that bottle of liquor I'd given him back in the dressing room, I had a feeling I knew exactly how he planned to accomplish that.

Tonight's disastrous event hovered over us like a dark cloud as the four of us milled into the living area of the opulent suite and flopped down onto the couches. With mouths shut, eyes looking anywhere but at each other, we tried to come to grips with the fact that we'd just been handed our asses on stage for the first time ever, and the disbelief began to set in.

Was this the end of TBD? Could a lead singer or, more accurately, a change in the lead singer really make or break us when we were still at the top of the charts? I didn't think that was actually possible, but after tonight it was becoming increasingly obvious that Trent had held more clout than I wanted to give him credit for.

Fuck.

"So..." Killian glanced over to the recliner I'd planted my ass in and arched an eyebrow. "You want to talk about what happened tonight?"

"No." Hey, at least I was honest.

"V, come on. We can't ignore it."

"I don't want to ignore it. I just don't want to sit in a fucking circle right now and hold hands while we all cry about it. That okay with you?"

Killian took in a breath, trying for patience, but I could see the telltale sign it was wearing thin. It was the tic in his jaw. I'd pissed him off enough over the years to know when he was getting ready to blow, and right now Killian was about two comments away from telling me to get the hell out of his face.

But that was too damn bad. Nothing was going to rein in my temper tonight. I'd kept a lid on it for Halo's sake as we made the trip back to the hotel, and I'd thought that maybe the alcohol would help. But even after downing half a bottle of whiskey and an entire pack of cigarettes, I felt the need to…punch something.

Killian ran a hand back through his hair. "Great attitude, Viper. You're not making this any easier, you know."

I didn't say anything to that, because really, what was there to say? I felt like shit, and no matter what Killian said to me, that wasn't about to change. Nope, I was quite happy wallowing in my misery, and if Killian wanted us all in a room to "discuss" things, then I guess they were gonna get dragged down into it with me.

"I don't know, Kill." Slade got to his feet and walked to the fully stocked bar in the corner of the room. "I'm kinda with Viper. I just want to get friendly with a bottle of booze and deal with this shit tomorrow."

"This shit?" Killian shook his head. "This shit is our livelihood, Slade. You think it's gonna look any better tomorrow when your head's pounding because you swallowed half a minibar?"

"Better than pounding because ten thousand people booed us off the fuckin' stage."

Killian's head whipped in my direction. "You. Shut the hell up."

Jagger propped one of his ankles up on his knees, his eyes

shifting between the three of us. "Maybe Kill has a point. I mean, yeah, tonight was shit. Like, total, utter shit. But we can't just get plastered and pretend it never happened."

"I can," Slade said, then tossed back a tumbler of vodka.

Jagger smirked as Killian ran a hand over his weary face, and I reached for the half-empty bottle I'd shoved down the side of the couch.

"Look," Killian said, "I don't want to sit around and talk about our feelings and shit. I think it's pretty obvious we all feel like hell. But just imagine how Halo has to be feeling right now. This is a first for us, after years of successful gigs, and no one likes being kicked in the balls. But this was his first experience *ever*. We need to pull our shit together so he doesn't walk."

Slade shrugged. "I mean, that'd suck, yeah, but if he walks, we could always find someone else."

"Someone else? Have you forgotten how long it took us to find Halo? And he was by far our best shot." Killian gripped the back of his neck. "That guy has one of the best voices I've ever heard, and if we don't get our heads out of our asses, he's gonna peace out on us before we can blink."

"My head isn't up anyone's ass," I muttered. "And with what happened tonight, I'm not going to be *getting* any ass anytime soon. How's your bed looking tonight, Kill? I don't see anyone waiting outside for you like they usually do."

"Fuck you."

"No, thanks. I don't dip my dick where I work." As soon as the words left my mouth, I wanted to take them back, and if Killian had been half the asshole I was, he would've taken the clear shot he had—but Killian didn't work like that.

"Watch yourself," Killian said in a tone I knew well. It was the warning he gave before he was done playing the peacemaker. The signal that you were a step away from him not giving a shit one way or another about how you were feeling. And if you pushed him there, well, the only way to get back was to grovel like a motherfucker.

Me, I didn't like to grovel. So I backed up a step.

"I don't know, Kill." Jagger ran a hand over his chin. "Maybe it would be better if he did walk. Then we could find someone who looks a little more like Trent? Or who's the same age? Maybe Halo is too...different."

The words made something inside my gut twist and revolt. It felt wrong to be talking about Halo like this when he wasn't there to defend himself, but I was hardly the one to be making any decisions tonight, not when I was three sheets to the wind. So instead of saying anything, I twisted the cap off the bottle of alcohol and tossed it on the ground.

"I'm not trying to be an asshole here," Jagger said. "But just because Halo is talented doesn't mean shit—obviously. He's not what our fans want. They want Trent."

And that was it right fucking there, wasn't it?

The fans wanted Trent.

The record company wanted Trent.

Bastard wouldn't get the fuck out of our way, even though he'd walked out.

"Well, that's too damn bad," Killian said. "Trent is gone. And he ain't coming back. We all have to deal with it, or this, this band we all love, we might as well kiss it the fuck goodbye."

I didn't want to acknowledge how the truth of Killian's words chafed my ego. After all, it had been the three of us—Killian, Trent, and me—who'd started TBD over a decade ago, and the fact that the rest of us couldn't sustain the band without Trent made me want to hurl the bottle in my hand across the room instead of finishing it off.

"Then what's the solution?" Slade asked as he dropped into the couch beside Jagger. "Where do we go from here?"

With his hands pulling at his dark hair, Killian got to his feet and paced the floor. All the rest of us could do was watch, because what was the answer here? If there was no Trent, there was no TBD. And there was no way in hell I was giving up what we'd worked so hard for because that asshole had walked.

With a sigh, Killian dropped his hands. "We pivot."

"We what?" Jagger said.

"We pivot. Change directions. Start over."

"Start over?" Slade's voice went high. "We've got half an album of new songs recorded—"

"That MGA's already trashed and burned by now," Killian finished. "We can't use 'em. We can't write songs for someone who's no longer here."

Shit. Was he kidding? That meant months of work gone.

"I think it's time we faced the inevitable." Killian shrugged. "We've got to bury TBD—"

"What? We're not fucking quitting—" I started, but Killian put his hand up.

"And rise again."

Rise again? And here I thought I was the one who'd had too much to drink. What the hell did that even mean?

"Like a zombie?" Slade said.

"Nah, man, like Jesus." Jagger nodded along. "Yeah."

I glanced between them, my lip curled up. "Why the fuck are you two talking about zombies and Jesus?"

"We're talking about rising from the ashes," Jagger said. "TBD's dead. Tonight made that pretty damn clear. We've got to start over."

"Dead?" I shook my head. "We're not dead. We just need to—"

"Change," Killian said firmly. "No one is gonna be able to take Trent's place; Halo was our best shot. So something's gotta change."

"Like what?"

"I don't know." Killian's eyes swept over the three of us. "I need time to think about it more, but this...this makes sense."

Did it? I wasn't so sure about that. Start over? Change? Throw away ten years of what we'd built? This was all becoming way too much for my brain to handle.

"I need to get outta here." Shoving up to my feet, I kept a tight grip on my bottle, as I went to walk past Killian to the door.

"Viper. We have to at least try. And if we fail, we fail. We move on."

I ran a hand through my hair, every fiber in my body resistant toward this idea, even though it was the only thing we really could do at this stage, or MGA would drop our asses.

"Are you with us?" Killian asked. The "us" didn't escape my attention, because he already knew the other guys' decisions without having to ask.

"Don't have much of a choice, do I?" I said, turning around to face him.

"You always have a choice."

"What, quit?" With a snort, I glanced at Jagger and Slade, who were watching us with caution. They really thought I'd walk? Because of this? "I'm not a fucking quitter. But I'm not promising anything, either. Can I go now?" I said, then raised the bottle between us. "I'd really like to finish this in private."

Killian nodded, and when I pulled open the door, he held it there and turned back to Slade and Jagger. "How 'bout you two get the hell out too? I'm done for the night, and neither of you are going to be able to help me forget myself for a few hours."

Knowing Killian could have one, two—hell, five—men up at his hotel suite within thirty minutes, despite what I'd said earlier, I threw a wave in his direction and meandered off down the hall.

I bypassed the door to my suite, not feeling like going in there and sitting in a silent room by myself, and instead took the elevator down to the lobby bar. I knew it was late, but it was Friday night—maybe there'd be stragglers and I could round up another drink.

I made my way to the doors of the bar, and when I noticed them shut, I was about to chalk it up to the perfect end to my shit-tastic day. But as I went to turn away, the faint sound of a piano caught my attention and had my feet rounding back so I could move closer. With the bottle in one hand down by my leg, I reached out with my other to see if the door was unlocked, and when the door pulled back, I stepped inside.

The bar was empty. There were no staff, no customers, completely and utterly empty. But the further I walked inside, the louder the music became, until I rounded a large pillar and my feet came to an abrupt halt.

Sitting at the baby grand piano with his head bent down over the keys was Halo. The softly glowing security lights were the only ones on in the bar right then, but I'd know those blond curls anywhere.

His almost-finished bottle of alcohol from earlier sat on the top of the piano, as his fingers flew across the keys, and he seemed oblivious to the rest of the world as he swayed in time to the music.

My feet moved of their own accord then, drawing me closer. The music he was playing was unlike anything I'd heard before. It was inspired and passionate, and, not wanting to interrupt this moment he was having, I stood as still as I possibly could, completely and utterly blown away by the sheer talent pouring out of Halo.

While we'd all been upstairs licking our wounds and drinking ourselves into a state of numbness, Halo had been down here losing himself in the one thing that should've brought all of us solace—his music.

Feeling as though I were intruding on something that was highly personal, I slowly backed out of the bar area to the door, my eyes not leaving Halo as he continued to play. He was mesmerizing, and I couldn't help but think that if the rest of the world would give him a chance, if they got to see him like this, to hear him *play* like this, there'd be no way they'd ever boo him off a damn stage again.

FIFTEEN

Halo

AFTER HAVING A few days to cool off, Killian called for a band meeting at his place.

I knew what that meant—I was out.

It wasn't something they'd want to do over the phone, so inviting me over, getting us all together so they could break it to me that I was no longer needed, was the most logical way. And even though my head knew what was coming, most of me stayed firmly in denial.

I took a spot on one of the leather couches in Killian's great room, where the rest of the band had gathered. The furniture had been moved into a semicircle so we could all face each other.

Great. Bring on the firing.

Killian looked around the room, nodding, and then rubbed his hands together. "Since we're all here, we can get started."

Yes, please make it quick and as painless as possible, I thought, as I shifted on the couch.

"We can all agree that what happened last weekend was a total shitfest," Killian said. Curses rang out, everyone nodding in agreement. "So the question is now, what the hell do we do about it?"

Here it was. I braced myself for impact.

"It's fairly obvious that Halo isn't the right frontman for TBD—"

My stomach dropped.

"But it's also apparent that unless Trent comes running through that door right now, no one's going to be who the fans want."

"Not like we'd take his fucking ass back anyway," Viper muttered, as the others nodded.

"Before we discuss options, I need to know if we're all in this. Whatever direction we go, we go together." Killian looked around the room, and when his eyes landed on me, he said, "So? You in this with us?"

My brows knitted together as I tried to understand what he was asking me. "So…hold up. You're not firing me?"

A hint of a smile quirked Killian's lips. "Hell no."

"But…" Had they lost their minds? Did they want a repeat of last week's show? Maybe that was it. They were masochists. "I don't understand."

"You're not goin' anywhere, Angel," Viper said, pinning me with a fierce look.

"That's right." Killian sat on the couch beside me. "The problem's not you, Halo. It's not us, either. But the combination? With the songs Trent's known for? It's not sitting well with the fans. So that means we need a new direction. A new sound, new everything."

"As long as it's not some country shit, I'm down," Slade said, eliciting a groan from Viper.

Killian smirked. "I think we can all agree on that. But we do need to find a new sound that fits all of us, so that's why I called us here today."

As the room plunged into silence, I watched as the other guys avoided Killian's gaze, looking everywhere but in his direction.

I was still wondering how the hell I wasn't already out the door.

"Anyone? Ideas?" Killian said, as the silence dragged on. After a few minutes, he began to whistle the *Jeopardy* theme song. "Seriously, nothin'? What'd you guys do the past few days?"

"Nicole," Jagger said.

"Drank a couple bottles of tequila and Netflixed five seasons of *The Great British Baking Show*." When we all jerked our heads in Slade's direction, he frowned. "What?"

"And I thought I was the gay one," Killian said, rolling his eyes.

"All right, so no one's given it any thought. Good start, guys. MGA will be so impressed."

"Fuck those guys," Viper muttered.

"*Those guys* pay our bills," Killian pointed out. "Without a record company, we're not getting very far, so maybe throw out a few ideas, yeah?"

Viper's mouth snapped shut, and we all resumed the quiet game.

Half an hour passed. An hour. Two hours later, and we were all still sitting around with nothing to show for it. I sure as hell wasn't about to throw out an idea first, especially since I still felt like the reason we were in this mess in the first place.

"All right. Let's take a break, grab a drink, smoke, whatever." Killian stretched his legs and then got to his feet. He and Slade headed downstairs while Jagger stepped out to make a call, leaving me and Viper alone in the vast space.

"I don't know about you, but I could do with some food." Viper made his way into the kitchen and grabbed a couple of bags of potato chips and a package of cookies out of the pantry, then set them on the counter.

"You got barbecue?" I asked.

Viper held up an unopened bag of chips. "Come and get it."

I rounded the island, and when he handed me the bag, I popped it open. As I tossed a handful of chips into my mouth, Viper said, "You didn't really think I'd let you leave, did you?"

I went still at the seductive edge in Viper's voice. Those words didn't sound at all innocent coming out of that lethal mouth, and as I forced my jaw to keep chewing, I took a good look at him.

Those penetrating eyes looked right back. Viper hadn't shaved in a few days, which others would probably say only added to his appeal, and as he finished off one of the chocolate chip cookies, some of the chocolate got left behind on his thumb. I was about to point it out, when Viper lifted his hand, his thumb disappearing between his lips as he licked it clean.

I swallowed and looked away. "Yeah, well, it's not like you get the only vote."

"You know better than that."

Did I? Yeah, I guess I did. The day I auditioned, I'd thought that my fate was in Viper's hands. Had he given a thumbs-down, I never would've been invited back, even if the others voted in my favor. Why that was the way, I didn't know, but it also said a lot about how I was still here.

"I saw you," Viper said, stepping toward me, his head cocked to the side so a few strands of hair fell against his cheek. "In Savannah. Playing in the lounge after hours."

"You did?" I thought I'd been alone. I certainly would've remembered Viper being there, even with as drunk as I'd been.

"I've never seen anyone play with as much passion as you do. You're fucking talented, Angel. Why didn't you tell us?"

"I'm—" My words got stuck in my throat, and I shook my head. "I was just drunk."

"If that's what you sound like under the influence, I'm dying to see what you can do without any interference. You need to show the guys."

"Show them the song? You liked it?"

"Angel." Viper's voice dropped down low. "I couldn't take my eyes off you."

There it was again. The provocative tone I never heard him use with the others, the one that slid over my skin like silk.

"You've got a few crumbs..." Viper reached for my face, his thumb—the same one he'd sucked the chocolate off a few minutes ago—brushing across the edge of my mouth, and all of a sudden he was inches away from me, close, too close—

I jerked away, turning my back to him so I could get some air. My face burned like I'd stepped too close to the fire and had moved away just in time. For fuck's sake, Viper had barely touched me, and my chest heaved like I'd run a marathon. *Get it together. It's not like he was trying to kiss you or take your clothes off.*

That may be true, but I was getting some seriously confusing signals here. Or was I? The guy flirted with everything that moved, so was this just the way it was with him, or was he hitting on me? I'd made it clear from day one that I was straight, but maybe I needed to remind him of that fact again?

I gripped my hair as I exhaled and turned back to face him. "Look, I appreciate your support. Really, I do. But if I'm going to be a part of this band, I feel like I need to make it clear that nothing's gonna happen here."

He didn't react. "Here?"

"Yeah. Between me and you."

Viper's lips quirked up at the sides, and something about his expression made my palms sweat.

"Okay."

"Okay," I repeated back to him like a moron, and then, just in case he didn't get it the first time, I added, "I'm straight."

Viper chuckled and nodded. "I know. That doesn't change the fact that what you played kicked ass. The guys'll like it."

Shit. Okay, maybe I'd read his signals wrong. "Uh, I don't know." I wasn't so sure about opening up that much here, in front of everyone. I wasn't sure I wanted to be that vulnerable.

Viper stepped around me, and as he headed back across the living space, he called over his shoulder, "There's a piano in the rehearsal room. You need to go and show them."

Just as his words trailed off, Killian pushed through the front door and looked in my direction.

"Show us what?" he asked, as he and the others headed back inside.

"Nothin'," I said quickly.

Viper gave me a pointed look. "Didn't sound like nothin' to me the first time I heard it."

Jesus Christ, Viper, shut up.

"I wanna hear it," Jagger said.

Slade nodded. "Me too."

And just like that, I was outnumbered.

"Well..." I chewed my lower lip as I walked around the island. "I was just playing around with something the other night."

"And you're only mentioning that now?" Killian said, as we headed into the rehearsal space.

"I didn't think it was your thing."

"Our thing?" Killian grinned. "Well, we're lookin' for a new thing now, so go for it."

My eyes darted around at the rest of the guys staring at me until they finally landed on Viper, who nodded toward the piano.

Okay. I guess I was doing this.

I took a seat behind the baby grand, and Viper backed away, giving me space. Thinking back to the melody, I exhaled and placed my fingers on the keys.

SIXTEEN

Viper

ALL RIGHT, ANGEL. Show 'em what you got.

Blowing out a breath, Halo laid his fingers atop the keys, and after several beats, he began to play the repeating piano riff I'd heard that night in the hotel lounge. His shoulders visibly relaxed as he went along, as though he'd managed to block us all out and only the music mattered.

Watching Halo was like poetry in motion. His hands glided over the keys with ease, his whole body following along where his fingers guided. I couldn't tell you how long it lasted, how long he played, but all too soon it was over, and as Halo lowered his hands from the keys, his eyes lifted to where the four of us stood a few feet away, staring at him with blank expressions—well, except for me. I had a smug-ass smile on my face, because fuck if he didn't sound as brilliant behind that piano today as he had the first time I'd heard him.

The silence in the room as he sat there looking at us was close to deafening, and I couldn't get a read on what the rest of the guys were thinking. Did they like it as much as I did? Did they think I'd lost my mind making Halo show them?

Whatever. It was badass, and surely they would realize that, once they wrapped their heads around just how different it was from our usual sound. I mean, that was what Killian had said he wanted. *Right?*

When the guys continued to stand there like shags on a rock, Halo stood and walked to where Killian's bass sat cradled in its stand. He gestured to it. "I can show you more? If you like?"

Killian blinked a couple of times, as though trying to understand what Halo was asking him, and I almost laughed. He was completely gobsmacked. And I could tell he was feeling the same way I had the first time I'd heard Halo play—blown the fuck away.

Killian nodded. "I didn't know you played."

"Yep," Halo said, his lips curling up at the edge now, as he picked up the instrument. He was beginning to enjoy this, showing us what he could do, and it was becoming more and more apparent there was a lot we didn't know about him. "Okay, so obviously this is all a little different from what you guys are used to—"

"Nothing wrong with that," I interjected. "Right, Kill? What was that about the damn zombies rising?"

"Right." Killian rubbed his chin. "Yeah, totally, we want a change."

Taking that as permission to continue, Halo ran his fingers up the neck of the bass until they were in place. Then he stroked his thumb down the strings, getting a feel for Killian's bass, before he shut his eyes and began to play. As he plucked away at the strings, Halo lost himself in the cadence of it, letting the tune build inside him, the same way he had on the piano.

When Halo looked up to see everyone staring at him slack-jawed, he knew he had our attention. No one was interrupting. No one was making obnoxious comments. We were all watching him with laser focus.

"Killian, you'd kill this," Halo said, as he continued to play and made his way to where Jagger's keyboards were set up, moving in behind them. He stopped when he reached them, knowing better than to touch another man's pride and joy without permission. Halo looked in Jagger's direction, and Jagger knew what he was asking without him saying a word.

Jagger nodded, and Halo let go of the bass and laid his fingers on the keyboard. As if the tune had continued to run through his head as he moved from one instrument to the next, Halo's fingers flew over the keys in a way most would find difficult to mimic after one listen through. But Jagger wasn't just anyone. That guy was pure talent behind any kind of keyboard, and when Halo and the rest of us looked at him, Jagger was grinning like a fucking loon.

"Dude." Jagger looked to Slade, Killian, and then me. "Is this guy for real? That's...that's fuckin' genius."

Halo looked at Killian, who nodded. But when he opened his mouth to speak, nothing came out—seemed I wasn't the only one who was impressed.

Slade twirled his drumsticks through his fingers as he walked in Halo's direction, then he gestured to his drum kit and said, "I suppose you're gonna tell us you can play those too, huh?"

I could hear the challenge in Slade's voice, and knew Halo would be able to see it in his eyes, and while most would be intimidated, it appeared Halo had decided it was time to stop holding back.

Halo held a hand out to Slade and gestured for his sticks. Slade snorted but gave them over, then looked at Killian. "Did you know you'd hired a fucking maestro?"

Halo gave Killian's guitar back to him, and as he took it from him, Killian slowly shook his head. "No. No, I did not."

Halo's eyes found mine, and if I'd thought he was hot when he was nothing more than the new lead singer, then watching him command every instrument in this place like he was born with it in his hand was one of the sexiest damn things I'd seen in my life. Add in the way he was looking at me with that crooked grin and excitement in his eyes, and I was going to have to excuse myself to hide the hard-on I was finding really fucking difficult to control.

Halo sat behind Slade's drum kit next and stretched his legs out, and with our full attention on him, he began to play, and soon enough the beat flowed out of him as naturally as it had on the other instruments, and someone cursed.

Halo looked up, his light eyes seeking me out, and when he caught me watching his movements, he looked as though my attention pleased him, something that was in direct contrast to his comments earlier.

Fuck. That look was all kinds of trouble, because Halo was looking for my approval. I didn't think he realized he was doing it. But as I moved closer, until I was standing only feet from him, a flush crept up his neck that made my dick really happy. So happy that if Halo dropped his eyes down to my jeans right then, he'd realize just how much I *approved.*

When Halo finished and stood up, Slade, Jagger, and Killian began to whistle and slow-clap, before they all looked in my direction.

Right. Three down. One to go.

Halo wiped the sweat from his brow with his sleeve, shrugged out of his jacket, then tossed it on a chair as he walked over to me, and as he drew near, all I could think about was how salty his skin would taste right now.

"Guess that leaves me," I said.

"Yep. May I?"

I glanced down to my guitar in its stand, and then back to Halo. "I don't know. No one touches my guitar."

Halo nodded. But then I smirked, reached for my Telecaster, and held it out to him. "But you seem pretty good with your hands. Just treat him gentle, yeah?"

With careful hands, Halo took it from me and strapped it over his neck, and then he took a deep breath, closed his eyes, and let his fingers fly.

As I stood there only inches away from him, I almost forgot the rest of the guys were in the room. Halo, running his fingers over the strings of my baby, was the hottest fucking thing imaginable. The way his body was moving against the back of it, his foot tapping along to the tune in his head, made it damn clear that by the end of this session I was gonna have to call someone up to get rid of this sexual tension clawing at me.

It'd been a long time since my dick had decided to become obsessed with a straight guy, but there was no denying it was interested now. The angel had ignited a fire I was finding really difficult to extinguish, and even though my brain knew he was straight, my cock didn't much care.

As Halo was finishing up, he opened his eyes and startled at whatever it was he saw in mine. His fingers stuttered over the strings momentarily, and then he caught himself and cleared his throat. "And then, uh...you'd do what you do best."

"And what is it you think I do *best*, Angel?" I said it in a way that made it clear I wasn't just referring to music.

"You'd slay everyone with a killer solo." Halo lifted the strap over his head and held the guitar out toward me.

"Oh? Not going to show me how it's done?"

"I'm sure you can handle it."

As I took the guitar, my hand brushed slightly against his, and before Halo let go, I lowered my voice so only he could hear my words. "Maybe I like watching you."

Halo's mouth opened, and then shut, and then he let go of my guitar and took a step back, and I was careful to hold the instrument strategically over the front of me.

"Well, hot damn," Jagger said, coming over and slinging his arm around Halo's shoulders. "That was insane."

"Hell yeah it was," Slade said, a grin stretching across his face.

I looked to Killian, who was smiling at Halo like he was the second coming of Christ, and if he kept this shit up, he just might be. "That was amazing. V, you heard this last week and are just telling us now?"

I shrugged. This wasn't my moment—it was Halo's.

"Brilliant. I can definitely see us working with this," Killian said. "I don't know about all of you, but I think we need to go out and celebrate. That's the best thing I've heard in days, and it's making me all kinds of excited."

"Settle down," Slade said, laughing. "Halo doesn't bat for your team. Right? You like the ladies like me and Jagger here."

Halo chuckled as he looked around the room, his eyes landing on me, as he said, "Right."

Jagger clapped him on the back. "That's okay, I guess. But make sure you don't double-dip any of our women, you feel me? It's kind of a rule around here. We don't want no woman who's had all the bees in her honey. It makes for a sticky situation."

"Jesus, Jagger." My dick instantly lost any kind of interest it'd had a minute ago, and as I put my guitar down, Killian said, "Why don't we all hit Easy Street tonight? To celebrate the fact we hired a fucking genius."

As all the guys agreed and started talking about how kickass Halo had just been, my eyes wandered back to the man of the moment, who was laughing along with them. But as though he could feel my stare from across the room, Halo's eyes drifted back to mine, and I inclined my head ever so slightly and reminded myself: *straight*. I couldn't help but think hitting up a bar tonight was an amazing idea. If only to find someone to help me fuck a certain angel out of my head.

SEVENTEEN

Halo

THAT NIGHT, WE commandeered a roped-off VIP section at a loud, packed bar called Easy Street, where rock hits from the seventies to the present day blared above the chatter. I couldn't remember the last time I'd had a night out with the guys, though I'd never been on the receiving end of the kind of attention we'd gotten just from walking in the door. It was like the disastrous show from last weekend never happened with the way everyone showered Killian, Slade, and Jagger with praise and everything their hearts desired. Best seat in the house? Check. Bottles of free alcohol? Check. Gorgeous men and women to entertain us? Check.

And though no one knew who I was, I hadn't been left out of the action. In fact, the only one who had was Viper, and that was because he hadn't shown up yet.

"Halo." Killian's arm went around the waist of the man he'd been dancing with—or grinding with, was more like it—and moved him to the side as he lifted up his empty glass. "Need a refill?"

I glanced down at my tumbler, only melted ice remaining, and excused myself from the three women who'd cornered me from all sides as soon as I'd sat down. Killian took my glass, chucked the contents off to the side, and then scooped in fresh ice and a heavy pour of vodka. As he handed my glass back, he lifted his chin to the women on the couch.

"Looks like you've got your pick. Will it be the Asian femme fatale, black beauty, or prom queen?" he asked.

I squeezed a lime over my drink and shrugged. "I'm not sure."

"Oh? If you need more choices, we can—"

"No, no, no. They're great." In truth, I'd been hoping to shoot the shit with the guys tonight, but they'd all taken up with others. Jagger had brought "his current lady love," according to Killian, and Slade was with a few women who had so many piercings that I'd given them a wide berth so I wouldn't get caught on them.

Killian clapped me on the shoulder. "Great, huh? Well, my man, no need to choose, then." As he gave me a sly wink, a wild burst of screams had us both jerking in the direction of the entrance. A mass of people surrounded someone, and as they attempted to move through the crowd, that someone's face came into view.

"About time he showed up," Killian said, shaking his head as Viper bumped fists, posed for selfies—scowling, not smiling, naturally—and signed exposed breasts that I knew he had no interest in whatsoever, though he definitely put on a good show of enjoying it.

Something about him looked different tonight. I tried to put my finger on what it was when Viper looked up, his eyes catching mine. There—that was the first thing. His eyes looked darker than usual, like they were rimmed in black. It gave off a provocative vibe that no one around him could seem to resist. He didn't look bothered in the least, and when a handful of security guards appeared out of nowhere to usher him through, he made sure to grab the tie of one of the men vying for his attention, bringing him along.

As they headed toward us, my eyes narrowed on the guy Viper had chosen. Who the hell wore a tie to a bar? Some stuffy accountant or whatever? That wasn't at all the kind of person I'd thought Viper would be attracted to.

"So good of you to make an appearance," Killian drawled as one of the security guards opened the rope for Viper and his...friend to step inside the VIP.

Dressed head to toe in black, Viper had left half of the buttons on his shirt undone, showcasing the tanned, well-defined chest usually hidden, and several thin silver chains of varying length hung around his neck.

Dangerous. That was the word that came to mind when Viper walked in and sucked all the air from the room.

"What'd I miss?" Viper said, his gaze sweeping around the space, and when it landed on the women behind me, he raised a brow. "Having fun, Angel?"

"You know it." I swallowed back some of the vodka, my head beginning to buzz slightly.

"Good. That's what tonight's for." He leaned in to my ear. "Some 'lose your mind and your pants,' *sexy* fun."

For half a second, I thought he was going to make a move. He was close enough. But as soon as the thought entered my mind, Viper moved away, turning his back on me completely as he rejoined his *friend*.

With Killian and the others preoccupied with their distractions for the night, I headed back to the couch, somewhat resigned to the way the night was going.

"There you are, gorgeous," the blonde, the one Killian had dubbed "prom queen," said, fingering the opening of my shirt when I sat down. Her tight, short dress left little to the imagination as she leaned in to give me a better view. "So tell us. How'd you hook up with these guys?"

"Yeah, what are you, like, *in* the band now?" one of the others said in my ear behind me as she scooted in close.

I took another sip of my drink. "Yeah, you could say that."

Black beauty scrunched up her nose. "You're not part of the *crew*, are you?"

"He's too sexy for that," prom queen said. "Aren't you, baby?"

Ugh, I hated the term *baby*, even from someone I was a lot more familiar with.

Jagger took the opportunity to stick his head in. "Ladies, meet our new lead singer."

All three of them gasped, clutching my arms, my legs.

"I just knew you'd be good with your mouth."

"You're the new Trent? Oh my God."

"You're even sexier than he was."

As Jagger backed away, he mouthed, "You're welcome," but my gut twisted. Sure, they'd been interested when they thought I was a TBD tagalong, but now? One of them had already unbuttoned my jeans and another was practically riding my thigh.

This should've been fucking heaven. Three beautiful women, a private area away from the crowd so we could do as we pleased. But…it all felt wrong. And in the back of my mind, all I could think was that everyone here in the VIP were nothing but groupies, hoping to get a few hours alone with any one of us. Was this what the guys went through every time they went out? Was this what was expected of me?

Goddammit, I wasn't drunk enough for this, and my glass was empty again.

I leaned to the side to get Killian's attention, but to my surprise, the VIP was empty. Out on the dance floor with security guards in tow were all the guys, except for—

"Need another drink there, Angel?"

Viper.

As he waited for me to answer, he set up a line of shot glasses and poured tequila over the top of them. He handed two to the stuffy tie guy beside him and then held one out to me. I took it gratefully as he refilled my glass.

"Why does he call you Angel?" The femme fatale giggled. "Is that your name?"

"His name's Halo," Viper snapped, handing me the vodka. "That's all you need to know."

"Mmm, Halo. That's sexy." Prom queen leaned in and sucked my lobe into her mouth, and I flinched but didn't push her away.

"You good?" Viper asked.

Was I? Suddenly this was the last place I wanted to be, but that was ridiculous. *Three hot women, Halo. Don't be a fucking dumbass.*

"Sure," I said, settling back against the couch as the girls crowded around again. Viper nodded and headed back to tie guy on the couch opposite me. After taking another shot, Viper wound his hand around the guy's tie and jerked him forward, taking his lips in a rough kiss.

Shit, I guess the time for talking is over, I thought, as one of the girls' hands inched closer to my zipper. *Relax and enjoy it. Viper's obviously enjoying it.*

He'd moved onto the couch, his legs spread wide, still tugging on that stupid tie. What'd he see in that guy?

The answer to that was simple. He was a somewhat attractive, eager, and willing male body. It didn't matter that Viper probably didn't know the guy's name, and if he did, wouldn't remember it tomorrow. Tonight was about pure physical pleasure—that much I was painfully aware of.

I tried to turn my attention back to the girls, but I kept catching glimpses out of the corner of my eye of what was happening only a few feet away.

Downing the rest of my vodka, all I could think was: *Please God, let me get drunk off my ass tonight.*

EIGHTEEN

Viper

___

FUCK. YES. THIS *is exactly what I need*, I thought, as Brett—*I think his name's Brett*—parted his lips and I slid my tongue deep inside his mouth. With the strong taste of tequila on his lips, he was the exact poison I needed to get my mind off the man who was sitting a few feet away from me, surrounded by ready, willing, and likely wet pussy.

Halo.

From the second I'd walked into the bar tonight, my eyes and dick had searched the angel out like a damn laser finding its target, and as I sat there now, it was taking some very heavy convincing from Brett to keep it occupied.

As a hand landed on my thigh and inched its way up toward the hard-on I'd been packing since I'd spotted Halo, I had to remind myself for the millionth time that he wasn't sitting there waiting for a moment with me.

"*Shit.*" Brett groaned against my lips, his eyes wide with that familiar starstuck look in them. He licked his lips as he scooted in so close to my side that I could feel his cock pressing up against my leg. "You're so damn sexy."

Yeah, that worked for me. I gripped his tie a little harder and nipped at his lower lip, making him tremble. "Why don't you come up here and tell me that."

"Up...there?" Brett asked, his eyes dropping to my lap and then coming back to meet mine.

"Straddle me," I suggested, tugging him a little closer, and it didn't take any more convincing than that.

Brett shifted up on the couch and lifted one knee over the top of my thighs, and when he was hovering above my legs, I tossed a crooked smile his way and ran a hand up his thigh. As my fingers dug into his hip and I drew him closer, Brett bit into his lip and squirmed against me, rubbing his erection up against mine.

"Oh fuck," he whispered, as I licked my lower lip. "This is—" Before he could finish his thought, I yanked on his tie, bringing his mouth into contact with mine, hoping that would silence him for the time being, because honestly, we both knew why he was there, and I didn't need him to kiss my ass to get into my pants tonight— it was already a foregone conclusion.

I'd known that from the second my dick had taken over all logical thinking, back at Killian's place this afternoon, that I needed to get laid tonight, and fast, and with the way Brett's hands were now trailing down my chest, I was positive that was about to happen really fucking soon.

Brett began to nip his way up my jaw line as his fingers continued south, and when I glanced over his shoulder to the opposite side of the couch, expecting to see Halo in a somewhat similar position—*but more...breasts in face and hands up skirts*—I drew up short when I saw his eyes locked on me.

Well, well, well, would you look at that. It seemed the angel was preoccupied tonight. And it made my stupid cock throb that he seemed preoccupied with *me*.

As Brett's fingers found the button of my jeans and his lips found my ear, I aimed a wicked smirk in Halo's direction.

Halo's jaw clenched, and I could've sworn he ground his teeth together, as Brett chose that moment to rock forward on his knees and rub his entire body up against my front. I grunted, the pressure against my cock feeling really fucking good, and let go of

Brett's tie to finally reach around and grab a handful of each of his ass cheeks. Brett moaned in my ear as I thrust my hips up off the couch, my eyes still locked on Halo's as the blonde on his right began kissing her way down his neck.

Fuck, he was gorgeous, with his jean-clad legs spread apart, cradling a now-empty glass in his hand like it was a damn lifeline. He had a scowl on his face I'd never seen before, and I didn't know what it said about me, but that irritated expression was making my already hard dick even harder.

Maybe it was because Halo was always so affable? I had no clue. But seeing him look like he wanted to shove the girls off him, and maybe tell me to go fuck myself, was really pushing my buttons.

Twisted? Maybe. But hell if I could help it. There was only one reason I could think of why Halo looked pissed off at me, and it had nothing to do with the threesome on his lap and everything to do with the fact he was finding it just as hard to look away from me as I was from him.

Just as that thought entered my head, Brett sat back on my thighs, blocking my view of Halo, and glanced down at the erection I had no hope in hell of hiding. He fingered the top of the zipper and gave me a coy look from under his lashes.

"Can I?"

I was close to saying, *Yes, as long as you move so I can see the guy behind you*, but considering how good he felt on my lap, I wasn't about to piss Brett off until we'd both gotten what we wanted from this moment.

Him: his twenty minutes with Viper.

Me: some kind of release from the lust that had been riding me from the moment I'd laid eyes on Halo.

I nodded and leaned forward to flick my tongue across the corner of Brett's mouth, and when he lowered his head to the task at hand, I looked at the man across from us.

Halo's eyes were on the fingers I was digging into Brett's ass, and when I squeezed to pull him closer, Halo's gaze flew up to mine and I winked. A flush spread up Halo's neck until it reached his face, and with the way he'd tied his hair back at the nape of his neck tonight, I could see every inch it covered.

I leaned back against the couch as Brett's hand found its way inside my jeans, and then he lowered his head and began to kiss his way down to the open neck of my shirt. Farther and farther he moved down my body, and with the way his tight fist was now milking my cock, I couldn't have kept my hips still if I'd wanted to. As his ass scooted back to the edge of my knees so he could suck a spot under one of my nipples, my eyes found Halo's again.

His lips were parted now, his legs were spread even farther apart, and blondie was rubbing her hand over his dick as he continued to watch us. I wasn't even sure Halo was aware what he was doing until Brett bit down on one of my nipples, and a groan escaped my throat.

Halo's hips shoved up from the couch against blondie's hand, and as his eyes roved up to my face, I grinned and mouthed, *Like what you see?* Halo blinked as though I'd snapped him out of some kind of trance, and when Brett flicked his tongue over my tingling nipple, I lowered my eyes back to his.

Brett smiled up at me, and I forced a smirk—the one I knew would drive him fucking wild—and then leaned down and pressed my lips against his. "You have a talented fucking mouth."

Brett's eyes shone with pleasure as his lips curved against mine.

"Why don't you show me just *how* talented it can be?"

Brett nodded eagerly as he slid off my thighs, lowering to the ground on his knees. When he reached for my open jeans to pull them down around my hips, Halo jackknifed to his feet, as though someone had goosed him on the ass.

My eyes flew up to his, and the annoyance and confusion swirling in them made it crystal clear Halo was fighting whatever it was he was feeling—and judging by the hard cock in his jeans, that was a whole fucking lot.

Before I could say anything—what, I didn't exactly know— Halo put his empty tumbler on the table and, without a thought to the women he'd left on the couch, made a beeline for the VIP restrooms.

Fuck. What the hell just happened?

As Halo disappeared out of sight, I glanced back to Brett and put a hand to his shoulder.

"Wait," I said, and then ground my teeth together, indecision warring. I knew I should just forget about Halo, let him do his thing. That was why I was here, but— *Oh, fucking hell.* "I'll be right back."

"Wh...what? Did I do something wrong?" Brett pursed his lips in a pout I knew would feel really good around my cock, but—

"No," I said as I zipped up and ran a hand through my hair. "You order yourself whatever you like, and I'll be right back."

Before Brett could say anything else, I shoved up to my feet and headed in the same direction Halo had run to, and when I saw the back hallway was empty, I shoved open the door to the men's room.

The deep blue light shimmered off the black tiles on the floor, and there was a wall of mirrors where the glass sinks were reflecting the opulence of the room. Off to one side was a vanity with a crystal vase with every size condom known to man, and beside that, a second one holding a variety of flavored lubes.

None of that was what I was looking for, though. What I was looking for was—

"What are you doing in here?"

Halo.

I turned away from the hallway that led to the facilities at the back, to find him standing in front of one of the couches in the aptly named "chill zone."

I swept my eyes down his body and noted his hands balled by his sides. "Maybe I needed to take a piss."

"Bullshit," Halo said, and my lips quirked at his tone—someone was *not* happy, and maybe slightly drunk. "Try again."

I'd never been one to beat around the bush, and with the tequila buzzing through me, I was even less inclined to keep a lid on it. So I moved closer until only inches separated us and shrugged. "I wanted to see where you ran off to."

"I didn't run off."

"Looked like it to me."

"Well, excuse me if I didn't want to sit there and watch you get your dick sucked."

"Why not?" I said. "You not into watching? You like to participate? I'd be more than happy to accommodate you, Angel."

Halo's eyes narrowed to slits. "I think I've been pretty clear that I'm not into guys, Viper. Give it a rest, would you?"

I shoved my hands into my pockets to keep them from doing something stupid, like grabbing his chin and making him admit that was a fucking lie. But when Halo dropped his eyes to my open jeans, I decided to go a different route.

"You didn't seem that interested in the women out there, so you can hardly blame me for being a little...confused."

It worked like a charm.

Halo's eyes flew back to mine. "I was interested."

"Could've fooled me." I let my gaze drop to his scowling lips and chuckled. "I bet you can't even describe the one who had her hand on your dick."

Halo's mouth opened and then shut. "I bet you can't describe the guy who was about to suck *yours*."

"You're right," I agreed, and then leaned forward on my toes, getting in his personal space. "I was too busy looking at you."

Halo's eyes widened until they looked as though they were about to fall out, and then he shook his head, blinked a couple of times, and, without another word, stepped around me and walked out of the bathroom.

Well, that'll give him something to think about later, won't it?

NINETEEN

Halo

WHAT THE HELL happened back there?

I clasped my hands behind my neck and stared up at the ceiling of my apartment, unable to get Viper's words from earlier out of my head.

"I was too busy looking at you."

Why? Why the fuck was he looking at me? He had a waiting list of men to choose from, so it wasn't like he was hard up for attention. Why bother with someone he knew was straight, especially when I'd reminded him more than once?

Groaning in frustration, I toed off my shoes and kicked them into the closet and then shrugged off my jacket, leaving it where it fell. Okay, so sue me, I wasn't interested in the women tonight. That didn't mean I was interested in Viper. Was that what he thought? That because I didn't want to ride the groupie train, I'd be down for whatever he had in mind?

The room began to spin, all the vodka I'd consumed tonight finally deciding to kick in full force, and I dropped back onto my bed.

Maybe that was the problem. I'd gotten drunk and imagined Viper looking at me the way he had. He'd obviously been enjoying his choice for the evening, even if tie guy wasn't anywhere near

Viper's league. It was annoying as shit to think Viper would even bother with someone like that, someone who was obviously using him. Then again, I supposed it was a trade-off.

But...why had Viper followed me? He'd been about two seconds away from having tie guy's mouth on his dick, so why blow off a sure thing to antagonize me? It didn't make any sense. Hell, I didn't even remember going in the bathroom or why, only that there was no way I could sit in the VIP and watch what was about to go down—which meant tie guy, literally.

The image of Viper on the couch with tie guy between his legs flashed through my head again. It hadn't been the man on his knees Viper was watching—it'd been me. And the truth I didn't want to acknowledge was that I'd been watching him right back.

This is fucking insane. I'm not attracted to Viper like that. To any guy like that. I closed my eyes, trying to conjure up a visual of one of the girls from tonight, but they came up only in the periphery as my mind focused in on Viper's rogue grin as he'd mouthed, *"Like what you see?"* It'd been like a rubber band snapping me in my face. I hadn't even realized I'd been watching them until that point, and I definitely hadn't noticed Viper watching *me* watching them.

That doesn't mean you're interested. Anyone would watch someone larger than life like Viper.

But the girls hadn't. No one else outside the VIP had either.

Fuck. I pressed the heels of my palms against my eyes, hoping to stop any other images from invading my mind.

Damn Viper. What the hell was it about that guy that pushed my buttons? Was it just that it was "Viper, rock god and guitar legend"? Or was it something else entirely? Something I didn't understand?

Sighing, I dropped my hands from my face, and when I opened my eyes, they landed on the laptop beside me. I sat up, bringing the laptop with me, and opened YouTube. I typed in "TBD" and chose the first video that popped up. It was from their last concert in London at Wembley Stadium, and as I scrolled through, it was obvious the person who'd uploaded the video had focused mostly on Trent, so I clicked off and typed in "Viper TBD" instead.

This time, video after video focusing only on Viper popped up. I clicked on the first one, determined to figure out what it was about him that had me feeling unsettled every time he was near. Hell, even when he wasn't. I'd left him back at the bar, along with the others, when I'd walked out of the bathroom, and that was where he should've remained, yet here I was, searching for him online.

My fingers hovered over the back button, but as a spotlight beamed on Viper as he began one of his guitar solos, I found my eyes glued to the screen. There was just something about the guy that was magnetic, whether he was onstage or walking into a room. Some people had that "it factor," that thing you can't describe but know it when you see it.

He swaggered across the stage, those piercing eyes making contact with the crowd as he played. Pure sex on a stick. He couldn't help himself. As his solo ended and the drums kicked in, he thrust his pelvis forward, his head falling back in a way that simulated pure ecstasy, and my cock throbbed in response.

It was so unexpected that the rest of my body went rigid. When Viper repeated the move, and it happened again, I could feel the heat creeping up my body, even though no one else was in the room to see my reaction.

Viper ran his hand through his hair and winked at the camera, almost like he could see the way my dick had hardened painfully behind my jeans. I reached down to adjust myself, and then thought, *Fuck it*, and opened the fly, but it didn't do much to relieve the pressure. I squeezed my cock over the top of my boxer briefs, and the shot of lust that ran through me at the move had my eyes practically rolling to the back of my head.

Holy shit...

My gaze fell back on the screen, and as it landed on Viper, I grew harder beneath my hand. My dick was utterly aware of one person on that stage, and while that should've been impossible, the evidence as the camera followed Viper across the stage told me otherwise.

Moving my hand up and down my covered cock slowly, I struggled to breathe as the realization hit me full force. I was harder than I'd been maybe ever, and even though I wanted to blame what I was doing on the alcohol, that voice in the back of my mind knew exactly what was going down. Guilt and embarrassment collided with the heavy dose of sexual desire coursing through my veins, and I halted my hand. My breathing came out in heavy pants, my mind conflicted.

Don't worry. He's not here. He'll never know...

Like the devil whispering in my ear, I pushed aside the confusion I felt. Shoving my boxer briefs down, I freed my cock and wrapped a hand around the hard length. I stroked down and then up, spreading the pre-cum from the head of my dick down my erection, giving me a smoother slide as I kept my eyes on the screen. Viper looked straight at the camera and licked his lips, and I moaned, my hips jerking up. God, I'd looked at his mouth before, but I'd never thought about the way it might feel against mine. He had full lips, and he sometimes sucked the bottom one between his teeth in a way that screamed tease. But Viper was no tease. He told you flat-out what he wanted, and I had no doubt that he got it 99.9 percent of the time.

Another guitar solo, and the camera panned down to Viper's talented hands. Talented on the guitar...talented in other ways? I imagined the way he'd wrap those long fingers around my cock and whisper against my mouth, *"Like me stroking your dick, Angel?"* in that arrogant voice.

That was all it took for my orgasm to come barreling to the surface, a seemingly never-ending wave that I rode long and hard, my hand—Viper's hand—milking every bit of cum out of me until I was spent, falling back against the pillow in a heap of sweat.

Goddamn, that was hot. That was...

My eyes searched out Viper on the screen again, but this time when I looked at him, a strange sensation fluttered in my stomach, and as the realization of what I'd just done hit me, I slammed the laptop shut.

Fuck. Oh *fuck*. I'd just gotten myself off to a man, and not just any man—Viper.

Jesus Christ... How was I going to look him in the eye now?

TWENTY

Viper

STORMING OUT OF the private elevator that led into my condo, I tossed my keys into the funky blown glass bowl my mother had given me this past Christmas, and marched over to the wall of windows that stretched the entire length of my living and dining room.

Tonight had veered into uncharted territory. When Killian suggested that we all go down to Easy Street to celebrate Halo's genius status, I'd agreed to go with one goal in mind: to fuck that genius right out of my head. But what had I done instead? Managed to let Halo fuck with my head.

Yeah, and how had he done that? By vanishing after our little *chat* in the restroom. After that, any thought of having my dick sucked by Brett was replaced by my obsession in finding out *why* Halo had left.

Was he running from me? Because of what I'd said? The thought wouldn't leave me alone. Or maybe he was running from himself, and what he was feeling. Because he'd *definitely* been feeling something.

It'd been written all over that angel face of his, on the parted lips and the thrusting hips he hadn't been able to keep still as he watched Brett writhe around all over me, and fuck, even now the memory of it had me reaching down to massage the stiff dick trapped inside my jeans.

I shut my eyes and let my head fall back as I imagined Halo standing there with me. His mouth on my neck, that silky blond hair brushing against my face, my lips, close enough that I could grab a handful of it, that I could take a deep inhale and let his fresh, clean scent envelop me.

Jesus. I wanted to drown in that scent. Roll around with him on my sheets until they smelled the same way he did, and when that image slammed into me, I groaned low in my throat and flicked open the button of my jeans.

I shoved a hand into my pants to fist the hard-on that seemed determined to stick around, and then I opened my eyes to stare out at the smattering of lights in Central Park. Where was Halo tonight? I had no idea where he lived, just that it was in the opposite direction from me, according to our one conversation about it that night at Li's. And thinking about *that* had me right back to imagining his mouth.

I yanked my hand out of my jeans and cursed. This was fucked. I hadn't been this wound up about someone in—well, ever. And the first time it decided to happen was with a straight guy? *Isn't that just fantastic.*

I told Killian this was a bad idea, and now I knew why. Tomorrow the guys were going to want to get together, talk about the new direction, think up lyrics and music, and all I'd be doing would be staring at Halo and remembering the way he'd eye-fucked me before he'd panicked and run away.

In short, there was no way in hell I was going to be of any use to anyone right now. I could honestly say that I'd never been more aware, and distracted, by my dick in my life, and all because of a guy with an angel's face and a No Trespassing sign.

Frustrated, I ran a hand through my hair and walked to the bar that separated the living room and dining space. I poured myself a glass of whiskey, snatched it up along with the bottle, and then made my way through to my bedroom.

Moving around the end of my California king, too wired to sleep, I headed to the corner of the room where there was a lounge and coffee table. I flicked on the lamp in the corner, grabbed the notepad and pen that'd been sitting on my nightstand, then took a seat in one of my favorite places in the condo.

Fucking Killian. This was all his fault. Hiring an angel to front our band. Making me look at that face every day and not be able to do jack shit about it. Well, it was time Killian knew exactly how I felt about that.

Throwing back the whiskey, I reveled in the burn, and when my dick kicked in response to the thoughts running through my head, I put pen to paper and wrote down the one thing I was feeling—hard.

TWENTY-ONE

Halo

THE NEXT AFTERNOON, we'd gathered back in the rehearsal space at Killian's, and from looking at it, I was the only one suffering a hangover. My tolerance was nowhere near the rest of the guys, but I'd needed the alcohol to get through last night.

Speaking of last night…

I looked to where Viper was laughing with Killian, and my actions from the night before came hurtling back with picture-perfect clarity.

God, why had I done that? I'd been so stupid. As I rubbed my hands over my face, I wondered how I was going to get through rehearsal without turning bright red every time Viper looked my way. No doubt he'd see right through me, and then what would I do?

"Hey, man, you okay?" Jagger asked. "Need somethin' for that hangover?"

"Uh, no. I'm good." More like in a load of shit, but that was nothing I was about to share.

We started things out by working on the song I'd brought to them yesterday. It was easy to keep my distance from Viper, but stopping my brain from tracking his every move or thinking about last night on repeat? That wasn't shutting off anytime soon.

It was after we'd come back from a quick lunch that I finally had to look Viper's way. If he'd gotten the hint I was ignoring him, he never said anything. He was the same old Viper, cracking on the guys with his sharp tongue and focusing on the music. As a matter of fact, the only thing different was the way he didn't invade my personal space...and I wasn't sure how I felt about that.

"I had an idea last night," Viper said when we'd gathered back in the rehearsal room. He held a sheet up that had his barely legible scrawl all over it. "I think Halo's song is great, and I think working on some tracks that are in the same vein would be a good direction for us to go. But what if we threw in one or two tracks that would sound more familiar to the fans that follow us over?"

"You got something in mind?" Killian asked.

Viper nodded and walked to where I stood behind the mic. It was the first time we'd locked gazes today, and as he stopped in front of me, my pulse sped up.

"Will you do the honors, Angel?" he said, holding the lyrics toward me.

I was still "Angel," but the way he said it held none of the flirtatious edge it had before.

"Sure." I took the ripped sheet of paper from him as he picked up his guitar.

"Something like this." Viper played a few notes as I skimmed the words he'd written, trying to get a feel for them—

Whoa. I blinked, reading them again. Holy fuck, the lyrics were filthy, in complete opposition to what we'd worked on that morning, and—

Had he said he wrote this last night?

Viper's face gave nothing away, but I knew mine had to. I could never hide the flush that came so easy to my skin, and definitely not when I knew exactly what this song was about. Or rather, *who*.

Me.

"What's the song called?" Killian asked.

When I didn't answer, Viper looked at the guys. "'Hard.'"

Killian opened his mouth to respond, but then glanced at me and seemed to think better of it. "Right."

"So I was thinking I'd start with this"—Viper played a guitar riff—"and then Slade, you'd come in with a fucking pounding beat. Like pure, headboard-banging sex, you feel me? And then Kill, the bass has gotta throb. Jagger, I haven't gotten that far yet, but you'd know better than me what sounds good." Viper continued to play and then nodded at me. "This is where you come in."

"I can't sing this," I said, shaking my head.

Viper stopped playing. "Sure you can."

"I don't think so."

"What's the problem, Halo?" Killian frowned.

"I think it's too risqué for our angel." Viper's lips twisted. "Don't worry. I'm sure you'll still get into heaven."

I shot a glare in his direction and looked back down at what Viper thought would be a good idea for me to say out fucking loud.

"Show me," Killian said, gesturing for the lyrics, and I handed them over. He nodded along as he read them, and when he was done, he let out a low whistle. "Christ, that face singing those words? Viper's got a point."

"You're serious?" I asked.

"Yup." He stood up and took his place to my left. "Show us what you got."

Singing a song Viper had written after our interaction last night and probably at the same time I'd been getting off to him? Yeah. Sure. No problem.

"Come on, Angel. Surely you've been frustrated in the past. Tap into that." To anyone else, Viper's words might've seemed innocent, but I caught his hidden meaning good and damn well.

How had I ever thought he was anything other than a pain in the ass?

As Viper began to play again, the others waited to hear what I didn't want to say, and when the asshole gave me my cue, I went through the motions.

. . .

"I WISH I could say I'm sorry
For the state you get me in
But nothing seems to help
This ache you cause within

I'VE THOUGHT about how to fix it,
What might do the trick
And fucking you for hours
Just might get it licked—"

"OKAY, HOLD UP." Killian held up his hand. "It's not gonna work if you don't put the frustration behind it. It's like you're reading the words."

"I am reading the words."

"But that's not how it works. You don't just read the words to your song."

"My song doesn't talk about blue balls."

Killian sighed. "Do the lyrics really bother you that much?"

I wanted to say, *Yes, because those lyrics are about me.* But dissing a song just because Viper wrote it wasn't being a team player, and it wasn't going to make any future songs I worked on any easier either.

"No," I said finally. "Start again."

TWENTY-TWO

Viper

I HAD TO ADMIT, when I'd been writing down the lyrics, I was frustrated, pissed off, and more than a little drunk.

But after hearing Killian's approval and watching Halo fumble around trying to finagle his way out of singing them, I was starting to believe this more than made up for the fact I'd had to come in here today and act like everything was fine and fucking dandy.

From the second I'd stepped into Killian's place, up until right now, I'd been trying really hard to keep my thoughts, and eyes, off the man standing beside me. Not an easy task when he was dressed in jeans that molded to that fine ass of his, and he had a navy-blue deep V-neck shirt that showed off skin I wouldn't mind running my tongue over, or you know, coming all over.

Since that option was clearly off the table with the way Halo had bolted last night at the mention of me in his personal space, I'd have to make do with watching him sing my little...ode to him.

That just might make the ache in my dick a little less painful.

"Hold up a second, would you, Angel? Let's see if we can't add some meat to this thing. Really make you feel it in your balls."

Jagger snorted. "Judging by those lyrics, you were *already* feeling something in your balls. What happened to the guy in the tie, V? Too stuffy? Not kinky enough for you?"

Not Halo enough for me, more like it. I ignored Jagger's question and flicked on my amp so I could really step up the sound on this thing for the silent man standing behind his mic, staring at me with a look I couldn't quite decipher.

In the space of ten minutes, Halo had gone from shock to disbelief, and right now he was looking at me like he'd never seen me before. His eyes were assessing, traveling over my face, my chest, down to where my guitar rested across my body, and when they came back and locked with mine, there was a light in them I would recognize anywhere—interest.

What. The. Fuck. I arched an eyebrow in his direction, and Halo blinked then quickly lowered his gaze to the paper he still had in a death grip, effectively cutting the connection.

"Yeah, you should've seen that guy's face when you left." Slade tapped his drumsticks on one of his knees. "Looked like you broke up with him."

Killian rolled his eyes. "V, break up with someone? That would imply he'd actually have to date someone first."

"How 'bout the three of you stop gossiping about what I do with my dick, so I can show you and Halo what I'm thinking for the beginning of this thing," I said.

The three on the couch stared at me as I bent down to fiddle with the dials on a pedal, and when I straightened, I said to Halo, "Okay, so I thought it could start out like this."

I closed my eyes and hit the strings as I pressed my foot to the pedal, the quiet tune from a second ago now snarling through the rehearsal room like a monster baring its teeth.

I fucking loved the way this sounded. I'd played around with it last night until I'd hit my mood and vibe just right. And this was it. A growl of pure lust. A tone that was thick and full of harmonics, as I played the full intro the exact way I would on a stage.

When I finished and opened my eyes, Halo looked a little...flustered.

"Fuck me," Killian said, getting to his feet. "*Jesus*, V. I don't know what got into you last night, but that's fucking unreal. Maybe you shouldn't get laid more often."

I shot him the finger. "Shut the hell up."

Killian laughed and then looked to Halo. "Come ooon, you know that shit's amazing, right?"

Halo nodded. "Yeah, it really is. I just..." He paused and looked in my direction. "How do you want me to play this? I mean, is the guy angry? Does he hate the person he's wanting to, um..."

"Fuck for hours?" I said. "If you can't say the words, how are you gonna sing them?"

"*Shiiit*," Jagger said as he stood and walked to Halo, his hand outstretched. "Hand it over, Halo. I want to see the rest of this thing."

"I'll sing them. I just want to know more so I can get inside his head," Halo said as he passed the paper to Jagger.

The air in the room suddenly felt about a million times hotter than it had a second ago, as I held Halo's direct stare in a stalemate of sorts. "He's not angry. He's frustrated. His dick wants something it can't have, and that's making him a little bit irritable."

"A little bit?" Jagger said as he finished reading the lyrics. "V, dude, I'm close to shelling out some serious cash to get you laid, my friend."

"What'd you think, Halo? You got it?" Killian said before I could tell Jagger to make sure whoever he bought and paid for had eyes the color of sea glass and blond hair that matched our lead singer.

"Yeah, I think so," Halo said.

"Good. That's good. I think if we can really nail this, we could call Brian down here to listen to these two we've been working on. See how he feels about them."

Slade, Jagger, and Killian moved back to the couch, and when I inclined my head in Halo's direction and he indicated he was ready, I started the intro again.

For a couple of hours we played around with the song, changing up melodies for the chorus once we reached it. We had

Halo try different notes on certain words—adding more emphasis or taking it away—but by the start of the third hour, I was done.

Something was missing here. I'd heard the song so clearly in my head, known exactly the way it needed to sound, and while it was okay, better than it had been when we'd started, it still wasn't packing the punch I knew it could.

"How about we call it for the day?" I sighed as I looked at the rest of the guys. "I'm tired, didn't get much sleep last night, and something's not working here."

Everyone but Halo nodded. Slade and Jagger headed out to Killian's kitchen for some food, as Halo picked up the bottle of water at his feet and took a few chugs.

Killian came over. "You okay?"

A frown pulled between my brows. "Okay?"

"Yeah." Killian lowered his voice. "Not sleeping. Not fucking. Writing lyrics titled 'Hard.'" Killian glanced over his shoulder to where Halo was sitting on a couch with the lyrics and a pen in his hand. "I'm not blind, V."

"You don't say." I shut my guitar case and picked it up.

"Look, the song's killer. But don't think for a minute I don't know who it's about." Killian ran a hand through his hair. "Tread carefully there. Give him a chance to get it right. He's good, but this is...a lot of song."

"Got it," I said. "Can I go now, *sir*?"

"Fuck you."

"If only you were my type."

I stepped around Killian and headed out of the rehearsal room, saying my goodbyes to everyone as I went for the front door. As I made my way to the elevator and pushed the button, I heard someone call out my name, and was more than a little shocked to see that Halo had stepped out into the hallway with his jacket and backpack in place.

"Yeah? What is it, Angel?"

As he walked down the hall, I noticed he still clutched the

lyrics in his fist like he was afraid he might lose them. "Are you angry with me?"

Angry? Why would I—

"Because I'm not getting this?" he said, holding up the paper.

"You're getting it. It's just taking a moment."

Halo looked down to the words and shook his head, and when all that blond hair shifted around his face, the scent of his shampoo filled my head and lungs. *Fucking delicious.*

"I'm not. I can't put my finger on why this is so hard for me."

When Halo raised his eyes to mine, a smirk crossed my lips. "Pun intended?"

"Wh— Oh," Halo said. "I guess. But something's not working, and I know you're disappointed. Do you think..." Halo chewed his lower lip. "Look, I don't want to be the reason this doesn't work out. Do you think you could maybe help me? Show me what you want?"

I eyed him for a beat, wondering if he even realized what he'd just said, and when the elevator door opened, I said, "I can show you exactly what I want, Angel. Let's go."

TWENTY-THREE

Halo

AS SOON AS the doors of the private elevator that led into Viper's condo opened, I realized my mistake.

When I'd asked for Viper's help in working out where I was going wrong with the song, it didn't occur to me that we'd end up at his place...alone. But as my eyes caught the floor-to-ceiling view of Central Park covered in a golden haze from the setting sun, I froze. With that view straight ahead, the lyrics in my hand, and Viper's close proximity, I was so screwed.

"I know the elevator has killer acoustics, but if you want my help, you should come inside," Viper said over his shoulder.

As the doors began to close, I stopped them with my arm and then stepped inside Viper's place.

Oh, this was bad. This was very, very bad. Viper strolled ahead of me, shrugging out of his jacket and throwing it over the back of his couch, and then he turned to face me as he pushed up the sleeves of his shirt.

He doesn't know about what you did last night. Just work on the song and get out. No big deal.

Viper crooked his finger for me to come closer, and I pushed aside my hesitation and walked forward into the living room—though as I looked around, I saw that, like Killian, he had an open floor plan, with a bar separating his living and dining areas. The walls on the side were glass, and the thought popped into my head that maybe his bedroom was too.

What the hell? I don't care about his bedroom. I don't want to see it. I don't want to think about it. Now I was lying to myself.

"Would you like a tour?" Viper asked, once again like he could read my damn mind.

I held up the lyric sheet. "I think we should work on this."

"Gotcha." He crossed to an electric-blue armchair and lounged back onto it. "Go on, then."

And now I had to sing these fucking words. *Great idea, Halo. Really. Brilliant.*

I cleared my throat and looked down at the lines Viper had written. It'd been hard enough getting through the song in front of the other guys, but now? With only Viper as my audience? Something about it felt too intimate, or maybe it was the fact that every time I looked at him, I could still feel the epic orgasm that had come from watching him.

"Make yourself comfortable," Viper said. "Sit if you want to."

Comfortable? Fat chance of that happening. I didn't need to get comfortable at Viper's place—I needed to fix my part of this song and get the hell out, so I stayed standing.

Viper shrugged. "Or not."

Cutting the small talk short, I began to sing, but I'd only gotten as far as the second line before Viper interrupted.

"You're starting it wrong. Yeah, you need that frustration later, but you've gotta build to that. Really think about the words here. You're turned on as fuck, and you're not about to apologize for it."

I swallowed and dropped my gaze back down. I heard what he was saying, but it was impossible not to think about Viper writing these lines. Blocking it out completely was the only way I could get through the song, but it wasn't giving Viper what he wanted. When I tried again, I closed my eyes, but he didn't let me get through the first verse before stopping me.

"Halo, I've seen you onstage practically fucking the mic stand, so what's the problem here?"

"I...don't know." Another lie, but what was I supposed to tell him? The truth?

"That's bullshit. You know how to bring it, but you're holding back. Why?"

I ran a hand over my face and sighed. "It's just not coming."

Viper sucked his lower lip into his mouth as he studied me, and then he pushed up off the chair. "Okay, we need to try something different. Tell me about your last fuck."

I coughed in surprise. "What?"

"Let me clarify: the last *hot* fuck."

"And that's important why?"

"Because that's what this song is about. A hot fuck. Or at least the promise of one."

Fucking was the last thing we needed to talk about, especially since the last hot one on my mind involved my fist and the man in front of me.

Viper let out a low whistle. "Damn. No hot fucks recently. That's a shame."

"I didn't say that."

"You didn't have to, Angel." He began to walk a slow circle around me. "Okay, what about this. I want you to close your eyes. Go on, do it."

I hesitated for a moment before doing as he asked.

"Good," he said. "Now think about what turns you on. If you were at home right now, what would get you off? Porn? Maybe a picture you keep in your bedside drawer? Or someone forbidden... someone you shouldn't want, but you can't help yourself."

Closing my eyes from having to look at Viper should've been enough to block him out, but with the way I could feel his breath on the back of my neck, and with the image he'd asked me to conjure in my mind, it was impossible to think of anything but him. Think of someone forbidden? There was nothing more off-limits in my world than getting myself off to Viper, for several reasons.

"Whatever you're thinking right now, go with it," Viper said. "Now try again."

Something in my expression must've given me away, but it was a good thing Viper couldn't see anything beyond that. Keeping my eyes closed, I thought back to last night when I'd lain in bed, stiff cock in my hand, and even now, I could feel the deep ache, the hunger I'd felt about someone I'd never expected.

The lyrics left my tongue, punctuated by soft moans that told the listener exactly how far gone my desire for the forbidden one went.

When I finished the verse, without interruption this time, I opened my eyes to see Viper staring at me with that same lust-addled expression I'd seen at the bar last night, but it flickered out, and he gave me a nod.

"Better. Much better. Keep going."

I hadn't memorized the chorus yet, so I looked down and kept on the same way, since Viper hadn't seemed to find fault with it, but three lines in and he waved his hands to get my attention.

"No. No, no. That's all wrong again. You did the verse right, but that hard edge you had earlier was what we need here. Like I said, you need to build it throughout the song."

I tried again, but even I could feel the way I shied away from owning the words. For fuck's sake, the chorus included the words "blue balls."

"Again. Harder this time."

But no matter how many variations I gave, Viper shot them all down, until finally he growled in frustration.

"No, it's just not right—"

"What the fuck do you want from me, then?" He wasn't the only one getting annoyed as shit.

Viper spun to face me and pointed. "That. That right there. Get pissed."

"Not hard to do around you."

He raised an eyebrow. "No?" He reached for the back of his shirt and pulled it up over his head, and as he dropped it to the floor, I took a step back.

"What are you doing?"

With a shrug, Viper stepped toward me. "It's hot in here."

"No, it's not. Put your shirt back on."

"No."

It wasn't the first time I'd seen Viper half-naked—he ripped off his shirt during almost every show—but it was only the two of us here, and I didn't need any more images of Viper to add to the erotic slideshow in my head.

"Viper. Put it back on."

With a walk so cocky it could only be described as a strut, he said, "Why? Is it bothering you? Annoying you? Do you feel frustrated that I'm not doing what you want me to?"

"Yes."

"Good. Because with this song, you've gotta make every single person in the stadium want to fuck you." He moved in even closer, his body only inches from mine and radiating heat I could feel through my shirt. "Can you do that?"

TWENTY-FOUR

Viper

AS MY WORDS lingered between the inches separating us, I was close enough to see Halo's eyes darken a fraction, and his Adam's apple bob as he swallowed in a gulp of air. I wasn't sure if it was my nearness, my nakedness, or the entire situation that had him all deer in headlights right then, but when he didn't immediately answer, I said, "Angel?"

"What?" The guilty response and the look that crossed his face made my cock punch against the zipper of my jeans.

"Can you do that?"

Halo nodded.

"Good." I turned away from him and made my way to the wall of windows that overlooked Central Park, then leaned my ass up against it and crossed my arms over my chest. "Show me."

Halo ran a hand back through his tangle of hair and took in a deep breath, and when he brought his eyes back to mine, there was a look of determination in them before he let them fall shut and he began to sing from the top.

With a safe distance now separating us, I took a moment to really look at the man who was moaning and groaning his way through the song I'd penned about him.

There was something incredibly hot about hearing that

smooth, husky voice of Halo's lamenting over the idea of fucking someone out of his system, and that was exactly what I needed him to bring to this song.

The need. The want. The ache that went with wanting someone you couldn't have. And if Halo opened his eyes right then, I knew he'd see all those things on my face.

Christ, he was sexy, and as he finally let go of whatever had been holding him back, Halo's body began to move along with the words falling from his lips. *Yesss,* he had it now, judging by the way my cock was reacting. I was hard as hell inside my jeans and couldn't have hidden it even if I wanted to.

Shoving away from the window, I made my way closer to him as the tone of his voice shifted, as it moved from a throb-worthy tease to my dick, to a throaty kind of purr that tugged nice and hard, and let me know he was working up to something that was going to make my eyes roll to the back of my head.

Fuck me. Whatever Halo was thinking about right now, whatever was running through the angel's head...I needed him thinking about *that* whenever he sang this song.

"Take your jacket off."

Halo's eyes opened and focused on me, and holy shit, he almost brought me to my knees.

Those light eyes were all but swallowed up by his blown pupils. The arousal from whatever he'd been thinking was stamped all over that flawless face of his, and as he shrugged out of his jacket, he continued to sing.

Halo tossed his jacket onto the couch, but kept his eyes locked on mine as I drew even closer, and I nodded slowly to let him know I was pleased by what he was doing, when really all he had to do was lower his gaze and he'd know I was super fucking happy with this new direction.

"Keep going," I said, and moved behind him, not wanting to break his concentration as he came to the chorus. I stepped in close, until I could feel the heat from his body against mine, as he dove headfirst into the chorus, this time with a raspy growl that was like strong fingers clawing at my back.

'Cause you make it so hard
  To think of anything but you
  You make it so hard my balls are fucking blue
  I want to get inside you, and show you exactly what you do
  Whenever your eyes invite me to fuck you like I want to

"Fuck." The word left my lips before I could bite it back, and Halo's head whipped to the side, a slightly wild look in his eyes, as though he'd been completely caught up in the song and the lyrics and whatever had gotten him so—Halo's eyes dropped to my lips—wound up.

Hmm. Now what have we got here…

Narrowing my eyes, I slowly stepped closer. Close enough that I could feel Halo's shirt brush up against my naked abdomen, and when our faces were but a breath away from one another, I said, "Second verse, Angel. You got it?"

Halo scraped his teeth over his lower lip, his breathing coming a little faster. "The words, I, uh…"

Jesus. The arousal swirling in his eyes was too much to resist, and with it all aimed in my direction, there was no way I wasn't going to take a goddamn taste. "How about I give you the lines, and you sing them back to me?"

Again, Halo's eyes fell to my mouth, and fuck it, I licked my lower lip to see what this supposedly straight guy was gonna do. When a low moan left his throat, that was enough for me. I threw any decorum I possessed out the window and planted a hand on Halo's hip.

When he didn't tell me to back up or move away, I leaned in close until our lips just about touched. "Feel my hands all over you as I slide inside your soul. Let me hear you scream for me when

I'm deep inside that hole. I'm gonna put my mark on you, so you smell me when I'm gone. I'm gonna make your body ache as dusk turns into dawn."

As I plastered myself against Halo's back, a shudder ran through his body. I tightened my fingers at his waist, and before he could do another damn thing, I wrapped my other arm around him to take hold of his chin. "Careful, Angel. Your eyes are telling me all kinds of crazy shit right now."

Halo's breathing came heavy as I dragged my thumb along his lower lip, and I knew he had to be able to feel my stiff prick up against his back. "If you're gonna say no..."

Halo's jaw bunched, but there was no *back off* look in his eyes like there had been every other time we'd gotten close, and when I leaned in and flicked my tongue over the corner of his mouth, a ball-tingling groan left the back of his throat.

Not needing any more permission than that, I crushed my mouth down over the top of Halo's, swallowing that sound when he made it again.

Christ. That sound was going to be imprinted in my mind for the rest of my damn life. It was frustrated, sexy, and needy, and when I tightened my fingers on his jaw, Halo turned his entire body into mine, and fuck, that was it.

I shoved my fingers into his hair and twisted, getting a good, tight hold, and when he parted his lips, I didn't wait around for an invitation. My tongue was in his mouth, tasting that sweet angel in a heartbeat, and when Halo grunted and grabbed for my waist, I slammed against him and walked him back to the wall of windows. When I had him where I wanted him, I shoved a leg between his thighs and bit at his lower lip.

"Shit." Halo panted as I slid my tongue along his upper lip. "This is..."

"Exactly what you fucking want," I said, and ground my erection against the very hard cock in Halo's jeans. "Have to say, Angel. This would've been much easier if you'd just told me from the beginning you wanted to fuck me."

"I—"

Halo's words came to an abrupt halt when I licked a path up his cheek to his temple, and when I put my mouth against his ear, I finished off the song that had gotten us both in trouble in the first place. "You make me so hard, I want nothing but you. And tonight I'm gonna corrupt you, the way I want to..."

"Fuck, Viper." Halo's hips bucked against my thigh as he hooked his fingers through the belt loops of my jeans and tugged me closer.

I brought my mouth back to his, and bit and sucked at his lips until Halo moaned and shoved his tongue in deep. Then he began to rub himself along my body like it had been designed for one thing and one thing only—to get him off.

Fine by me, I thought, as I lowered a hand between us and unbuttoned my jeans, then I moved to his. I wanted to get my fingers around him. I wanted to feel that throbbing cock pulse in my hand as I destroyed every single brain cell Halo had. And once that was done, I wanted to do it all over again.

Flicking the button free, I growled against his mouth. "I wanted to do this to you last night so fucking bad. But you ran away..."

Halo's frenzied eyes flashed at me, full of lust, full of a need it was clear he was still trying to understand. And I had no problem being the one to introduce him to this.

But when I unzipped his jeans, and glanced down at the hard dick trapped inside the denim, Halo reached for my hand and stilled me.

"Viper, Jesus. You've gotta stop. I..." His eyes dropped back to my mouth. "I need to think a minute, and—"

"Thinking's overrated and stressful." A rough groan escaped Halo as I cradled and squeezed the front of his jeans with a firm hand. "Fucking is much less taxing on the brain. And Angel, I'm a really good fuck."

Halo let out a rush of air but pinned me with the same determined look he'd had earlier, and I knew that *this* was over—at least for now.

With a clenched jaw, I dropped my hands to my sides and let my eyes roam down Halo. The messy hair, the flushed face, his swollen lips, and that hard fucking cock. "You gonna run?"

Halo shook his head, and I sighed and took a step back.

"Then you better think of something to do in the next five minutes to take my mind off the hard-on you seem to take delight in giving me whenever you're around. Otherwise, I'm gonna lose my fucking mind."

TWENTY-FIVE

Halo

IT WAS A good thing there was a wall to hold me up, because when Viper dropped his hands and stepped back from me, my legs almost gave out.

I stared at him in a daze. Chest bare, pants unbuttoned, his erection straining behind the open fly of his jeans. That wicked mouth of his that had been on mine...

A string of curses filled my mind, because fuck, had that really just happened? One minute I was singing, and the next we'd been devouring each other like we'd never get the chance again. The realization of what I'd done should've shocked the hell out of me. Viper had kissed me, and I'd kissed him back.

I'd kissed Viper. A *man*.

Not only that, but when he'd rubbed his erection against mine, my body had come alive, ready and more than willing to go wherever Viper wanted to lead. But how was this even possible? I'd never entertained the possibility of something sexual with a guy before, but with Viper? There was something about him that made my pulse speed up, sending all the blood rushing to my dick.

Fuck, what's happening to me?

"Angel, I'm about two seconds away from pinning you back against that wall if you keep lookin' at me like that."

I knew I needed to move, to put some space between us so I could think clearly, but shit. Even looking at him now had my cock throbbing. I wanted to reach into my jeans to relieve the ache, but that would just put us right back where we started.

My chest still heaving, I zipped and buttoned my jeans, and then I pushed off the glass wall, moving to the opposite side of the room.

Viper let out a shameless chuckle. "Smart move." Then he zipped his pants, leaving the button undone. "So what now?"

I bit down on my lip and forced my gaze away. The sun had set, the room fading into darkness but still illuminated by the glow of the lights from Central Park and the buildings surrounding it. It was beautiful, maybe the best view of the city I'd ever seen, and Viper got to look at it every day as he penned lyrics for TBD. Lyrics like the ones I'd been singing tonight. The ones he'd written about me.

No, don't think about that. Think about anything but that.

"You've got a great place," I said, and then cringed, because how lame was I?

Viper cocked his head, a hint of amusement on his lips. "You tryin' to tell me you want that tour now?"

"No."

"Liar."

I shrugged, not even caring he could see right through me then, and ran my hand along the back of one of the recliners. "So... you wrote the song here last night?"

"No. I wrote it in my bedroom."

"Oh." *Jesus, Halo, find your brain, would you?* "And, um, it's about...?"

Viper's eyes followed me as I stopped behind the recliner, using it like a shield. "You askin' me if I wrote it about you, Angel?"

Was I? I mean, I already knew the answer, but for some reason, I really wanted to hear him admit it. "Yes."

Viper's lips tugged up at the side as he walked to the bar, no doubt taking great pleasure in making me sweat this out as he pulled a bottle of vodka from the freezer. As he twisted the cap off the bottle, Viper ran those dark, suggestive eyes over me and said, "Yes."

Fuck. Okay. That was sexy as hell, and when my fingers dug into the back of the recliner, Viper's eyes fell to them, not missing a thing.

"You like that? That you make my cock hard."

"Jesus." I cleared my throat. "You don't beat around the bush."

"Correct," Viper said as he poured two glasses. "I don't beat any part of myself around a bush. But you? I definitely beat off to you last night."

Wow. Okay. Was this conversation really happening? I couldn't believe that I was standing in Viper's living room talking about him getting off to—

"It's your own fault." Viper cut off my thoughts as he picked up the tumblers and stepped around the bar, his destination clear—me. "From the second you showed up for your audition, I wanted to fuck you."

Over the past couple of weeks, I'd come to learn that Viper wasn't the kind of guy who hid behind fancy words, or hid in general. If he felt something, or wanted someone, he had no problem expressing it. So while I knew he was trying to shock me, I wouldn't have expected him to act any other way.

"You did?"

Viper stopped on the other side of the recliner and held a glass out to me, and when I reached for it and he didn't immediately release it, our eyes met in a kind of standoff. "I still do."

I swallowed around the lump somewhere in the back of my throat as I tried not to squirm under that direct gaze. Then something else occurred to me. "That's not why you hired me, is it?"

Viper snorted and released the glass. "That's why we almost *didn't* hire you, Angel. Trust me, you're in the band because you're fucking talented. The fact that I want to suck your dick is—*was*—a frustration I was just gonna have to deal with. But now..." Viper's gaze lowered to the button of my jeans, where, yeah, I was still hard. "Now it seems I might get to satisfy that particular problem."

"I don't know. That seems kind of messy."

Viper looked up at me, and it wasn't until right then that I realized why his eyes always looked so dark. It was his lashes. They were so thick and full it almost looked as though he had permanent liner rimming them.

"Oh, it would be messy, Angel. A sweaty, hot mess. And by the end of it, you'd want to do it all over again."

Keeping my eyes trained on his, I raised the glass to my lips and took a sip of the vodka. It was a strange sensation to feel so aware of your body and yet be so unsure of it at the same time. It felt as though every nerve ending I had was on high alert, and all because Viper was looking at me like he wanted to…what? Consume me?

As that thought slammed into me with startling clarity, the same kind of heat that had raced through me during my late-night escapades with YouTube licked along my veins, and I was reminded of why I'd sought him out in the first place. Viper had been consuming another just last night.

"What about tie guy?" I blurted out before I could think better of it, and when a frown pulled between Viper's brows, I immediately wanted to take it back.

"Who?"

My eyes widened a fraction, and when it appeared Viper wasn't going to clue in anytime soon that I was referring to the man he'd all but fucked in front of me last night, I knew there was no way to get out of this other than to jog his memory.

"The guy from last night."

Viper shrugged. "What about him?"

My mouth fell open, and before I could think of anything to say to that, Viper chuckled.

"You almost sound jealous, Angel. Is that what's going on here? You jealous?"

"No."

Viper tossed back the last of his vodka. "You sure?"

Yes. No. "Yes."

Viper nodded, but his lips twitched at my obvious irritation. "Because if it was jealousy, there's no reason for it. I left about five minutes after you, came home, and wrote a song about fucking you until I couldn't walk anymore."

I ran a hand over my face as I shook my head. Was this guy serious?

"Does that make you feel better?"

It did, actually, but I wasn't about to admit that. Unlike Viper, I didn't like to show my hand too early.

Viper smirked, like I didn't even have to say the words out loud—he already knew.

"So what about you?" He moved to the couch, set his empty glass on the side table, and then sat back, spreading his legs wide. "You left in an awful hurry last night and didn't even take your lady friends with you." He tsked, like it was such a shame, though I knew better.

"I'm sure they found someone else."

"You didn't answer my question." Viper rubbed his hand over his thigh and came to rest it by his pelvis, drawing my attention to his still-hard erection.

"I went home. End of story."

"Ah, see, I don't think so. Wanna know why?"

With one hand still gripping the top of the recliner, I brought the vodka to my lips, but before I took a sip, I said, "I'd love to hear your theory."

"Because I pay attention. You couldn't wait to get away from me last night, even though you couldn't stop staring at me. But something changed between the time you left and rehearsal today. What was it?"

"Eight hours of sleep."

Viper's mouth turned up. "I don't think so. Try again."

"How about you drop it?"

"Oh, defensive. Interesting." He patted the seat beside him. "Why don't you come tell me all about it?"

"There's nothing to tell. I went home. End of story."

"You know, you blushed quite a bit during rehearsal today, and right now your cheeks are red. It's a dead giveaway, Angel. Fess up."

Fucking Viper. He was way too perceptive for his own good, and though there was no way he could possibly know what I did when I went home last night, I had a feeling he knew he was on the right track.

I drained the rest of my vodka and then spread my hands along the back of the recliner. *Screw it.*

"I watched you last night," I said. "Online."

TWENTY-SIX

Viper

WELL, WELL, WELL. I'd known Halo was hiding something, but hearing him confirm he'd gone home to watch me? It stroked something else besides my ego.

"What did you see?" I said.

"One of your shows from the last tour. Whoever filmed it kept the focus on you."

"Do you like watching me, Angel?"

His blush deepened, and God, that was so fucking sexy. I loved that he couldn't hide his true feelings from me.

"Yes."

Christ. My dick strained against its confines, and I had to shift my position. But when that didn't help, I jerked the zipper down and palmed my erection. "Do you want to watch me now?"

Halo blinked at me, and for a second I thought he'd say yes. Then he shook his head, rubbing his face. "This is crazy. I can't... We can't... You're my bandmate."

"So?"

"So we can't do this."

"We're not doing anything with you standing all the way over there."

Halo sighed. "You know what I mean."

"Don't make it so complicated. I want to fuck you. You're definitely curious about what it'd be like to fuck me."

"So that's all you want? Just sex?"

"Not just sex. Hot, melt-your-fucking-insides sex."

"And then what?"

"Are you asking if I cuddle or some shit?"

Halo reared back. "No, that's not..." He threaded his fingers through his hair, clenching the curls.

"What else do you want?"

He sighed again, and when he dropped his hands, he said, "Dinner. That's what I want. I'm starving."

I supposed it was too much to ask if my cock would suffice, so I zipped my jeans and went to the drawer where I kept a stack of menus. I tossed them onto the counter as Halo followed me, still keeping his distance, as if he didn't trust himself to come closer. *Smart angel.*

He chose steak and potatoes from the restaurant downstairs, and twenty minutes later, I'd refilled our glasses and had the spread laid out between us. We sat across from each other at the dining table I rarely used. I could practically see the questions milling around in his brain.

A few minutes later, Halo stopped cutting into his rib-eye and looked me in the eye. "You do this a lot."

"Dinner dates? No, Angel. Not my thing."

"Not your thing," he repeated.

"Right. I'm more in the business of catch and release."

"Catch and release?"

"Mhmm. I catch someone's eye, bring him home for the night, and then, you know, release him back into the wild."

Halo scoffed, as I reached over and stabbed the piece of meat he'd just cut into. "In other words, you fuck and run."

Sitting back in my seat, I chewed my mouthful, swallowed it down, and reached for my drink. "I don't run anywhere, Angel. And the men who leave here aren't running either. In fact, most of them are lucky if they can walk."

Halo rolled his eyes. "You are so arrogant."

I leaned forward in my chair and scraped my teeth along my lip. "Just telling it like it is."

"And that's supposed to make me want to, what? Fall at your feet?"

I flashed a wolfish grin his way. "I'm nothing if not hopeful."

"You're insane."

"And yet you can't stop thinking about what it would be like to spend one night in my bed. Can you?"

Halo's jaw clenched, and he lowered his eyes back to his plate without answering.

"I'm going to take that as a yes."

"Of course you are."

"Of course I am. You practically came on my leg thirty minutes ago. I'm not about to let you forget that." I watched him closely as he diligently cut and piled the next mouthful of food on his fork as though it were a matter of life and death, and then I asked him something I could tell was bothering him, judging by this last line of questioning. "What's worrying you the most: the fact that you've never done this before or that I do it all the time?"

This time when Halo's eyes found mine, there was shock mixed in with disbelief. *That's right, Angel. Told you I pay attention.*

"Honest answer?" Halo said.

"Always."

Halo lowered his fork to the table and narrowed his eyes on me. "Both those things. I just got this gig. I don't want anything to fuck it up. Even if you do make me—"

When Halo cut himself off, I laughed. "Oh, don't stop there."

Halo picked his glass up and threw back a good, long swallow of the vodka. "Even if you make me hard, okay? As if you don't already know that."

"I do, but it's so fucking hot to hear you say it. I couldn't resist."

"Well, to me it's just…strange." Halo's mouth pulled into a

serious line. "I've never looked at a guy like that before, and now I can't stop thinking about it."

"Then don't stop."

"That's your answer?" Halo put his knife down. "That's a shit answer, Viper."

"Hey, I'm sorry if it's not what you want to hear, but that's all I got." And it was true. Why would you stop thinking about something if it felt good?

Halo pushed back from the table, and as he got to his feet, I looked up at him.

"Going somewhere?"

"Not sitting here I'm not," Halo said, his eyes boldly moving over my face, and this time, there was no uncertainty, no hesitation in the way he checked me out. "I'm gonna head home. This is... It's not getting us anywhere, and the guys are going to want to hear what we worked on tomorrow."

"I thought you said you wouldn't run."

"I'm not running," Halo said as he walked to the couch, picked up his jacket, and shrugged into it. When he turned back to look at me, he folded the paper with the lyrics on it and tucked it into his pocket. "But for now, since I *am* still able to walk out of here, I think I probably should."

As he moved back toward the elevator, I didn't once take my eyes off him, and when he pressed the button and the door slid open, I called out, "Angel?"

He put a hand out, holding the door for himself. "What?"

"I expect you to sing that song exactly the way you sang it tonight, and if you don't..." I ran my eyes over him and then brought them back up. "We'll just have to have another private rehearsal."

Halo sucked in a breath, the idea clearly appealing to him. But as if he knew what would happen if he stayed a second longer, he stepped into the elevator and let the doors shut behind him.

Smart angel.

TWENTY-SEVEN

Halo

I'D JUST STEPPED out of the shower the next morning, wrapping a towel around my waist, when there was a knock at my door. The alarm clock by my bed read eight thirty, far too early for Imogen to be up, so I quickly threw on a pair of sweatpants and went out to see who it was.

As I peered through the peephole, I got an eyeful of the man standing on the other side and had to do a double take. It hadn't been enough that I'd been up all night thinking about him after leaving his place, but now Viper had shown up at *my* place?

He knocked again, harder this time, and I unlocked the door and held it wide, wondering what had forced him out of bed so early to land on my doorstep.

A lazy smile greeted me as Viper held up a brown paper bag in one hand and a drink holder containing four cups in the other.

He'd brought breakfast too? Who the hell was this guy?

"You gonna let me in or just stare at me, Angel?" His gaze traveled down my naked torso. Shit. I hadn't even thrown on a pair of boxers or a shirt, and my hair was still wet and dripping down my back.

"What are you doing here?" I asked, as I moved aside to let him in.

"Rehearsal." Viper glanced around my small apartment, probably the size of his bathroom, and then set the food and drinks on the bar top separating my nonexistent kitchen from the rest of the room.

"Rehearsal's not until later at Killian's."

"Actually, it's gonna be you and me today," he said, leaning against the bar top and resting his elbows behind him. With his gaze on me again, traveling from my face down the length of my body, I was all too aware of my lack of clothes—dangerous, considering we'd been fully clothed last night, and look what happened.

"What do you mean just you and me?" I said. I moved back to my room to grab the towel I'd tossed on the bed then wiped off my chest and squeezed the water out of my hair. Then I threw on the first T-shirt I saw out of the closet and headed back out to see Viper frown.

"You really didn't need to do that," he said.

Oh yes, I did. Having Viper in my apartment was tempting fate already; I didn't need to add any more fuel to the fire.

Ignoring his blatant perusal, I made my way into the kitchen, the bar top between us—yes, another shield—and said, "You didn't answer my question. Are we not rehearsing with the guys today?"

"I told Killian you and I needed some more one-on-one practice."

"You did what?"

Viper tugged at the scarf around his neck, slowly pulling it off. "My song. Your song. Writing lyrics. Get your mind out of the gutter."

I knew better than to think he was here simply to work on the music. If his night had been anything like mine, he'd woken up hard and frustrated and having to take care of himself in the shower. Twice.

I fought back the image invading my brain and tried to change the subject by grabbing the bag he'd brought. "What's this?" I opened the bag to see an assortment of bagels and spread inside. "You brought...breakfast?"

Viper lifted his shoulder. "You get grumpy as fuck when you're hungry. I'd prefer to keep the demon fed if we're gonna work all day."

I eyed the four large travel cups. "And that?"

"I didn't know if you liked your coffee black or with the fancy shit in it." He opened the lid of one filled to the brim with black coffee and took it out for himself.

"Wow. *The* Viper brought me breakfast and coffee. Wait until the press gets a load of this."

Viper rolled his eyes, and I had to grin. He'd blown it off like it was no big deal, but Viper had indeed been paying attention, and this wasn't in his character make-up at all. He never went out of his way for anyone. Everyone else went out of their way for *him*.

I grabbed two plates from the tiny cupboard over the sink.

"Jesus, Angel, if I'd known it was gonna make you this happy, I would've bought you a fuckin' bagel last night."

After I put a couple of bagels on each plate and slid one over to him, I grabbed a knife from the drawer and reached for the honey walnut spread. "The steak was more than enough, thanks."

I could feel Viper's eyes on me as I smeared a liberal amount of the spread across both sides of my bagel, and as I brought it to my lips, he said, "You like the sweet stuff, huh?"

Before I thought better of it, I glanced at him and said, "Apparently not."

Viper's sinful lips curved against his coffee cup. "Hmm. Me, I'm developing quite a taste for it."

Sweet? He thinks I'm...sweet? I wasn't sure if I liked that, but my dick sure liked the way he was looking at me right then. A little too much. I took a bite of my bagel to distract myself, and after I swallowed, I said, "What makes you think I'm sweet?"

Viper put his coffee cup down and leaned over. "What makes you think I was talking about you?"

My eyes dropped to his dark stubble, and I couldn't help but remember the rough way it'd felt against my cheek when he'd run that taunting tongue of his up to my ear. Knowing that would lead me nowhere smart *fast*, I brought my gaze back to his. "Aren't you?"

With his glinting eyes fastened to mine, Viper reached across the bar, took the other half of my bagel, and brought it to his mouth. "Maybe."

As he bit down on the bagel and flashed a grin, I snorted. "There's a bagel right there for you, you know."

After he'd finished chewing, Viper nodded. "I know. But I like eating what belongs to you."

Shit. As innocent as that sounded, the look in Viper's eyes let me know nothing he was thinking was innocent. I wasn't sure how he'd managed to do it, but in the space of ten minutes, Viper had turned the chilly air in my run-down apartment to blistering hot. The air between us all but crackled.

I put my bagel on the plate and crossed my arms over my chest, resting up against the bar that sat between us. "So you're here to work on lyrics. And that's all?"

Viper took another bite of his—*my*—food and said, "Why else would I be here, Angel?"

"You're so full of shit."

Viper popped the last piece of the bagel in his mouth. "Is that any way to talk to someone who brought you breakfast? Maybe I was just being nice."

I highly doubted that. Nice and Viper were two words that did not go hand in hand. "Says the man who told me last night that dinner dates aren't his thing."

"They're not."

"And yet this is the second time you've bought me food."

"Third if we're getting technical," Viper said, and turned to look at the tiny living space behind him. "And from what I remember in high school, on the third date, the date usually puts out."

My cock jerked in response to that, and when I didn't immediately respond, Viper looked back at me over his shoulder. "So, what do you say, Angel?"

I picked up one of the coffees and walked around the bar, heading for the *seen better days* couch that sat across the room.

"Ah, a man of action," Viper said, following my lead. "I can work with a couch."

"You"—I pointed at the mismatched recliner in the room—"can sit there."

Viper shrugged out of his coat and then fell into the recliner, kicking out his long legs in front of him. "That's right, you like to watch. Can see me better if I sit over here, right?"

Should've known that would come back to bite me in the ass. "Are you done?"

Viper's gaze swept around the room, landing on the guitar case by my couch, the keyboard I had set up in front of the one window in this space, and, finally, the camcorder I had on the tripod aimed at the couch so I could record any music sessions.

God only knows what he's going to say about that.

But, surprisingly, Viper didn't say a word, merely brought his eyes back to mine and grinned as though he'd just stumbled on something particularly amusing. "Ready and willing whenever you are, Angel."

Somehow, I didn't think he was referring to writing songs.

TWENTY-EIGHT

Viper

THERE WAS SOMETHING about seeing Halo in his own place, freshly showered, barefoot, not rockin' a thing under those sweatpants—yeah, I could tell. It had my dick taking notice, but I'd meant what I said before. I *had* come here to work on music, though that wasn't the only reason. It was just the excuse I'd given Killian when I'd called him on the way over here to tell him we made progress last night and to give us another day or two to work out the kinks. We'd be meeting with Brian and one of the MGA guys on Friday, so we needed to finish working on the lyrics to Halo's song, but once we nailed that down...

I glanced back over at the video camera in the corner. That supposed angel was into some kinky shit, huh? I could definitely work with that.

Halo took a seat on the far end of the couch, unlatched his guitar case, and set the instrument beside him. "So what did you wanna work on first?"

"You finish writing your song?"

He shook his head.

"Then that's where we start."

Halo opened the drawer of the side table next to him and pulled out a worn notebook and a pen.

"You'll need to come a little closer if you want me to read that," I said.

He gave me a look. "Seriously?"

"Or you could work on it by yourself while I watch you." I stretched my arms behind my head and linked my fingers as I watched the indecision play out on Halo's face. When he lost the battle against himself, he cursed and moved to the opposite end beside the recliner. I stretched my legs out, hooking one of them behind his ankle, tangling us together, and his head shot up.

"Viper."

"Angel." I gave him a salacious grin. "You didn't mind working so close last night."

"Pretty sure we stopped working once you got that close." He moved his legs out of my reach and uncapped the pen between his teeth. "I got as far as 'I want to take you there' at the end of the chorus."

I reached for the notebook and read over the lyrics, and then I gestured for the pen. When he gave it to me, I made four lines underneath the last bit he wrote. "We need a bit more here. It's too short."

Halo chewed on his lip as he stared off into space, and I tapped the pen against the notebook to the beat, getting back into the work mindset.

"What about something like… 'With you, I lose my brain… something something insane.'"

"Is this a love song or are you writing about zombies?" I said.

"What's wrong with that?"

"Anytime someone sings about brains, it freaks me the fuck out. Next."

Halo sighed. "Why don't you help think of something, then?"

"What if you changed the words around, like: 'With you, I lose my mind…'" When Halo nodded at my suggestion, I wrote it down. "What else would you lose?"

With a pointed stare, Halo looked at me and said, "Control."

Control, huh? Fuck, my cock liked that, and I shifted in the recliner as I wrote it down.

"Which is it?" I asked. "You want to lose control or you can't help but lose control?"

A line formed between Halo's brows. "This isn't about me."

So defensive...again. "With songwriting, if you wanna make it good, you've gotta make it personal."

I could practically see the way he was thinking back to last night, back to the song I'd written for him. The one that told him exactly how I wanted to destroy his body in the best way.

Fuuuck. Drops fell down his neck from his still-wet hair, and I had to hold on to the arms of the recliner to stop myself from going over there and following them with my tongue. I'd gotten a taste of him last night, but it hadn't been enough. Not nearly enough.

Halo followed my gaze, reaching up to his neck in a self-conscious move, and when his fingers came away wet, my resolve crumbled.

I leaned forward, wrapping my hand around his wrist, and then I sucked two of his fingers inside my mouth. Halo drew in a sharp breath as I swirled my tongue around his fingers, making sure I got a thorough taste of him. A protest was forming on his lips, so though I hadn't nearly had my fill, I slowly withdrew my mouth and sat back, picking up the pen again like I hadn't just tongue-fucked his fingers.

"So after this line," I said, "maybe since you've mentioned what you've lost, you could have the last two talk about why or how or what you've gained instead."

Halo stared at me, probably wondering how I could be so nonchalant and back to business, especially when the heated look he was giving me told me he had lost his focus completely.

My lips twisted as I tried to hide my amusement. "Is that good for you?" He could take that any way he wanted to.

Swallowing, Halo dropped his gaze and then pushed off the couch, heading over to the tripod. Something about the way his hands shook slightly satisfied the craving in me, the one that wanted to see the angel desperate for what I wanted to give.

"This okay?" Halo asked, his finger pausing against a button. "I want to make sure we don't forget anything we work on."

"I'm into it if you are," I said, as the red dot flipped on, indicating it was recording. If it was anyone else, I never would've believed the camera setup was anything other than an exhibitionist fetish—which I had no problem with whatsoever—but with Halo, it was hard to tell.

As he sat back down, he pulled the guitar into his lap and began to play, singing along until he hit the last line we'd worked on. It didn't escape my notice how well he played, or what an intricate riff he'd come up with. And it wasn't just the guitar, either—he'd been the same way with every instrument the other day.

"Tell me, Angel. How'd you get to be such a little prodigy? Too much time watching music videos? Go to a fancy-ass school?"

Halo's mouth crooked, but his fingers never stopped moving. "Both. It helps that my parents are musicians. My sister and I never stood a chance."

"Musicians, huh?" Okay, that explained a lot.

Halo looked my way and nodded. "Yeah, my father's a professor at the New York Conservatory of Music, and my mother is a classically trained pianist. Cheryl Olsen." As he lowered his gaze back to his fingers to play around with a new bit he'd just added, he said, "She plays at Carnegie Hall a lot."

Well, I'll be damned. Halo was just full of surprises, wasn't he? "You fucking with me right now, Angel?"

Halo's fingers stopped, and he shook his head. "No. Why would I lie about that?"

Cheryl Olsen was one of the most brilliant musicians I'd ever heard in my life. She'd received numerous accolades over the years and was renowned as one of the most accomplished pianists of our time, and here Halo was telling me she was his…mother?

"Because your mom's super fuckin' talented, that's why."

Halo grinned and then started laughing, and the way that smile made his face transform from serious to stunning made something other than my cock ache.

"What?" I said, as he tried to get a handle on himself.

"I'm just trying to imagine her reaction to what you just said." That seemed to amuse him all over again. "Actually, I'm trying to imagine her reaction over the fact that a badass like Viper from TBD even *knows* who she is, period."

"Why? Do I seem that uncultured?"

Halo's mouth parted as though he were about to say something, but then he snapped it shut.

I shrugged. "My mom used to take me to Carnegie Hall whenever she was able to save up enough money for a ticket. It was kind of a thing with us."

Halo's eyes softened slightly. He was looking at me in a way I couldn't quite decipher, and wasn't sure I liked, so I refocused on the words we'd been playing around with earlier.

"Okay, then. Now that I know who you're related to, you better give me something fucking kickass."

"No pressure," Halo said.

"Take it away, Angel."

Halo's fingers moved over the strings again as he began to sing the chorus, and when he reached the point where we had stopped, he shut his eyes and finished, "You've gotten inside of me. To the darkest parts of my soul..." His eyes flew open and landed on me. "That's it. 'With you, I lose my mind. With you, I lose control. You've gotten inside of me. To the darkest parts of my soul.'"

And fuck if I didn't feel like he was talking about me, with the way his eyes were all but glowing with his excitement. I nodded, because really, it was all I could do. Halo was back to humming the chorus again as though testing out the words.

"Do you like that?" he asked when I still hadn't said jack shit.

"Yeah. It's good."

"Good?" Halo scoffed. "It's awesome. Don't play."

That confident attitude was all kinds of hot. "Like I said. It's good."

Halo tucked his hair behind his ear. "So glad you're impressed."

"Oh, I'm impressed, Angel. Really fucking impressed."

Halo's eyes zeroed in on mine and stayed there a little longer than necessary. The song we'd been writing took a quick detour out the window then, and so did any desire I had to continue working on it, as I lowered my gaze to the lips Halo was now worrying with his teeth.

Fuck. I wanted to be the one biting him there, sucking that lip into my mouth, but to do that, I'd need him closer—much, *much* closer.

TWENTY-NINE

Halo

VIPER WAS STARING at my mouth again. I'd caught him several times already since he'd been here, but this time his gaze lingered, and I couldn't say I wasn't affected. I still didn't understand how I could be so attracted to someone the complete opposite of anyone I'd ever been interested in before.

Where all of my past girlfriends had been smooth all over, from their lips to every inch of their skin, Viper was all muscle, every inch of him hard, including, frequently, the appendage between his thighs. I'd felt him against me at his apartment, his dick firm and unyielding, and I hadn't been able to get the feel of him out of my mind. Never before had I been interested in exploring another man's body, nor had I imagined them touching me, but with Viper? My curiosity was starting to get the better of me, especially right now, with his gaze still on my lips.

"Angel?" Viper's eyes didn't waver, and it suddenly occurred to me how used to the nickname I'd become that I answered to it now. More shocking, I actually kinda liked it. But the way Viper's voice dropped low told me something was about to go down, something less to do with working on music and more to do with the lust in his eyes.

Yeah, I needed to move, because Viper was about to strike.

I was on my feet before he could say another word, but he didn't let me get far. He reached for my hand, halting my steps and turning me back to face him.

"Running away again?" he asked. He didn't let go of my hand, instead tugging me toward him to stand between his spread thighs. "Do I scare you, Angel?"

"Yes." The truth fell from my lips easily, and a savage smile crossed Viper's face.

He let go of my fingers and moved his hand to the back of my thigh, squeezing the muscle there, testing me, and when I didn't move away, he repeated the move on my other leg. His hands were strong as they pulled me closer to where he sat, closer to the prominent bulge behind his jeans.

My cock kicked as Viper craned his head back to look up at me.

"So honest," he murmured, his hands sliding up to my ass. "What else are you thinking?"

"That this is fucking crazy." When Viper raised a brow at my blunt answer, I said, "But it feels good. Your hands on me."

"Mmm. And what about my mouth?"

Before I could respond, Viper angled his head down, holding my hips in place, and then his lips were on me, mouthing their way up my covered cock.

Holy fuck. I sucked in a breath at the unexpected move and reached out for something to hold on to. My fingers tangled in Viper's hair, and a low groan of approval vibrated through my dick as he worked his way from base to tip. I could barely breathe, the feel of Viper's mouth on me even through my pants like nothing I'd ever felt before. My cock was fully erect before he pulled away, and I missed the contact instantly.

Like he knew exactly the effect he had on me, Viper gave me a depraved smile and said, "You didn't answer. You like my mouth on you, Angel?"

God yes. Fuck yes. Why'd you stop? My voice shook with uncontrolled hunger when I answered, "Yes."

Viper brought my hips toward him again, this time nuzzling his face against my cock, teasing and tormenting, his hot breath scorching my skin through the material. Instinct took over then, my hips shooting forward to get closer, to get more of his mouth on me. But he continued to tease until I was burning up and my legs were ready to give out. I tightened the fingers I had threaded through his hair, forcing him to look up at me and giving me a chance to catch my breath.

But when I caught the blissed-out sexual desire in his black eyes, the only thing I could think was that *I* had put that look there. *I'd* given him that reaction, and the knowledge that Viper was so sexually attracted to me that we couldn't even get through a rehearsal made me feel fucking powerful. Forget the fact that I'd never done this before. I wanted Viper. My body wanted Viper. And as his lap beckoned, I thought about how hot it would be to straddle him the way tie guy had, only this time, Viper would know exactly who was making his dick hard. He wouldn't forget *my* name.

I lowered myself over Viper as his eyes widened slightly, like he was surprised I was making a move instead of running away. He shifted in the recliner, giving me room to put my knees on either side of him, and then, bringing my other hand up so both tangled in his hair, holding him in place, I sank down onto him.

A groan passed between us, and I couldn't tell if it was me, Viper, or maybe both of us, but damn he felt good. He was rock hard behind his jeans, and my own erection rubbed alongside his as he squeezed my ass to join our bodies together without an inch between them.

THIRTY

Viper

I WASN'T SURE what had gotten into Halo in the last five minutes, but the man currently straddled over my lap, moving his hips like a well-oiled piston, was no fucking angel.

What had started out as a tease on my end, a moment to see if I could push Halo into that place where he lost some of the control he swore he hadn't been writing about from experience, had wound up with the sexy angel's hands fisting my hair as he molded his body to mine.

It was fucking heaven—or hell, since his sweats and my jeans were still in place, because if I had my way, they would've been gone, and instead of Halo sinking on my lap like he just had, he would be sinking over my very stiff—

"Shit." Halo panted, his breath a whisper above my mouth as he lifted his head, his hips still moving, causing that brain-numbing friction to continue even as he took a time-out.

Not wanting him to think of a reason to end this, or all the reasons why this was a fucked-up idea—and really, it was in the grand scheme of things—I bit and sucked my way along his jaw line to his neck, and then began to kiss my way up under his ear.

The fingers in my hair tightened and twisted, and the bite of pain had me growling by Halo's ear, making his entire body shudder.

I'd done a lot of crazy, hot shit in my day, but feeling Halo's body writhing around over the top of me had me hornier than I'd been in my life. My cock was so hard for this guy it was a miracle I hadn't lost it already, and when I shifted on the chair and brought my face back in line with his, I said, "Give me your mouth, Angel."

A wild look entered Halo's eyes as he tugged at my hair again, angling my face the way he wanted it before he lowered his head and flicked his tongue along my lip.

When I parted my lips and he lifted his head a fraction, I hauled his body flush to mine. "Give me your fucking mouth."

Halo's lips curved as he shifted up a fraction on his knees, and then he crushed his lips down on top of mine. As he slid his tongue deep inside my mouth, my fingers trailed around the back of his sweats and then slipped underneath them to the freshly showered skin.

Warm to the touch, and still a little damp from his shower, Halo's skin was so smooth it made me want to rub my naked body all over it. I palmed his tight ass, spread his cheeks apart, and trailed my finger up and down his hot channel, and when I pressed the pad of my finger to his entrance, I drove my tongue inside his mouth, capturing his surprise.

Halo moaned and shoved back onto my hand, clearly liking what I was doing to him, and as we made out like a couple of horny teenagers, I knew every goddamn second of this would be used later...when I was alone.

"Viper, God, you gotta..." Halo raised his head, and as he sat back on my thighs and his bare ass filled my palms, he squeezed his eyes shut. "Shit."

"Mmm." I rocked my hips up against his, my eyes devouring the flush on his cheeks, the lips ripe and wet from mine, and when he opened his eyes again, I shook my head. God he was beautiful. "Fuck. If I had your face, I'd be a billionaire."

Halo freed his fingers and ran them down the back of my neck. "Is that your way of saying—"

"You're fucking gorgeous? Yes."

A smile tipped Halo's perfect lips up as he smoothed his hands over my shoulders, and while I wanted him to keep going further south, I had a feeling this was as far as he was willing to go today. I wasn't about to push him and fuck this up.

"Come on, Angel," I said as I removed my hands from his sweats. Away from temptation. "I can't be the first person to tell you that."

Halo ran his hands through his hair and sighed. "You just have a...certain way with words."

"Oh yeah?"

Halo nodded. "Yeah."

"Well, I must be sayin' something right. I've got you on my lap hard as a rock and your mouth looks like I've—"

Halo put a finger to my lips.

"What?" I said around the finger.

"You were about to ruin it by running your mouth."

I flicked my tongue over the tip of his index finger, and when Halo's hips punched forward, I reached up and wrapped my fingers around his wrist. "I think you like it when I run my mouth."

Halo looked at the mouth under discussion, and then nodded as he scooted back off my thighs and got to his feet, tugging his arm free. "Your mouth is..."

I reached down and palmed myself, adjusting the hard-on that Halo had once again caused and had yet to satisfy. "If you stop there, Angel, I'm gonna start thinking you're a sadistic little fucker."

Halo laughed as he too rearranged himself. "I was just going to say that it's rather talented when it's not busy mouthing off."

Despite the fact he was giving me the worst case of sexual frustration I'd ever had, I found myself laughing at the ballsy angel as he turned around and walked to—fuck me—his camcorder.

As Halo pressed a button I assumed was *off*, he glanced at me with a grin that was right on my side of fucking trouble. I had no idea what had made me think he was an angel when he could make me feel like I was burning up from a make-out session.

"And tonight," Halo said, "I'm going to have a really good time remembering that. So...don't ruin it."

I sat there staring at his teasing grin and couldn't help but wonder if this had been his plan all along. Either way, I wasn't about to complain. Well, not about the video, at least. But maybe the fact he didn't invite me to stay and watch it with him when we finished up later that day.

THIRTY-ONE

Halo

BRIAN ARRIVED AT Killian's at ten sharp Friday morning, his shiny black Oxfords squeaking on the marble floor. He wasn't a large man by any means, but his position as manager of TBD meant his ego more than made up for his lack of height. He'd brought along a rep from MGA, presumably to make sure we were on the right track.

Still annoyed by their last run-in, Viper ignored Brian, as well as the rep, leaving the niceties to Killian, and I kept my distance as well, not wanting to be singled out again for "ruining the band" or whatever it was Brian thought about me.

Today, we'd be playing them the two new songs we'd been working on. Somehow, Viper and I had managed to finish the lyrics to what we were tentatively titling "Invitation," though how I'd been able to concentrate enough to write anything after straddling his lap, I had no idea. Even now as I watched him tune up, his lips set in a serious line, I had the insane urge to walk over there and attack him.

No—I couldn't think about that right now, as hard as it was not to. The future of TBD rested on how we did today, and I couldn't afford another screw-up, or they'd kick me out for sure this time.

I turned away from everyone and paced as I hummed the

scales, warming my voice up. *Don't think about the pressure. Just focus on the songs. Think about the words...feel the music.* Easier said than done, considering what both these songs made me think of.

"How you doin' over here, Angel?"

I glanced over my shoulder to see Viper, and when he got a look at my face, he stepped around in front of me. "You gotta get out of your head."

"I'm not in my head."

"Yeah, you are." Viper touched a finger to my forehead. "I can see the wheels turning, but we need you focused. We need you thinking about the songs, the mood, the vibe..."

Which would be no damn problem if he kept on touching me.

Viper looked over my shoulder to where the other guys were busy warming up, and then brought his eyes back to mine.

"You need me to take you out into the hall and remind you what these songs are about?" Viper's voice was low enough that I knew no one else heard, but that didn't stop me from whipping my head to the side to double-check.

"What? Worried everyone in here knows you were riding me the other day until my cock ached?"

"Jesus," I said.

"Don't be. They have no idea." Viper leaned in a fraction and whispered, "But I do."

If I'd wanted to attack his mouth earlier, feeling his warm breath on my cheek just magnified that desire, like, one thousand percent.

"Mmm, yes. That look you have in your eyes right now, Angel..."

What? Pounce and devour?

"Use it, and then come find me later and use me." Viper punctuated his invitation with a flick of his immoral tongue across his lips, and as he moved around me, he made sure to brush his shoulder up against mine.

Use him? Shiiit. As if that wasn't going to be running through my head for the next however many minutes, hours, or whatever until we were done here. But Viper was right.

These songs *were* about sex. More specifically about being frustrated because you wanted it but couldn't have it. Not to mention losing your mind because the person in your bed was like a drug, and as I turned to watch Viper walk back to his amp and get situated, I suddenly had no problem feeling either of those two things.

That sinful man had managed to focus me in the best way possible—by all but stroking my dick.

"Right," Killian said as he, Brian, and the MGA rep came through the door of the rehearsal space, Brian texting away to someone he clearly deemed more important than the band he was there to see.

"You losers ready?" Killian said.

Slade snorted and flipped him off from behind his drums, as Jagger tugged his cuffed sleeves to his wrists, making sure he looked as good as he was no doubt going to sound.

Killian shifted his eyes to Viper next, who was eyeing Brian like he was a piece of dogshit, and said, "You good, V?"

When Viper said nothing in response but continued to glare in Brian's direction, Killian shook his head and looked to me instead. "You ready?"

No. But hell if I was about to tell Killian I had a sudden case of nerves.

Viper had vouched for me when we'd arrived today, telling the guys I'd nailed down these lyrics like I was born to sing them—his words, not mine—and that pressure from a second ago began to creep back in, almost choking me up.

I raised my eyes to Viper, whose lips crooked up, and I was instantly reminded of the way that expression had felt when he'd done it against my lips and I made myself tear my eyes from him. "I'm ready."

"Good." Killian clapped my shoulder and nodded toward the piano in the corner of the room facing the rest of the band. "Then let's do this fucking thing."

Yeah. Sure. Let's.

I walked around and took a seat at the piano, and as I stared down at my fingers, I willed them not to mess this up for me. I needed this to be perfect. Hell, I needed it to be better than perfect, and as I stroked my fingertips over the keys, I closed my eyes and lowered my head. Testing the first few notes, I worried my lip with my teeth and then looked to where Brian was standing by the door watching me.

His eyes were shrewd, his curiosity clearly piqued, as he'd stopped texting for the moment to see what the "newbie" was about to pull out of his ass. The MGA rep by his side merely stood with his arms crossed, leaning against the wall, face impassive, like he couldn't care less about being there. Or maybe that look meant he wasn't expecting much.

I glanced over at the guys, who all watched me, ready for my signal, since the first song began with a piano intro. After giving them a nod, I adjusted the microphone in front of me and then began to play the opening of "Invitation."

Any remaining nerves flew out the door once the guys joined in, rounding out the sound, and I relaxed into the music. My voice came out crisp and clear, and as I sang into the mic, I lifted my head to see Viper in my line of sight. His gaze was on me as he played, his back to our visitors, and as I sang the lyrics we'd written together, they took on a more intense meaning. Even from across the room, I could see Viper's eyes darken as I sang, "I wanna be the one that makes you fall from grace."

Viper had reworked that line yesterday, grinning at me in a way that told me it was exactly what he wanted to do. My dick had liked that a little too much.

As we launched into the chorus, I could see Brian out of the corner of my eye. He hadn't once put down his fuckin' phone since we started playing, which annoyed me to no end. I almost stopped the song right then to call his ass out, but the rational side of my brain won out and I focused back on Viper. His fingers were quick, his voice blending with mine as he joined in on background vocals.

With everyone playing their parts to perfection, it sounded unreal, and once again, it hit me that I was playing with *the* TBD, that we were singing one of my songs. How had I even gotten here? It seemed like I was still caught up in some far-fetched dream, but if that were true, then I had nothing to lose, did I? As the song came to a close, an idea I'd been thinking about for the last line crossed my mind again, and though I hadn't practiced it before, I thought, *Fuck it. Just go for it.*

I ended the song on a high note—literally—and when I looked up again, Viper's eyes had widened and then he mouthed, *Damn.* I grinned, pretty pleased at having pulled that off, and then I looked to where Brian finally lowered his phone, tucking it in his pocket, and then he clapped.

Wait...what? He was clapping? He hadn't even been paying attention, or so I'd thought. The man standing next to him didn't join in, but nodded in what looked like approval.

"Fuck yeah," Killian said, coming over to throw a fist bump my way. "Where the hell did that come from?"

I shrugged. "It just seemed like it would fit."

He shook his head then said to Brian, "What'd I tell you? We've got a genius on our hands."

As I rounded the piano, Brian came over and held his hand out to me, the look he was giving me a complete one-eighty from the one he'd shot my way after the show-that-won't-be-named.

"That was impressive," he said, as I returned his handshake. "What's your name again, kid?"

"It's Halo," Viper snapped from behind him. "Fuckin' write that down."

"You got anything else you wanna show me, Halo?" Brian asked.

I nodded. "Yeah, we've got another."

"Good. That's good." Brian smoothed back his slicked-down hair and motioned for us to keep going as he took up his spot by the door again.

This time when I sang, I wasn't able to look at Viper, since I was behind the mic stand beside him, but I felt his penetrating gaze on me the entire time, lighting my body from within and giving me the perfect amount of assertiveness to sing those filthy but sexy-as-hell lyrics.

Once we'd finished playing, Brian had nothing but praise for the direction we'd veered off to. The rep beside him said MGA would be in touch, but offered no more indication of whether he'd liked our new sound, and since it was MGA's opinion that mattered, not Brian's, we weren't sure where that left us.

But as for the rest of us? We knew we'd left it all on the floor, so if MGA didn't like it?

Fuck 'em.

THIRTY-TWO

Viper

THE SURPRISES COMING out of Halo at every turn were keeping the rest of us on our toes, that was for damn sure. If Brian and MGA couldn't see his worth, then they were idiots, because Halo had just poured his heart and soul out, and I'd be damned if they went stepping on him again.

For his part, Halo looked pleased as hell. The smile on his face hadn't disappeared once, and as he chatted with Jagger across the room, he'd occasionally look in my direction, and that smile would grow wider—and that stirred up a little something in me.

It must've been obvious what I was thinking, because Killian stepped in front of me, blocking my view of Halo.

"V," he said. "What are you doin'?"

I lifted my arm, showing I'd been tying up an extension cord. "Baking a fucking cake."

"That's not what I mean, and you know it. What's going on with you and Halo?"

"Nothin'."

"Halo isn't looking at you like it's nothing. And for that matter, neither are you."

I narrowed my eyes on him. "And that's your business why?"

"Because it's something that affects the band, that's why."

"I already warned you this would happen, Kill. You didn't seem to care so much then, did you?"

"I thought he was straight."

"Yeah, not so much."

With a sigh, Killian gripped the back of his neck. "Really? I thought after what happened with Trent, you'd somehow manage to restrain yourself."

I reared back at the low blow. "Fuck you for that."

"I didn't mean that, I just... We've got a good thing going right now. I don't want to screw this up."

"You mean you don't want *me* to screw this up." I scoffed. "Thanks, *friend*. I'll file that under 'things I don't give a fuck about.'"

"Just...be careful, okay? None of us need this to turn ugly."

"Jesus, it's nothing. We're not fucking, we're not dating—"

"But you want to."

"What, date?"

Killian rolled his eyes. "Yeah right. That's not in your make-up."

"Look, I've made it clear what I want from him. It's not up to you what happens next, so get lost with the fucking warnings. He did good today. How about you focus on that."

"Yeah, he did real good," Killian said, chewing on his lip as he looked over at Halo. "You think it's enough?"

"To keep our contract?" I shrugged. "If it's not, then they're not where we need to be."

"True. How much you wanna bet they make us sweat it out before we get any kind of feedback?"

I tossed the extension cord over the amp and reached for my bottle of water. "Fucking pricks."

"You know, you could try and temper your attitude around them. It might help."

"It also might help if I offer to suck their dicks, but you don't see me doing that." I screwed the cap back on the water. "Plus, it's your job to be all smiley-smiley and make nice. Not mine."

"And how exactly was that worked out again? I can't remember."

"Natural selection. I'm an asshole, you're less of one."

Killian rubbed the back of his neck and nodded. "Right, right."

"Hey?" Jagger called across the room, snagging our attention. "If Mommy and Daddy are done discussing their kids' performances, do you think we could all go out and get something to eat? I don't keep this toned physique all primed and ready for the ladies by sipping water and breathing air."

"Yeah. I need some meat in me," Slade said, making all eyes turn in his direction. "What?"

I strolled across the space, my eyes briefly flicking to Halo before landing on Slade. "Better be careful, man. You keep saying the shit you've been saying, and we're all gonna start wondering if you're switching sides."

THIRTY-THREE

Halo

IMOGEN: COME ASAP!!

The text came through as I pulled out leftover pizza from the fridge early Monday evening, the urgency in her message causing me to drop the container on the counter and grab my cell in one hand and a pocket knife in the other. I flew down the two flights of stairs to her apartment, taking less than thirty seconds.

I burst through her unlocked door, scanning the room for the source of the urgent text, my whole body alert and prepared for fight.

"Halo? What's wrong?" Imogen asked, eyes wide as she stared at me from where she sat on her couch with a laptop propped on her crossed legs.

As I looked around again, seeing nothing out of place, I frowned. "What's wrong? You sent me a 'come ASAP' text. I thought someone was attacking you."

"Oh my God." Imogen threw her head back and laughed. "I didn't mean that in a bad way, but it's good to know you can be here in two seconds if I need you."

"Uh, yeah. That's why we live in the same building. But if you keep crying wolf, I may not believe you if some shit actually goes down."

"Aw, don't be mad. I'm sorry I scared you," she said, not looking contrite at all. As a matter of fact, she looked…excited? Her eyes sparkled, and she practically bounced as she patted the cushion beside her. "Come here."

As the rush of adrenaline subsided, I shook my head. "Since you're not dying, I'm leaving."

"No, wait! There's something about you online."

I paused with my hand on the door and looked over my shoulder. "What are you talking about?"

"Just come here. You're gonna want to sit down for this." She motioned again for me to come sit beside her, and only because my curiosity was piqued did I agree.

"All right," I said, flopping on the couch. "What's so important I ran out without any shoes?"

"Wait for it." Imogen scooted closer, and after hitting a couple of keys on the laptop, she turned it in my direction. The video playing on the screen was shaky and focused on a floor, but in the background I could hear the opening notes of "Invitation" playing. The camera shifted suddenly then, zooming in on a piano and—

Me.

My feet fell to the floor as I jerked upright, stealing the laptop from Imogen. There I was, sitting behind the piano at Killian's rehearsal room the day we'd performed for Brian and that MGA rep. Hold up… They'd been filming us? I thought Brian had been texting on his stupid phone the whole time, but he'd actually recorded us? Was that even legal?

A few seconds later, the rest of the band joined in, the sound a rich and heavy throb, but for some reason, the camera didn't turn its focus away from me. Instead, it zoomed in, my face filling the screen as I sang.

I could only sit there stunned as I watched, so many thoughts running through my head, namely how Imogen had gotten the video. But the longer I watched, the more those thoughts disappeared and, always a perfectionist, I began to critique my performance. My voice was strong, though I noticed a few nerves right at the beginning, and I sang staring straight ahead in Viper's direction, ignoring Brian completely. The camera never veered away to show the rest of the guys, which I found curious, because if Brian was taping this, surely it was for MGA, and wouldn't they want to see the whole band?

But the song...damn. Viper and I had knocked that one out of the park, and even though I could hear a few things I wanted to tweak during our next practice, the overall effect was simply staggering. That song was a fucking hit.

"Look at you," Imogen whispered, fixated on the screen. "You're a star."

I opened my mouth to lob a self-deprecating remark, but right then, the me on screen launched into the ending high note I'd ad-libbed, and I could only stare. The video cut off then, and Imogen took the laptop away.

"I told you that you needed to sit down," she said.

Shaking my head, I forced words to come out. "How did you get that?"

"The Warden posted it on his Instagram last night, and now everyone's freaking out trying to figure out who you are."

"What?" My head began to buzz, the blood rushing to my ears, and I leaned over with my elbows on my knees and rubbed circles over my temples. "The Warden? Like the rapper? I don't understand."

"Crazy, right? He's got, like, one hundred and fifteen million followers. My baby brother is about to be super famous." She lifted the back of her hand to her head and leaned back dramatically, her long red hair spilling over her shoulder. "And here I thought it would be me. Le sigh."

"How did the Warden get that video? And why would he post it? Holy shit."

Imogen sat up, her hand resting between my shoulder blades in a comforting move. "Halo, this is a good thing. Breathe."

"It didn't even show the rest of the guys. I'm the one everyone booed in Savannah, so if this video's out... Oh fuck." There was no telling what kind of hate was being spewed my way if people saw this. Suddenly, I was unbelievably glad I didn't have any social media accounts.

"Whoa, you've got it all wrong. No one's booing you now, trust me." Imogen clicked the video off and typed in the Warden's Instagram. In his status, he'd written, *Need this record, stat. #onrepeat.* Then Imogen opened up the comments, and I moved away.

"No, I don't wanna see that," I said.

"Yes, you do, come back." She grabbed my arm, and when I shook her off, she rolled her eyes and started reading off the comments instead.

To my utter surprise, the responses to the video ranged from "Wow! Who is that and where can I buy the song?" to "Genius track. Voice that's half angel, half rock god. Dude's gonna be huge," and the more she read, the more I couldn't wrap my head around it. Now, whether she skipped over the shit ones was anyone's guess, and I was grateful if she had, but the sheer amount of comments and likes were mind-blowing. Over five million in less than twenty-four hours. Fuckin' hell. Over five *million*? As in five million people had heard our song, had watched that video?

"Can you believe it? Mom and Dad are gonna *freak*," Imogen said, shutting the laptop, a huge grin on her lips as she faced me. "Aren't you excited? You don't look excited."

"Yeah..."

"You don't sound excited either."

I snorted. "It's called shock. I mean, I didn't even know I was being recorded, and now millions of people have seen it?"

"You didn't know? Do you know who taped you, then?"

"It had to be TBD's manager, Brian. But I don't know how the Warden would've gotten a hold of it, unless Brian sent it to him, which is random as hell. I don't get it, Im."

Was this some kind of marketing ploy to fight back against the bad press we'd gotten after the show? Were the guys in on it too? Or, shit, did they even know?

"That *is* weird," she agreed. "But also freakin' awesome. This is it, Halo. Your big break."

I wanted to laugh in her face, tell her she was crazy, but a strange sensation settled in my stomach, and I wasn't too sure she was wrong. And if she wasn't wrong, then that meant everything was about to change.

THIRTY-FOUR

Viper

FUCKING HELL, IT'S cold tonight, I thought, as I stuffed my hands into the pockets of my leather jacket and trudged through the ankle-deep snow blanketing the sidewalk. Even with the beanie I'd pulled down over my head and the scarf I'd practically strangled myself with to ward off the frigid night air, the wind that whipped up every few minutes or so made the icy precipitation feel like tiny pinpricks stinging my face.

It was Monday night, and as always when I was in New York, I was making the commute from Manhattan to Dyker Heights, to check in on the one person in the world I loved above all others—my mother.

It was always such a trip coming back here, back where it all began, and as I passed by Killian's old house, I saw the flickering lights of a television playing inside the living room. His mother and father were sitting down to watch the nightly news, as was their routine even now, over a decade after we'd all grown up and moved away. It was strange, and comforting to know that some things would never change, even if everything else around you did.

Like the boy who'd lived in the house next door to Killian. The boy I now wished would go to hell. The boy who'd left us... Yeah, it was always a trip to be back here, all right.

The streetlights overhead lit up the narrow strip of snow-covered concrete as I made my way past their tidy little house and the rest of the block, where home after home stood side by side until I reached the one-family semi-detached brick home where I grew up.

Swirls of smoke drifted up into the night sky, and the porch light was on, as it always was when my mom was expecting me. The peaked entrance and roof were covered in the fresh white powder that was now coating my boots, and once I was up the three steps and on the small porch, I shook as much snow off as I could.

Before I could pull out my key for the front door, it was pulled open and my mom pushed through the wrought-iron security door with a smile on her face, wearing her usual pink robe with white flowers on it.

"David." The warm greeting made the chill in my bones instantly vanish, and so did the swift whack upside my shoulder that accompanied it. "Are you insane coming out here tonight? Walking around here in this kind of weather. Do you want to catch your death?"

"Damn, woman." I rubbed at my arm. "No. I always come home on Mondays. Plus, I didn't *walk* here."

"Really?" She planted her hands on her hip, her robe and matching slippers not detracting in the slightest from the fierce look in her dark eyes. "Then why are your jeans wet? Right up to mid-calf. God knows how much of that stuff got in your boots."

Okay, my feet are *fucking freezing.* "I walked from the station. Not from the city. And how about you yell at me about it in there? Where I can take my boots *off.*"

"Don't you get smart with me," she said, pointing a finger my way.

"I'm not."

"Uh huh. That viper tongue of yours came from me, remember?"

I smirked and wrapped an arm around her dainty shoulders,

tugging her into my side. "How could I ever forget?" I kissed her on the side of the head where her dark hair was tucked behind her ears. "But seriously, I'm freezing my ass off. You gonna let me in or what?"

She tsked me, but then pulled open the door. "Come on, then. In with you."

We headed inside, and as she left me to go into the kitchen, I unwound my scarf and toed off my boots, the inviting smell of homemade chicken parmigiana—my favorite—hitting my nostrils.

Mhmm, exactly. So much for thinking I wasn't going to show. She knew better.

After I hung up my coat, I walked across the parquet-floor dining room to the newly renovated, but small, kitchen, and when I stepped inside, my mom was right there holding out a glass of whiskey.

"Get that in you. It'll warm you up."

I grinned at her and threw back the smooth amber liquid that did exactly as she predicted, then gestured to the two plates on the counter with a tilt of my head. "Insane coming out here tonight, huh? Then who you cooking for?"

"Not you, if you keep giving me lip."

I chuckled and leaned back against the counter, placing the glass down beside me as she pulled open the third drawer and grabbed a pair of bright yellow oven mitts that had seen better days.

"You know the only way I won't be here on a Monday is if I'm—"

"Out of the state, country, or if the city has been shut down due to a natural disaster." She rolled her eyes. "I know. But some might classify this amount of snow as a natural disaster."

"Eh." I crossed my arms over my chest. "Then they didn't grow up in New York, did they?"

"Yeah, okay." She laughed. "You're real tough until you catch a cold. Then you act as though you're dying and who has to deal with it? Me, because Killian is—"

"An asshole?"

"David." She smacked me in the chest with her oven mitt. "That's not what I was going to say. I was *going* to say that he's far too smart to put up with you when you're being miserable and whiny. Plus, Killian's a doll. Always has been."

I thought about my conversation with Killian on Friday, the one where he'd questioned me about Halo and frowned. "Yeah, he's a real peach."

Mom narrowed her eyes, but before she could say anything, a timer buzzed and she turned off the oven. As she pulled open the oven door, the delicious aroma of breaded chicken cutlets wafted out into the kitchen, and she took out a baking dish covered in aluminum foil.

"Okay, what did you two argue about this time?"

"Huh?"

Mom uncovered the baking dish, grabbed the pot with her sauce in it, and spooned some of it on top of the chicken. "You and Killian. You seem…irritated."

"Nope. This is my standard mood."

"No, it's not. Not when you're here. Pass me the cheese, would you?"

I picked up the small bowl of grated cheese and handed it to her, and once she'd sprinkled it over the top and placed the baking dish under the broiler, she rounded on me and gestured for my empty glass.

After she refilled it, she asked again, "What'd you two argue about?"

"Nothing." When it was clear she wasn't about to let that be the end of that, I elaborated in the vaguest way possible. "We just had a disagreement about the new guy."

"Oh." She drained the pasta in the sink and then looked over her shoulder at me. "Angel, right?"

As Halo's stunning face came to mind, and the sexy way he'd moaned into my mouth every time it'd been under mine recently, I smiled against the glass. I was starting to think that nickname was all wrong for him, because the more confident he became, the more his "angelic" side was falling away.

"Yeah, but his name's Halo." When Mom frowned, I said, "I just call him Angel."

"Ah. And why do you call him Angel?"

"Stop being nosy, woman. You'll understand when you see him."

"Mhmm..."

"Anyway. Yeah, Kill and I had a disagreement about him." Like whether I was allowed to put my dick in him.

"Nothing major, I hope?"

I knew she was trying to be subtle, but it was obvious she was asking if it was something we'd be able to get past or something like…Trent. I thought back to the way Killian and I had left things and shook my head.

"Nothing major. We're cool, promise."

"Don't you lie to me."

I held three fingers up. "Scout's honor."

"You were never a Scout. They would've kicked your butt out the first week in."

"Hey. What are you tryin' to say?"

"Just that you're stubborn and don't like to follow rules." Mom opened up the broiler and pulled the chicken out. "You like doing things your own way, not as a group. Unless it's to help someone, then maybe you'd go along with it."

She was right. I hated following anyone's lead, which was her own fault, I was quick to point out. There was no one more independent and strong-willed than my mom. Something I was extremely proud and grateful for. But like me, she could be stubborn as a bull.

Case in point: she still lived in the same little house I'd grown up in, even though I'd offered to buy her a bigger, newer place anywhere in the world her heart desired. But she insisted that her heart was right here. In this quiet little street where she knew her friends and neighbors.

And who the hell was I to tell her she was wrong?

"Would you take these plates over to the table?" she said, grabbing a knife and fork from the drawer. "And turn on the television. I don't want to miss *Entertainment Daily*."

After putting the plates on the table, I snatched up the remote. Why my mom watched these shows was beyond me. I'd told her time and time again that ninety-nine percent of what they reported was gossip or trash, but she insisted. Always reminding me that it was called Entertainment *Daily*, not Truth *Daily*.

We took a seat, and as the overly manscaped host gushed all over the latest fashions at a movie premiere that took place this weekend, I tuned out and got stuck into the meal in front of me.

God, I loved my mom's cooking. I'd eaten my fair share of amazing meals over the past ten years, in the best restaurants, served by the top chefs. But nothing—and I mean *nothing*—would ever compare to a home-cooked meal made by my mom.

I twirled my fork through the pasta on my plate, and just as I was raising it to my mouth, the image behind the host changed to the next story and caught my eye. My hand froze where it was as my mouth fell open. It was a still shot of a man with blond hair seated behind a piano, and under that image were the words: WHO IS THIS GUY?

No. Fucking. Way.

"Hey, Mom? Can you turn this up?"

Mom hit the volume button until the announcer's voice was clear, and I sat there with my hand hovering above my plate, my brain trying to catch the fuck up.

"An Instagram post by the Warden has created quite a frenzy of excitement in the social media stratosphere. Not much is known about the origins of the recording that hit last night. In fact, the name of the singer isn't even known at this time. All that *is* known is that over five million people have viewed this clip of a blond man singing behind his piano, and have now made this video the most shared, liked, loved, and raved-about clip in years, and it's only been twenty-four hours. The question everyone, including us tonight, is asking is...who is this guy? Take a look, and see if you know him."

The show then cut to a shot of Halo—*fucking* Halo—sitting behind Killian's piano last Friday in the rehearsal space singing "Invitation." The recording was focused on him as he concentrated on the keys and opened the song with that fantastic riff I swore I heard in my sleep, and then as the rest of us joined in and Halo launched into the first verse, the camera zoomed in even closer but was careful not to capture any of us on film.

Goddamn Brian. That motherfucker had been recording us without telling us. What had he been thinking? But as Halo glanced across the top of the piano and gave that half smile of his that sent my pulse and cock to throbbing, I knew exactly what Brian had been thinking. He wanted to see the public's reaction to Halo without the influence of TBD there—and clearly, it had been a winning one, if I was to gauge it on this report alone.

Jesus. Had Killian seen this? Had Halo?

I dug in my pocket for my phone, but before I could call a number, my mom was speaking.

"David? Do you know that young man?"

Shit. I'd completely zoned out there for a minute. I nodded.

"Really? He's very good."

"Yeah. He is." I glanced back at the TV in time to see Halo lick his lip before the segment went to commercial, and before I hit Killian's number, I said, "That's our angel."

THIRTY-FIVE

Viper

KNOCK. KNOCK. KNOCK.

Two hours later, I found myself standing at Halo's front door with a bottle of whiskey in my hand, as I waited for the man of the hour to open up.

After talking to Killian on the phone, we'd both come to the conclusion that Brian was a scheming little motherfucker. But since the publicity swirling around Halo was unbelievable, we'd decided our manager could live to see another day...for the moment.

Somehow, I'd managed to make it through the rest of my meal and evening with my mom without being a rude asshole and going off somewhere to hide and watch this four-minute video in its entirety. But the second I'd gotten on the train and put my headphones in, I'd opened up that link and let Halo weave his magic, and that's exactly what he was—pure fucking magic behind that mic and piano.

Just thinking about it had my cock aching, and when the sound of a chain, and then a deadbolt, was undone, I tightened my fingers around the neck of the whiskey in an effort not to grab and attack.

As the door was pulled wide, and Halo came into view in a pair of light grey sweats and a black T-shirt, my lips pulled up. "Hey there, big shot."

I knew as soon as a flush hit his cheeks that Halo knew exactly what I was referring to as I pushed off the doorjamb and ran my eyes over him.

"You gonna invite me in? Or are you too busy replying to all your adoring fans to spare lil old me a moment of your time?"

Halo laughed. "I don't think there's anything little about you."

"So glad you noticed."

"That's not what I meant."

"Sure it isn't." I took a step forward, and when Halo didn't back up, I raised the whiskey and said, "Thought you might like to celebrate."

Halo's eyes shifted over my shoulder, and then came back to mine. "Are the rest of the guys with you?"

I slowly shook my head. "Nope."

Halo's lips parted, and this time when I walked forward, he backed up until I was in the apartment, kicking his door shut behind me.

"So I'm guessing you saw the video tonight," Halo said.

As I took a step closer and Halo continued his retreat, the adrenaline of this little cat-and-mouse game kicked in. Fuck, he was hot. Here in this place where he was most comfortable. The sweats and the curly hair that I wanted to fist my hands in gave him an I-just-tumbled-out-of-bed look that made me want to drag him right back into it.

"Oh, I saw it, Angel. On the TV, on my phone, in my fucking head every time I shut my eyes. I can't un-see it."

When Halo's back hit the edge of his tiny kitchen island, his breath caught and I reached forward to put the bottle down beside him. Then I left my hand in place, effectively caging him in.

"I would even venture to say about a million of the views now added to the tally on that thing tonight are from me. And you know what I saw other than you singing our kickass song behind a piano?"

This close, I could see the way Halo's eyes darkened, as his arousal began to take over anything other than the fact that I was now wedging my foot between his legs and getting as close to him as possible.

"What did you see?" Halo put his hands on my chest, and for a second I wasn't sure if he was going to shove me away or pull me closer. But when he gripped the material of my shirt as if to hang on for whatever was about to happen, I had my answer.

I ghosted my lips over the top of his, and when his tongue came out to try and tempt me to stay, I smirked and Halo moaned.

"I saw you watching me." I shoved my hips forward until my hard cock—that now seemed to want Halo and only Halo—rubbed up against his. "I saw you singing, and watching *me*."

"Fuck, Viper."

"Hmm." I kissed my way along his jaw, and then up to his ear and whispered, "Yes. That's exactly what your eyes were saying. Fuck me, Viper."

Halo twisted his fingers in my shirt and pulled me up so I was looking him in the eye. "That's not what they said."

"Yeah. But we both know that's what you want."

Before he could protest, I slammed my lips down on top of his, and Halo's opened, letting my tongue slide deep inside his mouth as his hands trailed down my front and slipped in under my jacket.

A groan escaped one of us, as I put my other hand on the counter beside him and rocked my body along the length of his.

"Damn, you looked sexy on that video," I said as Halo grabbed my ass. "Singing about losing control, losing your mind, while you eye-fucked me so hard my cock has ached ever since."

Halo sank his teeth into his lip as he thrust his hips forward. "What... No random stranger offered to fix you up?"

"No random stranger will do. You see, my cock, it seems fixated on a certain angel."

Halo's eyes roamed over my face, his expression unreadable, as I brought a hand up off the counter and trailed my cool fingertips under the hem of his shirt.

"Shit," he said. "Your fingers are freezing."

"They won't be for long." I ran them along the edge of his sweats to the drawstring that was neatly tied and sitting low on his waist.

With my eyes locked on his, I hooked a finger through one of the loops and slowly dragged it free. Halo's breath left him on a rush, and when he let go of my ass to brace his hands on the counter behind him, I took a step back and lowered my eyes down to what I was doing.

The soft fabric of Halo's sweats was doing nothing to cover the stiff length inside, and when I had the drawstring loose, I raised my eyes to see Halo's fastened on what I was doing. The tip of his tongue was running along his top lip, and when my hands froze, Halo raised his head, his eyes asking one thing: *Why'd you stop?*

Dropping my hands, I took a step back and said, "Take off your shirt."

Halo swallowed, his Adam's apple bobbing in his throat as everything he was feeling flashed across his face. Lust. Uncertainty. Need. And desire. But it was clear what the most dominant feelings were as Halo reached for the hem of his shirt, drew it up his torso, and threw it to the floor.

As his smooth skin came into view, I reached down to readjust my throbbing dick. I couldn't remember the last time I'd teased myself so hard before I actually gave in. Things came so easily to me these days that I could practically point at someone and know I could have them in my bed in under five minutes, and out in fifteen. But the angel? He was different.

Something about Halo made everything inside my body feel alive, and I had a feeling fifteen hours or days wouldn't satisfy the fire he was stoking in me.

"You know," I said, and took the steps to bring me back within touching distance, where I dipped my fingers in under his sweats. "They always say you shouldn't drink on an empty stomach." As I curled my fingers around the hard-on inside the angel's pants, his jaw clenched, and I squeezed. "And I *am* kinda hungry..."

Halo's chest rose and fell as he looked down between our bodies, where my hand was working his cock nice and slow.

"But you know what else?"

Halo cursed. "What?"

I released my hold of him and hooked my fingers in the edge of his sweats. I pulled them down until I was at his feet and he was staring at me with untamed lust igniting those light eyes. Then I flashed him a feral smile and said, "I was always taught to eat my meals at a table."

THIRTY-SIX

Halo

I COULD BARELY BREATHE as Viper straightened, his powerful body aligning with mine, and then his lips brushed below my ear.

"On the counter, Angel," he said, his breath on my neck a whisper that made me shiver.

Overwhelming. That was the first word I'd use to describe what was happening. I lifted myself up onto the counter, my bare ass hitting the cold surface and making me flinch, and then Viper's hands were on me, tracing up my thighs as he stepped between my legs.

Not for the first time since we'd met, I wondered how we'd gotten to the point where I craved not only Viper's attention, but now his hands and mouth on me. I kept waiting for the ball to drop, for the fact that Viper was a man to sink in and make me run.

But running was the last thing on my mind right now.

As he lowered his head, Viper's mouth bypassed my stiff-to-the-point-of-painful erection, and instead, his tongue ran a path along my inner thigh. The move was so unexpected, the skin there so sensitive, that I bucked beneath him, causing him to chuckle against my leg. Then he repeated the move on the opposite side, his lips coming so close to my dick that I could feel his hot breath there, but then he was gone, straightening so we were face to face.

"I think I like making you squirm, Angel," he said.

I don't know if it was the cocky tone, or the way he was looking at me with hunger in his eyes, but I found myself making the first move for once, holding either side of his face, and angling my head in toward his for a searing kiss I felt all the way to my bones. Viper opened for me without hesitation, diving in deep, each of us starving for the other. My cock jerked between us, desperate for his attention, and lucky for me, he didn't make me beg. Keeping his lips fused to mine, Viper wrapped his hand around my erection, warm and tight, and when I moaned inside his mouth, he squeezed.

God, just him touching me had my eyes rolling in the back of my head, but Viper wasn't content to stop there. No, he was just getting started.

He pulled away from me, his lips pink and slightly swollen, and then he lowered his head, his breath ghosting over the head of my cock. So, so close, but he was still teasing, making me desperate for him.

"I've been waiting to taste you from the minute I saw you," he said, looking up at me with heavy-lidded eyes, a look so sexy I knew it would be burned in my mind forever. Then Viper's mouth was on me, his tongue swiping over my slit, making me gasp. When he repeated the move, my hand shot out to grip his hair, and Viper seemed to take that to mean I wanted more—fuck yes, I did—and his mouth sank slowly down onto my cock. Warm, wet, and tight, the sinful heat of him was enough to make me come right then, but the threat of embarrassing myself by blowing my load after two seconds kept my dick in check. Barely.

"Shit, Viper." I panted as he swallowed every inch of me. I couldn't stop watching the dark head between my thighs, trying to reconcile that it was *Viper* giving me more pleasure than I could remember having in forever. His mouth moved back up my hard length, his hand following after in firm strokes, a double whammy designed to drive me crazy.

But it was when his fingers grazed my balls that my hips jerked up off the counter, and deviant that he was, Viper cupped them in his palm as he sucked me down again.

God, it was too fucking much. I tugged at his hair like they were the reins to stop his mouth with, but he ignored it completely, probably because it wasn't "stop" or "slow down" coming out, but curses and unintelligible groans, all of which drove him forward with single-minded purpose.

The strings that held my self-control together were already thin where Viper was concerned, but now they were practically nonexistent. I could feel the impending surge, a massive wave beginning to crest. My breaths became unsteady, my body jerking as I undulated against his mouth, getting closer…closer…

Had it not been for Viper's hands holding me steady as an orgasm so strong I almost blacked out hit, there was no way I would've been able to keep myself on the counter. My head fell back, and I couldn't feel anything other than the powerful climax and Viper's mouth, sucking every bit of me down his throat. As if he'd gotten a taste of something he liked and wanted more of, Viper moaned around my dick, greedily swallowing until there was nothing left.

My whole body was shaking as Viper tore his mouth away, licking the head of my cock one last time before lifting his gaze to mine. He looked momentarily satiated, though I could still see the desire lurking in the depths of his eyes.

He hooked his hands behind my knees and hauled me forward to the edge of the counter, bringing our bodies flush against each other. With one hand still tangled in his hair, I pulled his head back, taking in the heat that now stained Viper's fierce cheekbones, the hair that lined his jaw and surrounded the sultry lips that had just been wrapped around my cock. Viper was all man—a sexy-as-fuck man. Or, as I was currently thinking, a sexy man I wanted fucking me.

That realization had my lips slamming down on Viper's, and as he opened to me, I could taste myself on his tongue. His hands slid up my bare back, pressing me against him, and the surprising thought that entered my mind then was: *I want to be even closer.*

When I lifted my head to take a breath, I looked between us. I was completely naked, my pants and shirt on the floor, but Viper had managed to stay clothed, and having seen at least the top half of him, that was a tragedy.

"Your clothes are still on," I said.

"There's a reason for that." When I quirked a brow, he nipped at my lower lip. "Because if they come off, someone's getting fucked."

Another shiver rolled through me, because holy shit, what would that be like?

Viper leaned back, cocking his head to the side. "You're not looking too angelic right now, Angel."

I grinned. "You're enough to corrupt anyone."

"Ah, so you're like a fallen angel?"

Hmm. That seemed a pretty apt description of me at the moment, didn't it?

Viper's gaze fell down my naked body, and with a groan, he pushed away from the counter. "You need to put your fucking clothes on unless you want this to go any further tonight, and I"—he rounded the counter and picked up the bottle of whiskey—"could use a fucking drink."

I couldn't hide my surprise as I slid down off the counter and picked my clothes up off the floor. Viper wanted to stop? He was walking away without getting anything out of it on his side? Had we stepped into some kind of alternate universe?

"But...you didn't..." I didn't even know how to voice what I was trying to say, but Viper knew.

"Trust me, I know," he said, and when he saw I still wasn't dressed, he rubbed a hand over his eyes and turned his back on me. "Clothes, Angel."

I quickly threw on my T-shirt and sweatpants, wondering why

the sudden halt. Part of me felt a little disappointed, especially after watching the video of the two of us together and how hot that had been, but the truth was that I wasn't sure I was ready for all that "going further" entailed. Hell, I was still coming down off the high of what we'd just done; reality hadn't set back in yet. By all means, I should've been the one putting a stop to things, so having Viper put his foot on the brakes, albeit grudgingly, made me wonder what exactly was going through his head.

One thing I knew for certain, though: this thing between us was far from over.

THIRTY-SEVEN

Halo

"EVERYONE HERE? WHERE'S VIPER?" Brian stuck his head out of the rehearsal room. "Viper! If you could grace us with your presence, that'd be great."

When Brian turned back to face the rest of us, he shook his head and checked his watch.

"You in some kind of hurry, man?" Killian asked, where he lounged on the couch beside me with his legs casually crossed at the ankles. We'd all been called together by Brian the day after the "Invitation" video had gone wild, presumably to figure out what the hell happened next.

"Time is money," Brian said, turning on his heel, and as he opened his mouth to yell again for Viper, the man in question shoved past him into the room, nearly knocking Brian off-balance. When our manager didn't say a thing as he steadied himself, Viper smirked and flopped into a chair opposite Killian and me.

Jesus. After last night, I could barely look Viper's way without heat creeping up my neck, because damn, him between my legs had been the hottest thing I'd ever experienced. As if he knew what I was thinking, Viper grabbed the end of the toothpick in his mouth and slowly slid it in and out several times until I made myself look away or risk giving myself away.

"So," Brian said, straightening his tie and then sliding his hands into his pockets. "I think we can all agree that the video I sent the Warden has paid off quite well. You're welcome, by the way."

"Recording without consent is a dick move," Viper said. "You pull that shit again or post anything online without our approval and there won't be a fuckin' next time."

"V." Killian shot him a *shut the fuck up* look. "Let's hear what he has to say. I'm sure Brian had a good reason for being a sneaky motherfucker and posting a private session."

Brian paled. "What? You guys should be thanking me. Over five million people saw that video—"

"Over seven now, actually," Viper said. "Which means you owe Halo about seven million apologies, considering it was his face you focused on."

I sank down a couple of inches, not wanting to draw any more attention to myself, since it seemed like I was always in the center of the damn maelstrom.

"You're not serious," Brian said, his hands balling at his hips. "I did you assholes a favor. Your career was going up in flames, but now everyone wants to know who Halo is. He's gonna save you."

Save them? This coming from the guy who told the band to fire me?

Slade pointed a drumstick Brian's way. "Not fuckin' cool."

"Yeah, you should apologize," Jagger agreed.

For the first time since he'd entered the room, Brian looked at me. With nowhere to hide, I straightened and waited to see if he'd bow to their demands. Personally, I didn't need any kind of apology. The song going viral was the coolest thing that'd happened in my lifetime other than joining TBD, but I could understand the invasion of privacy being an issue for the others. They'd had to deal with this kind of thing far longer than me, so when Brian puffed himself up and threw a quick "sorry" in my direction, I nodded, ready to move on.

"Good," Killian said. "Now what is it you wanted us here for?"

Clearly thrown off his game, Brian ran a self-conscious hand over his tie and tried to regain his upper hand. "Due to the response the video has generated, MGA wants you in the studio to record 'Invitation' tomorrow. They want to get it out to radio, stat, while it's hot."

Holy shit...my song—our song—was gonna be on the radio already? My eyes found Viper's, and I couldn't stop the grin on my face as he nodded in approval.

"That's not all," Brian went on. "I also showed them the second song, and they've agreed to give you guys studio time to get the album done. You've got three months, and you can utilize any MGA property. The only stipulation is you lock that shit down, give them an album they can do something with, and you leave this week."

Viper waggled his brows at Killian. "Miami?"

"Hell yes," Jagger said. "I'm over this snow shit."

Killian looked at me. "What about you, Halo? Think you can write some songs in Miami?"

Uh, I could write a song in a cardboard box if it was going to be on the radio or on a TBD album, but I tried to rein in my excitement and play it cool.

"Yeah." I shrugged. "Miami works."

"Good. Be at the studio tomorrow at noon, and then pack your shit for the weekend." Brian turned to leave, but then seemed to remember something. "Oh yeah. You've got a *Late Night with Carly Wilde* performance Friday. Make sure you've got a new name when you show up."

"A new name?" I said. *And a TV performance? Shit.*

"New band name. TBD's dead. Try to come up with something a little more original this time, guys."

With that, Brian slammed the door shut, and a few seconds later, Killian's front door also slammed shut.

"Man, I fucking hate that guy," Viper said. "I don't give a shit if he's been with us since the beginning. Money's made him a douchebag."

"He's not my favorite either, but he just gave us a decent deal and MGA's still interested," Killian said.

I was still focused on the last bit Brian had said. "So you guys were serious about changing our name? We won't be TBD anymore?"

Killian reached over to squeeze my shoulder. "Startin' fresh, my man. Any ideas?" He looked at the others. "What about you guys?"

I had a feeling this wouldn't be an easy decision, considering I heard the guys chose TBD—"to be determined"—as a placeholder while they thought up a name, and it ended up sticking.

"Maybe something that incorporates the first letter of our names?" Jagger said. "What word can we make outta that? We've got K...H...V...S...J..." He stopped and frowned. "Not one fuckin' vowel?"

"Moving on." Killian drummed his fingers along his thigh in a steady rhythm. "What about something to do with New York, since we all grew up here?"

"Us and millions of others. Really unique there, Kill." Viper snorted and threw his toothpick in Killian's direction. When it missed and hit me instead, Viper narrowed his eyes and cocked his head to the side, studying me. You could practically see the wheels turning in his head, whatever was going on in that brain of his nothing good, and when a wicked smile crossed his lips, I braced myself for whatever was about to come out of his mouth.

"Fine. What have you got?" Killian said.

"Oh, I've got somethin'." Viper didn't take his eyes off me as he inclined his head in my direction. "Look at our frontman. What does he look like to you?"

When everyone turned toward me, I shot Viper a dirty look, but that only made his smile grow.

"Those golden curls, that angelic face, his name. But underneath lurks a man who writes and sings filthy lyrics. A...*fallen angel*, wouldn't you say?"

As the reference to what Viper had called me last night after the epic blow job hit my ears, I glared his way and opened my mouth to disagree with his suggestion, but Killian beat me to it.

"Fallen Angel... Dude, that's perfect."

Out of the corner of my eye, I could see Slade and Jagger nodding along.

"He really does look like a fallen angel," Jagger said. "And being the face of the band, especially after the video? The ladies are gonna go apeshit."

"The guys too," Viper said, shooting me a wink that had my stomach flip-flopping, as if everyone knew exactly what he was referring to. But of course they didn't. How could they? They thought I was straight. They'd never suspect I'd be tempted by our devilish guitarist, or at least not that I'd give in.

"So we're all in agreement? The band is now Fallen Angel?" Killian looked at the group of us, everyone throwing out a version of yes, and when he got to me, I gave Viper another look. He seemed pretty damn pleased with himself, stretching his hands up over his head and lacing them behind his neck as he smiled my way.

Great. Our new name was forever going to be a reminder of Viper's lips wrapped around my dick.

"Fallen Angel it is," I said.

"Damn. That might've been the quickest decision we've ever made," Killian said. "Now let's go practice this shit before we lay it down tomorrow."

THIRTY-EIGHT

Viper

"OKAY, GUYS, YOU have ten minutes until you're on, got it?" Brian's eyes swept around the green room of *Late Night with Carly Wilde*, which we'd occupied several times over the years back when she had a daytime talk show. And when he realized we were all there except for one, his eyes skidded to a stop on Killian. "Where's the kid? Why can't you all ever be in one place, on time?"

God, I hated it when Brian called Halo that. *Kid.* It was condescending, not to mention really fucking rude, considering that *kid* was about to be the person who ensured Brian's paycheck this month.

But before I could voice my opinion, Killian spoke up, likely sensing my desire to rip Brian a new one.

"He just went to hit the head. He'll be back in a minute."

Brian glanced at his watch, then looked toward the door Halo had disappeared through five minutes ago and said, "I don't care if he's back in eight. As long as he's here when they come to get you guys."

"Jesus, Brian. Relax, would you." Jagger poured a shot of tequila from the fully stocked bar, and then held it up. "You want one of these? Maybe two or three?"

"Hell," Slade said. "Give him the whole fucking bottle. You need to chill, man."

"Chill?" With a hand on his hip, Brian rubbed his other fingers across the bridge of his nose and then said in a lowered voice, "I don't think you realize what's at stake here tonight. I will 'chill' when you five get on that stage, wow the audience, and remind them all why they fell in love with you. *Tonight* needs to be perfect. *You* all need to be perfect."

Was he fucking kidding with this shit right now? Talking to us as if we didn't know what was at stake? This was our livelihood. Our jobs. Christ, he had some nerve.

Shoving to my feet, I was about two seconds away from putting a fist in the bastard's face, when Killian intervened by grabbing my arm.

"Viper was just about to go and find Halo and let him know it's time. Right, V?"

If the choice was between that or murdering Brian, I knew which I preferred right then.

"*Right*, V?"

I aimed an *eat shit* look in Brian's direction, and when he rolled his eyes, I ground my molars together. "Right."

As I turned to leave the room, I took the shot Jagger still held in his hand and slammed it back, and when he offered the bottle, I took it from him. Not for me, but just in case Halo needed a shot of liquid courage.

It'd been a couple of days since we'd finished up the recording of "Invitation," and with tonight's interview, the track about to hit, and the trip to Florida all happening at a whirlwind pace, none of us had really had a chance to stop and think about everything going down.

That wasn't so much of an issue for me and the guys—we were used to the chaos that sometimes surrounded our lives—but for Halo? I had a feeling that things were starting to catch up with the angel.

Pushing through the door of the men's room, I wasn't at all

shocked to find Halo standing at the far end of the vanity in front of the mirror, staring at himself as though he were looking at a stranger—and tonight, he probably felt like one, at least to himself.

To me, however, he looked sexy as fuck. In black boots he'd left half unlaced, jeans that were ripped in all the right places, and a fitted white shirt he'd only buttoned to mid-sternum, the man standing in front of the mirror with the disheveled curls and luminous sea green eyes looked like a man who people would lose their fucking minds over.

Add in the black leather jacket, and when Halo stepped on that stage tonight, every person sitting in the audience, and at home in their living room, was about to fall in love.

"How you doing in here, Angel?"

Halo looked in my direction, and when his eyes fell to the bottle in my hand, he said, "Do you always carry a bottle of alcohol around with you?"

I raised the tequila and shrugged. "Maybe. I thought you could do with a shot before we hit the stage."

"Ugh." Halo scrunched his nose up.

"Or maybe not." I put the bottle on the vanity and walked to where he was back to staring at himself in the mirror.

"I already feel like I'm going to be sick," he said. "That will not help."

I'd figured as much, but as I stared at Halo's profile, I couldn't for the life of me imagine why someone like him would ever be nervous. He was...magnificent.

"Angel." When Halo didn't respond, but kept staring at himself, I moved around behind him until he could see my face in the mirror beside his. "You are going to kill it out there tonight."

Halo's eyes searched out mine, and I could see the real worry there, the real...fear.

"I don't know, I... What if it's like it was back in Savannah? We all thought I was going to kill it there, and look what happened. I killed it. As in TBD is dead because of me."

Without even thinking about it, I grabbed Halo's arm and spun him around so he was chest to chest with me. Then I took hold of his chin and said, "TBD is dead because of Trent. Not you. Do you hear me?"

When Halo remained mute, I dragged my thumb over his lip and followed the path with hungry eyes. "*You* are giving us a second chance. Your music kicks ass, your lyrics are hot as fuck, and this face with that voice? Angel, you're about to be a fucking superstar. Enjoy that. Be proud of it."

When Halo slowly nodded and shifted closer to me, I groaned.

"And keep that look that's in your eyes now, would you? It'll make me uncomfortable as shit, but it'll be perfect when you hit the stage."

"What look's that?"

Knowing my own limits, I dropped my hand from his face and took a step away. "Ask me after we're done here and I'll show you." I walked back toward the door and snatched up the tequila. "Final chance."

Halo walked my way but shook his head, and I was relieved to see the fear from a second ago had been replaced with a new sense of determination. "You really think my music kicks ass?"

I grabbed on to the door to open it for him and nodded. "I do."

The smile that lit Halo's face made something in my stomach tighten.

"Then what do I care what the rest of the world thinks?" he said. "That's good enough for me."

As we walked back to the green room, it was to see the rest of the guys coming out the door. When they spotted us, they all started shooting the shit with Halo, pumping him up for what was to come, and I hung back a little, hearing Halo's words over and over in my head.

I had to admit, it felt really fucking good to know that I was the reason Halo was now standing tall and looking like he had won some goddamn prize, and as one of the assistants began to mic us up, I made sure to keep my eyes off him. Killian was standing close enough that he'd see any kind of thought or feeling that was on my face, and the last thing Halo needed was Killian calling me out on my wayward dick.

"Okay," Killian said, as he clapped Halo on the arm. "Ready for this?"

Halo scoffed. "Uh...no." Then he flashed a charming smile. "But I'm gonna rock it."

"Of course you are, man." Jagger peeked out of one of the curtains and then looked back at us. "And if you get nervous there's a serious hottie, front row, on the right. Miniskirt, legs for days, blond hair."

Never in my life had I wanted to be called on stage for an interview more. And when Halo grinned at Jagger and said, "Nah. You can keep the blondes, they aren't my type," I almost asked one of the assistants if she could bring that bottle of tequila back.

"How about he looks at Carly," Killian said, as he shoved Jagger in the shoulder. "Since she's the one doing the interview?"

Before anyone could chime in with anything else ridiculous, a woman with tight red curls stuck her head behind the curtain.

"You guys are on in five, four, three," then she mouthed, *Two, one,* and before Jagger was shoved out from behind the curtain, he whispered to Halo, "What about redheads?"

Then Carly Wilde's voice came over the speakers. "Please welcome to the stage, everyone, Fallen Angel."

THIRTY-NINE

Halo

"CHAMPAGNE, SIR?" THE flight attendant asked as I buckled myself in on MGA's private jet the next morning. *Private jet. Will I ever get used to this?* Answer: I certainly hoped not.

As Viper made his way down the aisle, he swiped a champagne glass from the attendant's tray. "Might as well keep the party goin'," he said, winking my way before downing half the contents. For a heart-stopping second, I thought he'd choose the seat beside me, but he sauntered past, claiming the cream leather couch on the opposite side.

I blew out a breath and smiled at the flight attendant whose nametag read *Shirley.* "Thanks, Shirley, I'd love one."

Last night's performance on Carly Wilde's show had gone phenomenally well—nothing like our Savannah show—and we'd spent all night celebrating at a dive bar. My head pounded, but I drank the champagne gratefully. Hair of the dog and all that.

"'With a new name, a new sound, and a new lead singer, the band formerly known as TBD made its first live appearance last night on *Late Night with Carly Wilde*, and it was nothing short of spectacular.'" Killian grinned as he read to us off his phone. "'Just last week, the world saw its first glimpse of new frontman, Halo, when the Warden posted a secretly recorded video of the singer performing what will surely be a hit if the reactions on social media are any indication. With the face of an angel and the voice to match, Halo stunned the late-night crowd, breathing new life into the powerhouse that was TBD, and all but ensuring the rockers of Fallen Angel a future spot among the greats. We're anxiously awaiting the debut album, release date still to be announced…'"

Killian had been reading off articles the entire drive to the airport, and while I was ecstatic at the response, I couldn't stop focusing on the work we had ahead of ourselves.

"We just have to write and record an entire album in three months and make it kickass. Worthy of being one of 'the future greats.' No big deal," I said.

"You," Viper said, pointing my way. "Drink. Stop fuckin' stressing."

"Yeaaah, we're goin' to Miami." Jagger rolled his hips like he was grinding in a club—shit, maybe in his head he was.

"And what does that mean? You don't stress in Miami?" I said.

"Damn right," Killian said. "Impossible to stress in paradise. We're gonna write, record, drink, spend every spare second on the beach—"

"And prowl at night." Jagger high-fived Slade, and I had to shake my head. Easy as that, huh?

The pilot came on over the intercom, announcing we'd be taking off momentarily, and as the others buckled themselves in, Viper cocked his head at me.

"You still look nervous, Angel. I bet I know something that'd take your mind off those worries." With the heated stare he was giving me, my eyes widened. What the hell was he doing?

Viper swung his champagne glass back and forth, holding it by the stem, and then he grinned. "Once we take off, how about I introduce you to the mile-high club?"

My mouth fell open. Did he really just say that in front of the others? Uh, what was I supposed to say to that? I knew what I *wanted* to say, but…

A chuckle met my ears, Killian shaking his head and throwing one of the pillows in Viper's direction. "Ignore him. He asks everyone," he said.

"Everyone, huh?" I said, raising a brow as my shoulders relaxed. "Anyone ever take you up on it?"

Slade snorted. "Oh yeah."

"The flight attendant from the trip to Chicago," Jagger said. "Had to grab my own damn food on that trip."

"And the manager from... Who's that band that opened for us in Dallas? Something stick..." Killian snapped his fingers and pointed at Viper. "Stage Trick. That's it. He wasn't even supposed to be on the damn plane."

Slade laughed. "Shit yeah. And then—"

"Okay, we're done here. Thanks for the trip down memory lane, assholes," Viper said.

"Someone's gotta remind you. With so many to remember, it's gotta be a little crowded up there." Killian tapped the side of his head, and under his breath, Viper cursed.

So Viper got around. That wasn't exactly news to me. I'd known what I was getting myself into, but hearing the others talk about it so casually, jokingly, made me glad about his status, because it was taking the focus off what *I* was doing with him. Or *half* doing at this point.

Like he knew what I was thinking, Viper shrugged, and as the guys continued, I settled back in the most comfortable plane seat I'd ever been in. A plush recliner was hands down the way to travel, and as the plane began to race down the runway, I found my eyelids growing heavy from the lack of sleep. In a few hours, we'd be away from the cold of New York and welcomed into the warm, sunny arms of Miami, and I couldn't fucking wait.

"WAKEY, WAKEY, SLEEPIN' beauty." The low, rough sound of Viper's voice by my ear had my eyes opening.

Sometime during the three-hour flight, my mind had veered off into dangerous territory. I had gone from a relaxing sleep to a wicked-hot dream. One where Viper had taken me to the back of the plane and introduced me to the mile-high club that he seemed to be a VIP member of.

As his face came into view now, my eyes automatically searched out the lips that had just spoken. The ones I could still feel on my neck from the dream, as he'd followed me into the larger-than-average restroom, shoved me up against one of the walls, unzipped my jeans, and taken me.

My cock kicked at the thought, clearly liking the idea of having Viper in control of me, as I recalled in vivid detail how those lips had felt as they'd moved to my shoulder, his teeth biting into the tense muscle there—

"We're here," Viper said, his mouth curving in a crooked smile, as though he knew where my mind had gone, and when my gaze flew back to his, I realized just how close he was and where we were, and immediately shifted away from him.

Viper chuckled, and that didn't do anything to help my…condition.

"Relax, Angel." Viper took one of my curls and wound it around his index finger. "The others are out in the car."

I glanced over his shoulder to make sure he wasn't screwing with me; Viper wasn't exactly the king of discretion. But when all I saw was an empty plane, I brought my eyes back to his and said, "Then we should go. Shouldn't we?"

"Probably."

"Probably?"

"Yeah, probably. The guys have been waiting a little while now, but when I came back here to get you, and heard you groaning in your sleep"—Viper tugged on the curl around his finger—"I decided to sit here and watch you for a minute…or five."

Oh my God. If the ground wanted to open up and swallow me right now, that would be A-okay with me.

Deciding to deny, deny, deny, I shook my head. "You're full of shit. I wasn't groaning."

"Mhmm. Yes, you were." Viper ran his eyes down to my very obvious erection and said, "What were you dreamin' about, Angel?"

Like I was going to tell him. "Nothing."

"Liar." Viper rubbed the hair between his thumb and forefinger, his eyes narrowing on me. "Okay. We'll play your way for now. You'll tell me eventually."

That made me laugh. "Pretty sure of yourself there, aren't you?"

Viper leaned in close and put his lips to the corner of my mouth. "Not pretty sure. One hundred percent sure. I'm also sure of you. So unless you're gonna tell me that the thrill of flying in a private jet got you all kinds of fucking excited, I'm going to place bets that the hard cock between your legs right now is for me."

A rush of air left my lips, and I turned my head to try and get a taste of his. But Viper moved out of reach, releasing my hair and standing tall, and when I looked up at him, he smirked.

"Hold that thought till we get to the house."

Shit. "Then what?"

Viper palmed the front of his jeans, drawing my eyes to his arousal.

"Then you're gonna tell me what you were dreamin' about." Viper ran a hand through his hair. "You got five minutes, Angel. Don't make me come back here and get you."

That had been enough of a warning for me, and thirty minutes later, Slade was pulling the black Cadillac SUV that had been waiting at the private hangar to a stop in front of a set of wrought-iron gates that fenced off a driveway so long that I couldn't see the actual house.

The drive between the airport and what I now knew to be Indian Creek Island had been eye-opening, to say the least. For one, the sun was out, miracle of all damn miracles. I was used to the blizzardy mess that was New York right now, and the idea that I'd be able to sit outside and soak up the warmth of the sun in February was really damn appealing. Second were the sheer sizes of the houses we'd been driving by to get to our final destination.

Jagger had been acting like a tour guide of sorts, explaining how Indian Creek Island was the most exclusive place to live in the Miami-Dade area. With approximately forty-one homes on this slice of paradise, it offered luxury *and* privacy to MGA's clients and artists, and for the next three months, this was home.

I felt like I'd tripped and stumbled into an alternate universe—a really fucking great one.

"It's good to be back in Miami," Killian said as Slade wound down the window and punched in the code.

As the massive gates yawned open, and Slade put the SUV in drive, Jagger leaned across the second set of seats and said, "Wait till you see this place, Halo. It's totally sick. Twelve bedrooms, ten bars, a swimming pool and Jacuzzi, a sky bar—"

"A recording studio," Killian said, twisting around in the passenger seat. "A 3D movie room."

"A helipad," Slade added, as I peered out the window at the lush green foliage and palm trees that lined the entryway. "And anything it doesn't have, you can get with one call."

"Paradise," Jagger said, and when I looked out the front windshield, an enormous palatial estate seemed to appear in the middle of all that greenery, as though it had sprung from the earth the same way the plants had.

Slade brought the car to a stop at the front entrance, which looked like some kind of Spanish bell tower. As I climbed out and craned my head back to take in the sheer size of it, I heard doors being slammed shut behind me as the guys continued talking about sun, sex, and—

"I call dibs on the guesthouse, losers." Viper slung a massive duffel over his shoulder and then picked up another before heading to the stairs.

"That's not fucking fair. You had it last time," Slade said, as he hiked a backpack up his arm.

"Don't matter. Rules are rules. Whoever calls it gets it." Viper walked backward, a shit-eating grin on his face as he stared at the four of us who were standing at the back of the Cadillac.

Jagger grabbed his Louis Vuitton suitcase from the trunk and extended the handle. "Eh, less awkward that way. Now we don't have to pretend to remember every new guy we run into in the kitchen."

Viper flipped him off. "Doesn't save *me* from tripping over every new chick out by the pool doing a downward fucking dog at the ass crack of dawn."

"What can I say? I like someone who's a little bit flexible." Jagger laughed and then wrapped an arm around my shoulders. "Don't worry, Halo. There's plenty of rooms to go around—"

"And plenty to choose from so there's a few doors in between," Viper called over his shoulder, and while I knew the others would take that to mean so I wouldn't have to hear Jagger, my mind went directly to how they wouldn't hear me...with Viper.

FORTY

Viper

DID YOU FINALLY PICK A ROOM?

It was around an hour after we'd arrived at the mansion that I tossed my bag onto the California king in the guesthouse and kicked off my boots. After taking a look around the main floor, we'd decided to go and settle into our respective corners and get some much-needed shut-eye before meeting up for our first meal in the big house later that afternoon.

But since Halo had already taken a three-hour catnap, I had a feeling the angel would more than likely be awake. Not two minutes after I'd sent the text, I got my answer.

Angel: I did. How's your luxury suite out there by the ocean?

I walked over to the French doors I'd opened as soon as I'd let myself in and looked down to the small waves that were crashing onto the sand.

Fucking amazing. Wanna come see?

And while the view *was* amazing, I found my eyes glued to the three little dots on my phone.

Angel: The ocean?

Something about that comment made my pulse speed up,

because it was obvious Halo was thinking about something other than the goddamn sea. **If that's what you wanna look at.**

There was a pause for a moment, and while I could've let him off the hook—fuck that. Halo had been the one to open this line of dialogue, and I wasn't about to let him run and hide. **Come down here, Angel.**

Three dots appeared, disappeared, and then—

Angel: I don't think that's a good idea.

Bingo. **Why? You're just going to look at the ocean.**

Angel: Now who's lying?

If he thought I wasn't about to own up to that, think again. **Me.**

Fuck. I reached down to massage the heel of my palm over my dick as I leaned a shoulder up against the door. **What room are you in?**

Angel: I'm not telling you that.

But you want to, don't you, Angel? Just like you want to come down here and see my...view.

A couple of minutes went by, and just when I thought Halo might've decided he was done with the conversation, up popped—

Angel: I really fucking do, which is...crazy.

Ah, okay. This...*this* I could work with. **Crazy how?**

Angel: Crazy as in, I can't stop thinking about your damn mouth for one. And what it did to me the other night.

Oh, I liked that. I liked that a whole fucking lot. My first taste of the angel had left me wanting more.

And what is my mouth doing now whenever you think about it?

Three dots. No dots. Three dots—**Angel: Kissing me... sucking me...spouting off shit that I shouldn't find hot but...do.**

Jesus. Halo had my cock so fucking hard from this exchange that I reached down to flick open the button and unzip where I stood. I needed some kind of relief, and if he wasn't going to come to me, then the next best thing would be to come thinking about him.

Was that what you were dreaming about on the plane?

Angel: LOL. That's driving you nuts, isn't it?

YOU are driving me nuts. Not to mention making mine ache, I replied, and then added, **I haven't jerked off this much since I was in fucking high school.**

Angel: So I heard. Apparently you just fuck whoever is close by.

Come down here and that'll be you.

I wasn't sure what kind of response I'd get to that, but then Halo wrote back, **See, that shouldn't make me hot, but damn, it really does.**

I shoved a hand into my jeans and wrapped my fingers around my aching length, and, no longer able to text, I hit the call button and brought the phone to my ear.

The second it connected, before Halo could say a word, I said, "What were you dreamin' about on the plane, Angel?"

"Shit." Halo's response was part moan, part curse, and much deeper than his usual cadence.

"Angel?"

The heavy breathing in my ear told me I wasn't the only one turned on, and when Halo finally said, "You," my fingers tightened around my cock and a low growl escaped my throat.

"What about me?"

"Viper…"

"Angel. *What* about me?" As I waited for his answer, I walked back into the room and stretched out on the massive bed, jeans now pushed down my hips so my cock was firmly in hand.

"I was thinking about you and the, um, mile-high club."

You've gotta be fucking kidding me. I'd thought the guys yapping about all that would've turned Halo off. Apparently not. "And what about it?"

When Halo groaned in my ear, I clamped my fist around the root of my dick and cursed. Damn, whatever it was, that groan sounded fucking promising. "Angel?"

"Yeah." Halo panted in my ear.

"What were we doing?"

"You were behind me..."

My eyes fell shut as I imagined Halo somewhere up in the big house with his hand wrapped around his dick, as he imagined—

"Your hand was working my cock, and you were...inside me."

Oh fuck. I hadn't expected *that*. But I sure as shit wasn't about to let it go. "Is that something you want?"

"I...uh...yes? I think so."

"You think so? You'd better be sure."

I heard Halo take in a ragged breath.

"Come down here," I said.

Halo let out a strained laugh. "No way."

I squeezed my eyes shut, my frustration and lust at an all-time high before I reined it in. "Okay, fuck. What else was I doing to you? In this dream."

Halo didn't miss a beat. "Biting me."

My hips bucked up off the bed, my slick dick now sliding easily through my hand as my climax raced down my spine. This scorching call was only seconds away from being over.

"Where?"

"Where?"

"Yes. Where was I biting you? I want to know so the next time I get you alone near a goddamn wall, I can shove you up against it, get my hand around your cock, and leave teeth marks on—"

"My shoulder," Halo said, and then that sexy growling sound he made when he came reverberated through the phone and into my ear, triggering my own release.

As I looked down at my sticky hand, I crooked my head until the phone was pressed tight to my ear and said, "Angel?"

"Viper."

"The view's nice down here, but I can think of an even better one."

"Mmm?" he mumbled, like he no longer had the energy to get the words out.

"You, naked, in my bed, and making those hot-as-fuck sounds when you come. Tomorrow, you're mine."

FORTY-ONE

Halo

"ALL RIGHT. I'M OUT." Jagger stood up from behind his keyboards and stretched his arms up over his head until they cracked. Then he looked over at Slade. "You comin'?"

As Slade got to his feet, Viper's fingers paused over the strings of his guitar. "Whoa, whoa, whoa, where the hell do you two think you're goin'?"

"We've been at it all day, and the sun's going down soon," Jagger said.

"So?"

"Sooo, I need to find myself some inspiration."

Viper snorted. "Does that inspiration come in a bikini?"

"Damn right it does. You guys wanna come? Halo?"

I automatically shook my head. We'd been working on a new song for hours without a break, and while we'd made some real progress, I wanted to push on a bit more, see what else we could squeeze out.

Viper shook his head as well, and when Jagger's gaze landed on Killian, he said, "Come on, Kill. You know you wanna hit the beach. That lifeguard we saw was giving you major fuck-me eyes."

Biting down on his lower lip, Killian looked between us.

Always the most responsible in the group, the one to keep us all on task, it shocked the shit out of me when Killian got to his feet.

"I'm in," he said, setting his bass in the stand. "We got a lot done today. A break might give us a refresher."

"Mhmm." Viper cut his eyes at Killian. "All work and no play makes a cranky gay."

Killian rolled his eyes. "That mean you're coming?"

"Who said I haven't been playing?" When Viper grinned, Killian glanced at me and then back to Viper.

"Guess that means you've been enjoying the guesthouse." Killian flipped him off as he followed Slade and Jagger out the door. "Halo, you sure you don't wanna come with?"

I shook my head, too focused on what we'd been working on to think about stopping now. "No, I'd like to see if I can work out the last verse. You guys go ahead."

"If you change your mind, you know where to find us." With a wave, Killian and the others left, leaving Viper and me alone in the vast studio. Located in the basement of the mansion, the studio was decked out in all the latest technology—perfect for the producers who were set to join us next week, though they wouldn't be staying here with us.

"Well, well, well." Viper strummed his guitar. "Looks like it's just you and me."

Without the others, the large space suddenly seemed intimate. When Viper stood up to come closer, I held my hand up.

"Stay over there or we won't get anything done." I knew that to be the truth as much as my next breath; Viper's final words to me last night had been "Tomorrow, you're mine," and even though that sent a thrill shooting straight to my cock, I needed to focus on the song. The pressure from all those damn articles waiting for our album weighed on my shoulders, and I wasn't going to be the one to let them down.

"Okay, Angel." Viper settled back down in the recliner, laying his guitar across his lap. "You've got one hour."

"Might take longer than that."

He shrugged. "One hour."

"And then what? Bikinis?"

Viper snorted out a laugh that only drew my attention to his full lips, the ones that had pulled from me my sleeping fantasy like a confession, and when he saw where my eyes were focused, his tongue came out to swipe along his lower lip.

"If you want that hour, you better stop lookin' at me the way you are right now, Angel."

Fuck, how was I supposed to concentrate now that his sexy-as-hell release from last night was all I could hear? There had to be a way to get *that* in a song, because it was the hottest thing I'd ever heard.

"What I wouldn't give to be inside that head of yours to see what you're thinking," Viper murmured when I didn't look away.

"I was thinking of the way you sounded last night. How I've heard you but I've never seen you come."

"Fuckin' Christ. Are you shitting me right now?" Viper's hand disappeared under his guitar like he had to adjust himself, and then he growled as his head fell back. "Read off the last goddamn line or we're leaving."

His reaction had me grinning, because who wouldn't be proud of affecting Viper to the point of torture? *Might have to do that more often...*

But later. Because right now, there were words to write. "Smacked down...they've got you right where they want you. Hands bound..." I scratched through the next line. "I don't like what we had after that, so let's start there."

With his head still back and his eyes squeezed shut, Viper said, "What do you suggest?"

"Um." I chewed on the end of my pen as I ran threw a few options in my head, but none of them seemed to fit just right. *Tomorrow, you're mine. Gah, fuck. Get out of my damn head, Viper.*

Viper opened one eye. "What was that?"

"Uh, nothing." I glanced down at the lyrics again, tapping my pen along the notebook to the beat, hoping the perfect line would appear out of thin air. "Something tumbling, tumbling..."

As we sat in silence, the quiet was deafening, especially with the others not humming along or cracking a joke or messing around on the keyboard.

"It's too quiet in here," I said, sighing.

"I can fix that." Viper sat up, and as he began to play the song, I sang along with what we had down so far, but then stumbled over that damn fourth line. I cursed, which only made Viper chuckle. "You're too hard on yourself. You don't have to be perfect in here."

"Yes, I do."

"This is the place for mistakes. Just throw out whatever you've got."

"I don't have anything. That's the problem."

"Then you're thinking too hard."

I glared at him. "I don't see you coming up with anything over there."

Viper cocked his head to the side, and then began to play:

"That Angel, what a tease,

But damn he loves me on my knees,

Makin' him say more, Viper. More, please."

I laughed, shaking my head. "You're fuckin' ridiculous."

"You mean fuckin' talented. You can say it. 'Viper, you're a talented motherfucker.'"

"Because you can churn out inappropriate Seussicals? Hardly."

"I wasn't talking about my songwriting skills," he said, running his hands through his hair, and though it wasn't his intention, I found my gaze following those strong hands as they landed back on the guitar, one wrapping around the neck of the instrument and sliding its way down, just like he had with my cock—

Ugh, hell, this was not working today, or maybe it was just that I could no longer work one-on-one with Viper without thinking of him outside the band. Like in my kitchen...in Viper's living room...in...me.

Ever since I'd watched the recording of the two of us in my

apartment, the one where I'd straddled Viper and he'd teased my ass with those talented fingers, I couldn't help but wonder how it would feel to have him go further.

And why did he have to look so damn tempting all the time? I'd gone from never noticing a guy before to being laser focused on everything about Viper. He wore ripped jeans today, a pair so faded it looked like he'd had them for years, and every time he stood up, they rode so low on his hips that I knew if I put my fingers through his belt loops and tugged, they'd fall right off. And damn, wasn't that a delicious thought.

"Look at that. Time's up," Viper said, glancing at a nonexistent watch on his wrist before setting his guitar to the side.

That shook me out of my reverie. "What? Why?"

"I told you to stop looking at me like that. You can't manage to do that, so your hour's up."

FORTY-TWO

Viper

THE ANGEL COULDN'T say I didn't warn him, and judging by the lack of protest as I got to my feet, I didn't think he was about to tell me to stay put a second time. So I wasn't surprised in the slightest when Halo's eyes went on a round-the-world trip of my body from head to toe and every inch in between—and right now, there were several extra inches than usual.

Well, that wasn't exactly true. Around Halo, those inches were becoming the norm, especially since the guys had left and I'd caught him watching me with a new kind of hunger in his eyes. One that was pretty damn close to mine, if I had to place bets.

Halo had gone from looking at me with curiosity and confusion, to openly checking me out, and that made both me, and my dick, ecstatic. Last night had clearly been a turning point for the angel, judging by the blistering looks and that comment he'd made about wondering what I'd look like coming, and there was no way I was about to let this opportunity, this opening Halo had given me, pass me by.

"I'll behave. We might be able to get a little more done today," Halo said as he looked at me from behind the safety of the closed piano, which was on the opposite side of the room to where I'd been on the couch, and that just wouldn't do anymore.

"There's no way we're going to get anymore done," I said as I walked over and stopped at the end of the piano.

"You don't know that."

"Yeah, I do. Nothing good comes when you're forcing it, Angel. Let it go. We can come back tomorrow."

Halo let out a grumble and tossed the notepad on top of the piano, then he looked down to the keys as though they'd help him find what he was missing.

Aww, the poor guy was frustrated—join the fucking club.

"Look," I said as I made my way to him. "Why don't we get out of here for a while? The guys were right—it'll help clear your head."

Halo turned on the seat and angled his face up until he was looking at me. "Get out of here? No offense, but watching women in bikinis is not going to inspire me right now."

I chuckled and placed a hand on the piano so I could lean down until our lips were but an inch apart. "Thank God for that, otherwise this will be really awkward for you."

Before Halo could ask what, I tangled my other hand in his hair and took his mouth with mine, taking the kiss I'd been denied until this very moment. Halo's lips parted in an instant, his tongue sliding over my lip to enter my mouth. I twisted my fingers in his hair and groaned, and as though he knew what I was thinking, Halo began to move.

He pushed up to his feet, his mouth never leaving mine, as he took a step closer to me, his hands going for the waist of my jeans, his fingers sliding through the loops to tug me to him until I had his back against the piano, and my front against his—but then Halo stopped.

"Angel?"

"I'm sorry," he said, putting a palm to my chest. "I'm just all up in my head right now."

I took a step back and shoved my hands into the pockets of my jeans to give him the space he seemed to need, and let out a sigh. "You need to relax."

Halo laughed and shook his head. "Yeah, this is not helping that plan at all."

"It will," I said. "Eventually."

"Right. But until then, you're in my head, MGA is in my head, the millions of people who watched the video are—"

"Hey, hey, hey," I said, moving back into his personal space so I could take hold of Halo's shirt. I could sense the anxiety attack waiting to happen, and found myself trying to ease his panic. "Breathe. I have an idea. One that might relax *and* inspire you."

Halo took hold of my wrists and stared into my eyes. "Pretty sure I felt your idea of relaxation pushing up against me a second ago, Viper."

I chuckled and raised a hand so I could trace one of my thumbs over his cheekbone—because fuck me, I couldn't stop myself. "Feel free to use me to relax any time you want, Angel."

"Such a generous offer. I appreciate you sacrificing yourself for my needs."

"Hey, I'm all about lending a hand to help a fellow man." I let go of him and took a step away, knowing if I stayed within touching distance, this would end the way it usually did whenever Halo was around me in private these days.

"Just a hand?" His lips curved.

"Or a mouth. Or anything your...*heart* desires."

"Not sure it's my heart controlling my desires right now, but I'll think about it and let you know."

What was that song I was singing earlier? *That Angel, what a tease.* "Sooo if we aren't going to be working and we're not going to be fucking, we need to get the hell away from this empty house and the twelve bedrooms in it."

Halo laughed as he pushed off the piano. "Have you got any suggestions?"

"Some friends of mine are in town; you might've heard of them. The Nothing?"

Halo's grin disappeared as his mouth fell open. "Are you kidding?"

I realized that I'd somehow stumbled on something he really wanted. "Not kidding, no. We opened for them back when we first started out. I'm buddies with the lead singer and I could get us some tickets. Would that inspire—"

"Yes." Halo nodded. "Hell yes."

"You don't even know what I was gonna say."

"I don't care. You just asked if I want to see The Nothing. The only answer you're going to get from me tonight is yes."

A smile slowly curled my lips. "Well, that's certainly good to know."

Halo swallowed, his eyes shifting over my shoulder to the door, as though checking no one else was with us, then they came back to me. "Would the rest of the guys be coming with us?"

"No. Just you and me. That cool with you?"

Halo took a breath and then bit down on his lip, and I had to dig my fingers into my palms in an effort not to grab him.

"What will you tell them?" Halo asked, and it took a second for me to get my mind off his mouth and back to the conversation.

"Who?"

"The guys."

"I'm not gonna tell them shit."

Halo's brows pulled together. "You don't think they'll think it's weird? Us going to a concert together, without them?"

"Uh, no. Should they?"

Halo shrugged. "I don't know. Killian, he…"

When Halo's words trailed off, I shook my head. There was no way he wasn't going to finish that sentence. What had Killian done? Because if I found out he'd said something to Halo, I was going to track him down whether he was with that damn lifeguard or not.

"He just gave me a look today before he left. It made me think he might know about this." When Halo moved his hand between us, I took hold of it, halting it midair.

"So what if he does?"

"You don't think he'd care?"

"More like I don't give a fuck if he does. Kill doesn't tell me where to put my dick, and I don't tell him where to put his. We get along much better that way."

"And you want to put it…?"

An indecent smile tugged at my mouth as I raised Halo's hand to my lips and nipped at his fingertips. "Wherever you let me, Angel."

FORTY-THREE

Halo

LATER THAT NIGHT, a black Escalade arrived at the mansion to pick up Viper and me to take us to the American Airlines Arena in downtown Miami, where The Nothing were headlining. The others had spent most of the day out, and when they'd come back, they weren't alone, which meant they weren't at all interested in joining us for the show. I wasn't sorry about that, considering I'd be getting several hours with Viper, including the time spent alone in the back of the SUV, something I was now enjoying despite my earlier freak-out.

It hadn't hit me until this afternoon how crazy my life had become in the last few weeks. I still hadn't adjusted to the speed and urgency of the music world that I'd been swept up into. I hadn't anticipated the pressure that would come with not only fronting such a huge band and rebuilding from the ground up, but also going from being a nobody to being the "next big thing"... whatever that meant.

And the craziest part of it all was the surprising and intense sexual attraction I was having for the man sitting beside me, which was eclipsing everything else to the point where almost all I could think about was him. I'd never been one to let another person consume me, but Viper wasn't just anyone, was he? He was a rush like

I'd never felt before. When he walked in a room, my eyes immediately found him. If I heard his voice, I wanted to seek him out. And when his attention was on me, no one else existed—and I liked it.

The farther we drove from the mansion, the more my worries over the music and the band faded away, until all I could see was Viper.

With a privacy shield up between us and the driver, Viper and I sat together in the back, his foot casually hooked behind my ankle, the only place our bodies connected. As the lights of the city passed by in a blur, and with no one else around to see, I let my eyes roam over him.

Damn, he looked sexy tonight. He'd changed into a pair of non-ripped jeans and a black T-shirt, and he somehow looked like he'd stepped off the pages of *Rolling Stone*. It didn't even seem to matter what he wore, Viper just had this swagger, this vibe coming off him that made you sit up and take notice when he walked in the room —or simply sat beside him in the car.

"Look all you want, Angel," Viper said. With his face turned toward me and lit from behind, he was a dark shadow, but I caught the flash of white teeth when he grinned. "You can touch, too."

Tempting. He was so very, very tempting, and it wouldn't be difficult at all to close the inches between us and explore the parts of his body that I'd denied myself earlier. But if I did that, we'd never make it to the show, and if we didn't make it to the show—

A familiar piano riff broke into my thoughts, and as I realized where it was coming from, I jerked up in my seat.

"Shit," I said, fumbling with the buttons beside me, trying to find the one I wanted.

"I got it." As Viper pressed the right button, the song grew louder, filling the interior of the car, and I stared at him.

"That's us," I said, breaking into a huge grin. "That's *me*. On the radio. We're on the fucking radio!"

Viper chuckled, but the music was so loud I couldn't hear him. He seemed to like watching me, though, as I drank in the fact that

"Invitation" wasn't just a song in my head anymore, wasn't just a song we played in the studio without anyone else around. It was out in the world now, playing on radio stations, and holy shit, I couldn't get over the fact that we were sitting there listening to the final version we'd recorded and that others were listening to it too, right now, at the same time.

As the song ended and the next one began, Viper turned the music back down.

"Pretty fuckin' cool, huh?" he said.

"Are you kidding? That was... It was... Shit, I can't even talk."

"Take it all in. You only get to hear your first time once."

"Isn't it always like that? Like, every time the new stuff comes out. Doesn't it blow your mind you're on the radio?"

"It used to." Viper cracked his window open before grabbing the cigarette over his ear and the lighter from his pocket. He lit up, sucked in a long inhale, and then blew the smoke out the window. "Guess you get used to it."

"No way. I could never get used to that."

Viper's lips curled as he brought the cigarette to his lips again. "That's 'cause you're a romantic."

"A romantic? Me?"

"Yeah, you know, walkin' around wearing rose-colored glasses. It's all new to you. Exciting." Viper blew another stream of smoke into the night air.

"That's not a bad thing," I said, feeling a little defensive. "It's a huge freakin' accomplishment to be on the radio or to get to play on a stage where people actually show up to listen to you. That doesn't happen for most musicians, and it sure as hell never happened to me before. I'm allowed to be excited. Sorry, Mr. Cynical."

"Don't be sorry. I like that about you."

"You do?"

"Yeah. You remind me of how it should feel." He cracked a smile. "I'm a jaded asshole, what can I say?"

"Jaded, yes. An asshole...eh. That wouldn't be the word I'd choose."

"No?" Viper's eyes glittered in the dark. "What would you choose?"

There I'd gone, opening my mouth and backing myself into a corner without thinking it through. "I haven't decided yet."

"Ah. Need any help?" Viper's hand moved to my thigh and began a slow slide up, and when his fingers grazed over my dick, I sucked in a breath.

The intercom flipped on, the driver announcing our arrival at the arena, and Viper gave me a slight squeeze before pulling his hand away. He popped open the door before the driver could, and as he got out, I took the moment to adjust myself. Couldn't go meeting the guys of The Nothing with a raging hard-on.

The driver had pulled around to the back of the venue beside a couple of tour buses, and when we got out of the car, a guy who introduced himself as the tour manager gave us a couple of backstage passes and led us inside, where the halls were filled with frenzied staff hurrying in all directions. More than a few did a double take when they saw Viper, but it must've been an unspoken rule that no one was to stop us, because we were led straight back to The Nothing's dressing room. It'd been set up according to their rider, which Viper had told me used to include "normal shit like bottles of booze and fast food," but, along with their growing success, had morphed into a full bar of high-end liquor, black curtains that covered every wall, red light bulbs replacing the white, and, in the center of the room, a huge, solid glass tank that encased a fifteen-foot boa constrictor.

"Oh shit," I said, taking a step back from the tank.

"Scared of snakes?" Viper smirked. "Don't worry, the only snake that's gonna bite you tonight is standing right next to you."

I pulled my gaze away from where the boa constrictor was stretching itself out along the side of the tank to see Viper's devilish grin.

"Come on," he said, his hand brushing against mine before he led us past the tank to where the members of The Nothing were being interviewed by a reporter I recognized from *Entertainment Daily*. When they saw Viper, the reporter was promptly ignored, the band getting up to greet him with slaps on the back, fist bumps, and curses. I stayed back a little, trying not to be starstruck, but hell, I'd been listening to these guys for over a decade. And they just so happened to be friends with Viper. Would this ever be anything but surreal?

"Guys," Viper said, moving to the side and gesturing my way. "This is Halo, our new frontman."

"No fuckin' way," Dex, the lead singer, said, shaking my hand, and then he stepped back to give me a once-over. "Jesus, you couldn't get someone who wouldn't make me look like an aged pig beside him, could you?"

Viper laughed. "Fuck no."

"I saw you on *Late Night*," Chris, the drummer and songwriter of the group, said, coming over to greet me with a handshake as well. "Epic song, man."

I blinked at him, a thank you on my lips, but unable to come out, because fuckin' Chris from The Nothing just said my song was good, and I could die now.

"I saw it, too. Several times," the bassist, Jonny, said, his eyes dropping down my body, checking me out with no subtlety whatsoever. He took in a drag of his joint, holding it in for a moment, and then blew the smoke out. "That pretty mouth of yours really knows how to sing."

"Uh, thanks," I said, thrown a little off guard by his blatant perusal. Unlike the reaction I had when Viper ran his eyes over me, I found myself uneasy under this guy's gaze.

"If you want to stick around after the show, my cock would love to see just how talented it is."

Beside me, Viper tensed and went to take a step toward Jonny, but I put a hand on Viper's arm, halting him from coming to my defense.

"Jonny, isn't it?" I said. "I was a big fan of yours…in middle school."

"Oh shit," Chris said, snorting out a laugh and slapping Jonny on the back as laughter broke out around us.

"It's like that, huh?" Jonny said, his eyes narrowed on me so hard they were practically slits. "Good luck filling Trent's shoes, kid." He put the joint back between his lips and walked out, leaving an awkward silence in his wake—especially when we realized the reporter had caught every bit of that exchange.

"Sorry about that," Dex said, rolling his eyes. "He's been such a cheerful bastard since he's been out of rehab, what can I say?" To the reporter, he said, "Don't write that down."

The reporter looked up as if caught, and then scratched out the last few lines on the page.

"He's always been a fuckin' dick," Viper said, and Dex shrugged.

"We've fired him more times than I can count, but he always worms his way back in." Dex leaned around me to say to the reporter, "Don't include that shit either."

We grabbed drinks and hung out with the remaining members, bar Jonny, until they had to head onstage. Again, the word "surreal" popped into my head, because even as normal as they were, cutting up and recalling inside jokes with Viper, they were still the larger-than-life guys I'd grown up listening to, and no matter how many times I pinched myself, it still wasn't sinking in that I was a part of it all.

Before we headed out to watch the show from the wings—a first for me—Chris said, "You guys free after the show? The hotel's shutting down the top floor for us. Free booze, lots of willing bodies—and don't worry, Jonny'll have other distractions."

"Um…" I glanced at Viper, who shook his head.

"We've got other plans," he said, and when Viper's eyes met mine and I saw the primal look in them, suddenly, the last thing I wanted to do was stick around after the show. That look was full-on sex, and had both my cock and pulse throbbing. Because whatever Viper had in mind, it was clear he wanted to do it without others around...and fuck, I wanted that too.

"If you change your mind, just give them the password 'boa' at the door. Good to meet you, Halo, and good luck." Dex and Chris both said their goodbyes, and as we followed them out to the wings, Viper's fingers slid beneath the loop of my jeans, pulling me back into him.

"I told you, Angel," he said in a low whisper. "Tonight, you're all mine."

FORTY-FOUR

Viper

THE HEAVY BEAT blasting from the megawatt speakers of The Nothing's impressive stage was making the floor in the wings vibrate as they belted out one hit song after another, causing their fans to lose their fucking minds.

They'd been at it now for nearly an hour and a half, and I wasn't sure what was louder, Chris pounding on the drums or the screams from the fans below as they chanted out every single lyric at an ear-piercing level.

One thing I was sure of was the total rush I got from watching a kickass band tear up a stage with music that made your entire body hum and your mind think of one thing only—sex.

Hot, raw, break-the-headboard sex. Add in Halo, who was standing in front of me, his ass brushing up against my dick as he shouted the lyrics to songs that had no doubt accompanied couples to beds, to the backs of cars, hell, to restrooms at clubs when things got out of hand, and my entire focus had shifted from the guys on the stage to the guy standing in front of me.

Halo was looking totally fuckable in his jeans and white linen shirt that had been playing a game of look-but-can't-touch with me all night. With its three-quarter sleeves and open V-neck, the shirt should've been a deterrent, considering all that it covered. But when the light hit him just the right way, every delicious inch of him from the waist up was displayed, and I wanted my hands and mouth back on him as soon as fucking possible.

Glancing over my shoulder, I took in the dark corridor to the left of the stage area that led to a set of stairs behind an exit door. I'd found them by accident during a performance TBD had done here, when I'd been wanting to go outside for a smoke before we hit the stage. Instead, I'd ended up in a maze of tunnels beneath the arena that were like a rabbit warren. The perfect place to go so no one could find you.

As the song drew to an end, I turned back in time to see Chris and Jonny tossing back shots and Dex switching out his guitars, and I knew they had to be coming to the end of their gig.

Halo looked over his shoulder at me, his face flushed from singing and jumping up and down like the rest of the fans. The thrill of the night was evident in his eyes as a bead of sweat trailed down his temple.

"*This* has been fucking awesome," he said, his exuberance contagious as he ran a hand through his hair, and when the leather straps on his wrist came into view, my eyes fastened on them, and I had a sudden urge to see him sprawled out naked on my bed with his hands tied—bound to me.

This young, fresh-faced *angel* had me more turned on than I could ever remember being, and all because he'd smiled at me— but what a smile it was. It was obvious that tonight had done the trick. All the anxiety from earlier was gone, and as I took a step closer to him, I said, "Heard enough?"

Whatever Halo saw in my expression had him slicking his tongue over those perfect lips as he nodded, and without another thought, I grabbed his wrist and led him down the dark corridor.

As I made a left, marching toward the exit door, I towed him along behind me. He didn't put up a fight, not even a token one, as I shoved through the door and led him down the cement stairwell inside.

The sound of stomping feet could be heard from the arena

floor above, and when we reached the bottom of the stairs where the rabbit warren began, I tightened my grip on his wrist and made a sharp right, pulling him out of the dimly lit walkway and into a shadow-filled alcove, where I backed him up against the wall and placed my hands on either side of him.

"What is this place?" Halo's breathing was more rapid, his eyes a little wild, then he rocked his hips into mine.

"Somewhere private," I said, just as The Nothing let loose on their latest single. It blasted through the arena like a cannonball, and Halo grabbed at my hips.

"Somewhere I could...use you, maybe?"

"Is that what you want?" I said, wanting to make sure I was reading him right, because I was about two seconds away from devouring him.

Halo leaned forward and nipped at my lower lip. "Mhmm. Are you ready to sacrifice yourself?"

I chuckled against the angel's taunting mouth. "Well, as long as it's for the good of man and all."

"It'll be good for one man, that's for sure." Halo's fingers tightened on my ass. "So what'll it be? Your hand, your mouth, or...?"

"Careful, Angel. Your deviant side is showing."

"Yeah? Well, maybe I'm sick of being good. Maybe I want to be...bad tonight."

Hell if I didn't want that too, but... "You don't know the first thing about being bad."

"Well, if anyone could teach me, it would be you. Right, Mr. Cynical?"

I removed my hands from the wall and reached for the ones he had on my ass, then I licked the sweat from his temple and said by his ear, "I thought you'd never ask."

Taking a step back, I pulled Halo away from the wall and spun him around so I could muscle him forward, until his front was flush with the concrete.

As I ground my stiff cock up against the crack of his ass, I took

Halo's hands and planted them above his head. "Keep 'em there. I wanna look at you."

Halo made a sound like a purr, as I smoothed my hands down the length of his arms and burrowed my nose in the back of his hair. He smelled amazing, like shampoo, soap, and sweat, and when my hands skimmed over his ribs to his hips, Halo bucked back into me.

I slid a hand around to cup the erection threatening the zipper there, then I jammed my hips forward, shoving into him the way I wanted to when we finally got rid of this denim. "You like that you can make me hard. Don't you, Angel?"

"Yes," Halo said. "I really fucking do."

"Hmm." My fingers curled around him and squeezed. "Good. 'Cause I gotta say, it drives me crazy the way your body responds to me. It doesn't even know what it wants yet, but it's beggin' for it."

Halo pressed his forehead to the cool concrete and groaned, as I drew my fingers up his zipper to the button of his jeans and flicked it open.

"Jesus." He turned his head as I got the zipper down, and when I pushed my hand inside to find his dick, my name left his lips.

"Remind me," I said against the thin material of his shirt. "That dream you had on the plane, where I took you into the restroom and fucked you—"

"Oh God." Halo slammed his eyes shut, his erection jerking in my hand.

"You said I bit you." When Halo didn't respond but his jaw bunched, I growled. "Angel?"

"Yes. I—" Halo's words cut off on a sharp inhale, as I ran my thumb over the plump, wet head of his cock. "Fucking hell, Viper."

I chuckled, but the sound was strained even to my own ears. I was wound up tight, ready to finally get inside the angel if he'd let me, and since he was about two tugs away from coming all over my hand, I thought I just might have a shot.

"You said I bit you," I repeated, and this time Halo nodded as though he'd lost the ability to speak. But when his eyes found mine, I noted how dark they were, how needy. Halo was as on edge as I was—exactly where I wanted him.

"On your shoulder, right?" My eyes dropped to the spot in question. "My cock in your ass and my teeth in your shoulder. That's hot as fuck. Look at you, dreamin' about things you know nothing about. You still want that?"

Halo's entire body shuddered in response as he nodded. "Yes."

I slowly stroked my hand down to the root of his shaft, and when I got there, I tightened my grip.

"Good," I said, and let him go. "Then let's get the hell out of here. Because if you're gonna use me, then you're gonna do it naked in my bed, where I can finally come all over you when you're done."

FORTY-FIVE

Viper

"WANNA CHANGE YOUR MIND?" With my key in the lock of the guesthouse, I glanced over my shoulder to where Halo stood with his hands jammed in his pockets.

The lights around the pool shimmered across the water and lit his hair up like a halo, and when he shook his head and said, "No," I wondered if that was him talking or the two shots he'd tossed back in the SUV on the way home.

We hadn't said much since we'd left the tunnels back at the arena, but the entire drive home, I'd been achingly aware of Halo's eyes roaming all over me. My face, my chest, my hard-as-hell cock, which I had no hope of hiding, and when he'd reached for the whiskey and thrown back a shot of the liquor, I could only begin to imagine what was going on inside that head of his.

When I didn't immediately unlock the door, Halo cocked his head and said, "Do you want to change yours?"

A smirk tugged at the corner of my lips as I looked down to my erection. "What do you think?"

Halo walked forward until he was so close that the night breeze was having a difficult time getting between us. "I think you should open the door before one of the guys comes out here and you're left to write yet another sonnet to your...frustrations."

Can't say I didn't warn him, I thought, as I turned the key and shoved open the door. I stepped aside so Halo had to walk by me to get in, and as he went, I took in a deep inhale, the scent of him intoxicating every single one of my senses. I couldn't wait to strip him down and get all up on him. I wanted to taste, touch, and fuck every single inch of him. But I also knew I had to play this just right. This was a first for Halo, and while he had given every indication that he wanted it, I needed him out of his mind begging for it before we got there.

I shut the door and made sure to engage the lock—the last thing I needed was a midnight visit from one of the guys if the mood struck them—and when I turned back to find Halo standing at the foot of my bed, I told myself to calm down.

"If I didn't know better, I'd think you were nervous," Halo said as he looked around the room.

"But since you know that's a fuckin' lie, what is it that you think I am?"

Halo looked over his shoulder to the messy bed that took up most of the living space in the guesthouse and said, "Tense," and when he brought his eyes back to mine, he added, "Charged. Wound up tight."

"I'm trying to be...polite."

"Who asked you to be polite?"

That was it—fuck standing by the door. If ever I'd been given a green light, it was right then, and I made my way over to Halo, took his chin in my hand, and said, "I hope like hell you mean that, 'cause that was about as polite as I can be."

When Halo's eyes sparked and his lips morphed into a grin just this side of triumphant, the sound that left my throat was close to feral as I reached for the back of his neck, tangled my fingers through his hair, and then crushed my lips over the top of his. Halo's mouth opened under the assault in an instant, and his hands came up to grab at my shirt as his tongue found mine and he groaned at the contact.

He tasted like whiskey and sex as he trailed his hands down my stomach to the bottom of my shirt, and when he slipped them under the black material, I wound an arm around his waist to grab at his ass.

I hauled Halo's body in as close as I could get him, and as I ground my hips up against his, he yanked his mouth away from me and said, "If I'm gonna use you, you need to take this off."

It took my brain a second to realize what exactly he wanted off, but when he began to shove my shirt up my torso, I smirked. "You seem to be doing a good job. Why don't you take it off?"

Letting go of him, I looked down to where his hands had stopped, and then back to his flushed face, before I raised my arms above my head. Halo lowered his eyes to where his hands were balled in the material, then began to slowly inch my shirt up my body. When he got to mid-chest, he glanced at me from under his heavy lids, and whatever he saw there had him bending down to put his lips to the center of my sternum.

At the touch of his warm breath on my skin and the—*fuck me—* wet flick of his curious tongue, I dropped my arms down so I could slide my fingers into his hair. Halo made a low hum in his throat as he kissed his way over to my left nipple, shoving the material up higher, out of his way, and then the angel became bolder, tracing his tongue around the flat surface he'd found.

"Christ." I tightened my fingers in his hair and tugged his head back so he was forced to look up at me, and the smile that slid across Halo's mouth made my cock jerk behind the zipper of my jeans.

"I've wanted to see you again with your shirt off ever since that night at your place," Halo said as he straightened, and I released my hold to let him take the fucking thing off. When he tossed it on the ground, Halo's eyes ran down over me, and his scorching gaze was a tangible thing as my skin heated everywhere those hungry eyes touched.

"You made me nervous that night. I was so confused about you." Halo reached out and traced a finger from the base of my neck down between my pecs, and when I grabbed his wrist, halting him, he grinned.

Tugging Halo close, I pressed a rough kiss to his mouth and said, "And are you still confused?"

Halo took my other hand and drew it to the front of his jeans, where he thrust his hips forward. "Do I feel confused to you?"

No, he fucking didn't. He felt like a man who knew exactly what he wanted, especially when I squeezed the outline of his cock through his pants, gliding my hand up and down his thick length.

"Thank fucking God," I murmured against his mouth as I flicked open the button of his jeans and then slid the zipper down. "If you were just a tease after all this, I'd throw myself off a bridge."

A low chuckle left Halo's throat as he felt his way up my chest, exploring the contours of my body. "So different," he said, his fingertips moving down to curl around the waist of my jeans. He had my pants undone in a hot second, his hand trailing underneath my boxer briefs to wrap around my dick like a second skin. "Mmm. I like the way you feel."

Shit. There was no hesitation in Halo's voice now, only a sense of wonder, like he was surprised to find how much he liked the way another man felt. Goddamn, he'd barely touched me, and I was desperate for more.

I let out a groan as he began to stroke my cock, my lips slamming onto his, my tongue urging his on in a way that said, *More... harder...faster...*

"Oh fuck," Halo said, ripping his mouth away to look down at where he gripped my dick, no longer stroking, but fingering the curved barbell that pierced the head of my shaft.

I held my breath, waiting to see what he'd do, and the angel didn't disappoint. He let go of his hold on me to tug my boxer briefs and jeans all the way down to the floor, and then he looked up.

I gripped the base of my dick, pointing it in Halo's direction so he could have a better look. "See something you like, Angel?"

He wet his lips, his eyes going from the piercing up to my face and back again. "Will it hurt?"

Such an honest question coming from those wide, curious light eyes. "It'll feel so fucking good you'll never want me to leave."

Halo's gaze fell back to my cock. "Really..." Then, before I knew he was going to do it, his tongue came out to lick a path along my slit, and my hips bucked up from the surprise. He glanced up at me and asked, "Is this okay?"

"Angel, anything you want to do to me is more than fucking okay." I barely got the words out again before Halo repeated the move, this time also teasing the barbell with his tongue in a way that made my eyes nearly roll back in my head. But I forced them to stay open, to stay focused on the man on his knees tasting, experimenting, and damn near tongue-fucking my cock.

One of Halo's hands replaced the hold I had on my dick, gripping the base to hold my erection steady as he teased, while his other hand gripped the back of my thigh.

It was a perfect image, one I wanted to burn into my mind for all time. The only thing that could possibly top this was getting inside the angel, all that silky skin naked and beneath me, covered in sweat.

He was driving me out of my mind, and it was all I could do to put my hand on his arm and pull him up to his feet, but that was what needed to happen if he wanted me to come deep inside him and not down his throat.

"As good as that feels, I need you naked. Now." As I gripped Halo's linen shirt and hauled him toward me so I could taste myself on his lips, the thin material ripped, and it took me all of two seconds to decide *to hell with it*. It didn't take much for the shirt to tear apart easily in my hands, and I tossed the remains on the ground as Halo stared at me, a mixture of lust and amusement on his lips. "Unless you want me doing the same to your pants, I'd suggest you get them the fuck off."

Slivers of moonlight peered in around the closed slats of the blinds, but even in the low light, I could make out every naked inch of Halo as he stepped out of his jeans and kicked them away. I crooked my finger at him, and he followed my command, walking forward until we were toe to toe, both of us naked, our bodies humming with anticipation. Damn. I was finally about to get what I'd been dying for.

"Get on my bed, Angel."

FORTY-SIX

Halo

AT VIPER'S REQUEST, my heart pounded, all the blood rushing straight to my cock. Every nerve ending in my body was alive with awareness, even without Viper touching me, and, feeling brave from the slight buzz of alcohol running through my veins—and horny as hell—I let my fingers brush against his erection before walking to the California king that was front and center in the room. It was as if it'd known who its owner would be and had made sure to be the focal point as soon as you walked inside.

A growl left Viper's throat as I climbed onto the bed, giving him a prime view of the ass I knew he was dying to get inside. Fuck, I wanted that too. I wanted Viper however I could get him, and after the way he'd worked me up at the concert, not to mention all the foreplay over the past few weeks, all I'd been able to think about was what it'd feel like to have him penetrate me *there*. In the place no one had ever been inside. I wanted Viper to be the one I let into my body, because a. I'd never been so turned on by anyone in my life, and b. because I knew Viper would make it fucking amazing.

I felt the bed dip behind me, and I looked over my shoulder to see Viper with one knee on the bed and his hands braced on the mattress. His eyes were on me, all over me, and it was then that a ripple of nerves coursed through my body. But as soon as they'd come, they were quickly driven away when he leaned forward and licked a path along one of my ass cheeks. My head dropped forward as he repeated the move on the other side. His teeth grazed along the wet path, nipping at my skin, and I found myself pushing back toward him, wanting more of his mouth on me.

Viper's tongue disappeared, but only for a moment, because then he was hovering over me, licking his way up my spine, leaving goosebumps in its path.

"Damn delicious," he murmured, as his mouth moved to my right shoulder, and as I felt him bite into the skin there, his left hand reached under me to grab a hold of my cock. The sensation of pleasure chasing away the pain was a new one, and I thrust into Viper's hand, wanting the friction of his strong grip to take the edge off the ache he'd been building in me all night.

"Is this how you imagined it?" Viper said, his teeth sinking into a spot above the last one.

"Fuck yes," I said. Only in my dream, I hadn't dared imagine it happening in Viper's bed, but here I was, facedown, his cock trailing along the crack of my ass, giving me the slightest hint of what was to come.

With my dick hard and heavy in his hand, and after hours of pent-up sexual frustration, it didn't take long before I could feel my orgasm threatening. But as I tensed, Viper backed off completely, his mouth and hands gone, his erection no longer sliding between my cheeks.

I must've groaned in irritation at the loss of him, because Viper let out a low chuckle as he walked to the nightstand and opened the drawer.

"Feeling a little needy, Angel?"

"I never took you for a fuckin' tease," I grumbled, rolling to my side to watch him and taking matters into my own hands by gripping my cock. Viper tossed a condom on the bed and took out a bottle of lube before closing the drawer.

"Did I tell you to move?" he said.

"You left."

"I'm not goin' anywhere. On your hands and knees, Angel."

God, the sight of Viper standing beside the bed, body fully on display and his Prince Albert piercing catching the moonlight, made me want to do anything but turn away from him. In that moment, with the power radiating off Viper, and those defined muscles tensed beneath his olive skin, he embodied the part of the bad boy, the sex god come to take what he wanted—and that just so happened to be me.

My cock jerked in my palm as my eyes roamed over him, and then, hungry for what he would give, I got back on my hands and knees. Viper flipped open the bottle of lube as he climbed up on the bed, and I reached for my dick to give it a firm stroke, because while this was all completely new to me, the thought of what and where he was about to put his slicked-up fingers had my toes curling before he'd even touched me.

"Don't even think about making yourself come," Viper said from behind me. "I get to do that tonight."

My body trembled at his words, which sounded like both a promise and a threat, but either way, I pinched the head of my cock in an effort to quell the climax that was threatening to explode.

Viper must've caught the move, because a low laugh met my ears at the same time cool fingers teased the top of my crack. "See, you are good. You even take orders."

I opened my mouth to say God only knew what in return, but Viper chose that moment to stroke his slippery finger between my ass cheeks, making them flex, as I grabbed the duvet beneath me instead.

Okay, that felt—when Viper did it again, but this time pushed the pad of his finger over my hole, I automatically shoved back —*really damn good.*

"You like that, Angel?"

My white knuckles and throbbing dick seemed to indicate yes, and when I looked over my shoulder to see Viper staring at me, I realized he was waiting for an answer.

I nodded. "Yes."

When he repeated the move, he kept his eyes locked on mine until the pressure against my entrance felt so damn good I had to squeeze my eyes shut.

My cock was leaking all over my hand, as my head fell down and I tried to calm my body. But Viper was hellbent on keeping me on edge as he continued to massage me in a place no one had ever touched me before.

Jesus. I'd known coming to Viper's bed was going to change me in ways I'd never be able to come back from. Not only because he was a man, but because a simple touch from him gave me more pleasure than I'd ever experienced in my life.

As if to emphasize that point, Viper teased me once, twice, and then he was pushing more firmly against me until his finger slipped inside, and my entire body clenched in response.

"Fuckin' hell," he growled, as he massaged his other hand over my ass cheek, relaxing me, spreading me a little farther apart. "You okay?"

Was I? I had no idea. My mind was spinning at the feeling of having something of him inside me, and when that thought hit, my cock pulsed in my hand and I had my answer.

"Yeah, it's just...different."

"Good different?" Viper slowly withdrew the digit but didn't pull it free, before he slid it back inside. "Or bad different?"

My eyes slammed shut as all the new sensations flooded over me and registered. "Good. It feels so good."

The sound Viper made was half groan, half growl, as he removed his hand and reached for the bottle beside him. When the cool liquid hit the heated skin of my crack, I cursed as the muscle there automatically flexed in response.

"Christ. It's taking every ounce of control I possess not to drill you through that fuckin' mattress right now, Angel."

Those words and Viper's tone should've probably shocked me,

but as though my body was hard-wired for his, my balls tightened to the point where I had to clamp a fist around myself to stop my release.

"You like that idea," Viper said, as he stroked two fingers down the same path he'd taken a minute ago. "Get through tonight, Angel, and we can revisit it. Promise."

God, what would that be like? To have Viper... *What did he say? Drill into me?*

But before I could think more about it, Viper was easing two fingers inside me and slowly twisting them, widening them until —"Ah, *fuck*"—he'd hit what had to be my prostate, because it felt unfuckingreal.

I shoved back on him, wanting to feel it again, and the sinister laugh that came from over my shoulder told me that that was the exact reaction Viper had been aiming for. For the next few minutes, Viper continued to drive me out of my ever-loving mind. Teasing and tormenting me, bringing me right there to the brink, only to pull me back from the edge. Then finally, when I thought I might just kill him, Viper pulled his hand free.

Out of the corner of my eye, I saw him reach for the condom he'd tossed on the bed earlier. As he snatched it up, my body trembled, my entire being now craving his in whatever way he wanted to give it—and when I heard the telltale sound of him ripping open the packet, I let go of my cock and braced my hands on the mattress.

Oh my God, this is really about to happen. I'm about to have sex...with Viper, and if there'd been any doubt in my mind about who it was that had gotten me so wound up, the strong hands now gripping my hips made it crystal clear.

As I stared at the pillow a few inches up the bed from me, I noticed the indentation in it from Viper's head, and wondered if this is where he'd been last night when he'd called me up and came in my ear.

The thought had me moving back into him, and when Viper's fingers dug into my skin, I groaned.

"You ready, Angel?" The question wasn't one I could typically imagine Viper asking. But the fact he was taking the time to make sure I was still on board was exactly why I knew he wasn't the asshole he'd said he was earlier.

Viper cared enough to make sure that this was just as good for me as it was for him—if not, he would've been shoving his way inside me regardless of my response, and that only made him hotter.

"Yes," I said, though my voice sounded ragged even to my own ears. "So ready."

Viper smoothed a palm over one of my ass cheeks. "That's the perfect fuckin' answer."

It was the *only* answer. I'd told him earlier that I'd only be saying yes to him tonight, and one of these days, Viper was going to have to start realizing I meant what I said.

As Viper spread me apart, I felt the head of his cock tease up and down the slippery strip of skin he'd worked over, allowing me to become familiar with having him there, feeling his presence in such a monumental way behind me. I rocked back against him, enjoying the sensation of having something hard to rub up and down against, and as my movements became faster, Viper's fingers dug harder into my skin.

"Fuck. If you move like that when my cock is inside you, I'm not gonna last long enough to shout your damn name."

I grinned at the torment in Viper's voice—not that he could see—because the idea that he was as affected by me as I was by him was one hell of a rush.

"I've gotta get in you," he said as he pushed the tip of his shaft to my opening. "If you want to stop—"

I looked back over my shoulder. "I won't."

Viper's jaw clenched before he lowered his eyes back to what he was doing, and when the wide head of him breached that first tight ring of muscle, my body froze. The burn was instant, the pressure insane, but the promise of what I knew would be on the other side of the discomfort, like when Viper had bit into my shoulder but then drove away the pain with pleasure...? *That* was the feeling I was chasing, and I knew he'd deliver.

I gripped the covers under me as Viper slowly entered my body, and just when I thought the discomfort might surpass my desire to find the oasis I knew was on the other side, Viper shifted down over me and wound an arm around my waist.

As his naked skin came into contact with mine, his fingers wrapped around my softening cock and stroked. The pleasure I felt was instantaneous, his touch making the lust that had taken a detour come roaring back to the surface, as he settled in behind me and began to work me over.

He kissed along the top of my shoulder and up my neck to my ear, and when Viper sucked on my lobe, I automatically shoved back.

"Goddammit, Angel. How am I ever gonna leave you now?"

My dick jerked as my ass clasped the cock deep inside me, and the curse that left Viper told me whatever I'd just done felt really fucking good.

He drew out of me slowly, every millimeter pure torture until he pushed forward again, filling me up. With Viper's front flush against my back, I reveled in the way his strong body felt against mine, and as he went to pull out again, I reached back and grabbed his thigh, holding him there.

Viper hummed his approval against the base of my neck. "Doesn't look like you want me to leave either." He began to rock his hips back and forth slightly, little thrusts that sent me gasping. My head fell forward as I dug my fingers into his thigh, the new sensation almost overwhelming in how good it felt. "Mmm, I like that too."

As he continued to drive into me, he circled his thumb over the head of my cock, spreading the pre-cum down the length in a slippery slide. It was almost too much, Viper filling me from behind while he worked my dick. But it wasn't until he bit down on my shoulder again that I was sent flying over the edge. I had no choice then—I had to let go and let the tide carry me where it would.

"That's it, Angel," Viper said, his voice thick and gravelly. "Your ass is so fucking tight it's strangling my dick."

I shuddered, the tremors of my orgasm racking my body into oblivion, and I found I couldn't hold myself up anymore. With my cock spent, I collapsed onto the mattress, and Viper pulled out of me completely, the weight of him disappearing. Before I had a chance to mourn the loss, his strong arms looped around me, flipping me to my back.

"I died," I said. "You killed me."

A cocky grin appeared on Viper's face as he angled his head toward mine. "Can't wait to kill you again, Angel."

Then his lips slammed down onto mine, a brutal meeting of the mouths that flamed quickly and died all too soon when he tore his mouth away and sat back on his knees.

"I believe I owe you something," he said, rolling the condom off his rock-hard length. Then he took his dick in his hand and played those talented fingers up and down his length the way he did his guitar.

Jesus, he's sexy as sin. Viper put on a private show for me, his eyes taking me in, the cords of his neck straining, a sheen of sweat covering his mouth-watering body. I knew what was about to happen, because I'd asked for it. I'd been imagining it since I'd heard Viper come in my ear.

Viper jerked himself faster, bringing himself closer to the brink. His dark hair fell into his eyes, his breathing became jagged, and as much as I wanted to put my hands on him then, I craved the way he'd fall apart in front of my eyes.

"You're so fuckin' hot," I said, unable to stop the words from coming out of my mouth. I was mesmerized. "I could watch you fuck for hours."

Viper's body tensed, his hand erratically sliding over his cock as hot jets of cum hit my stomach and chest. A heady shout filled my ears as Viper's orgasm roared through him, seemingly never-ending, and as he fell forward on top of me, he burrowed his face in my hair and took a deep inhale.

As the adrenaline subsided, and all talk ceased, the only sounds I could hear were the ocean waves outside and Viper's heavy breathing by my ear. The weight of his body pressed down on mine, and I could feel the rapid beat of his heart, as reality came crashing back in.

I just had sex with Viper... *Viper*. And it had blown every other sexual experience out of the water. I hadn't expected that. I'd known it would be intense, because Viper was, but the experience of being taken so completely by a man like him, and loving every second of it, surprised me. I'd assumed one night with him would be enough to quell the aching desire he brought out in me, but I'd been wrong. Using, and being used by, Viper had only left me craving more.

God, this was gonna be complicated. I thought I'd walked into this with eyes wide open. I knew Viper. I didn't have any delusions about who he was or what he wanted, because I thought I'd wanted the same.

But as I lay there in the aftermath, with Viper's steady breathing against my neck, I realized I knew nothing. Because coming into Viper's bed hadn't only changed my life—it had shown me what I'd been missing.

Thank You

Thank you for reading HALO! We hope you enjoyed our smokin' hot rock stars!
Make sure to join us for the continuation of Halo and Viper's relationship as they tackle their attraction and rise to fame head-on.

VIPER
Fallen Angel Series #2

COMING MARCH 25th, 2019

followed by

ANGEL
Fallen Angel Series #3

COMING APRIL 25th, 2019

**Love HALO? Leave a review!
Reviews are vital to authors, and all reviews, even just a couple of quick sentences, can help a reader decide whether to pick up our books.

If you enjoyed this book, please consider leaving a review on the site you purchased from. Halo and Viper may even give you a sneak peek of their new album if you do!**

Special Thanks

We've been wanting to dive into a rock star series for quite some time, and the stars finally aligned for us to bring you the guys of Fallen Angel! These sexy rockers are just getting started, so we hope you'll continue their journey in VIPER.

We'd like to thank the following talented humans for helping us bring HALO to life:

- Hang Le for the gorgeous Fallen Angel Series covers, banners, and teasers
- Sarah Jo Chreene for some fun surprises coming your way with this series (shhh we can't tell yet)!
- Arran for an always entertaining edit
- Judy's Proofreading for being our final eyes on HALO

A special thanks to the Naughty Brellas who named the guys of Fallen Angel!

Jay Ell ("Halo")
Jayne John ("Viper")
Brittany Cournoyer ("Killian")

Vandy Marie Bauer ("Jagger")
Sharna Morris ("Slade")

A huge thank you to the bloggers who support our work by taking time out of their busy lives to share our releases. You're the real rock stars. <3

Finally, if you're reading this, we'd also like to thank YOU for picking up this copy of HALO. We're so grateful to be able to write these stories in our head for a living, and that is only possible with your continued support. A million thank you's and big bear hugs.

xoxoxox,

Ella & Brooke

About Ella Frank

If you'd like to get to know Ella better, you can find her getting up to all kinds of shenanigans at:

The Naughty Umbrella

And if you would like to talk with other readers who love Ella's Chicago Universe, you can find them at:
Ella Frank's Temptation Series Facebook Group.

Ella Frank is the *USA Today* Bestselling author of the Temptation series, including Try, Take, and Trust and is the co-author of the fan-favorite contemporary romance, Sex Addict. Her Exquisite series has been praised as "scorching hot!" and "enticingly sexy!"

Some of her favorite authors include Tiffany Reisz, Kresley Cole, Riley Hart, J.R. Ward, Erika Wilde, Gena Showalter, and Carly Philips.

Want to stay up to date with all things Ella?
You can sign up here to join her newsletter

For more information
www.ellafrank.com

About Brooke Blaine

About Brooke

Brooke Blaine is a *USA Today* Bestselling Author of contemporary and LGBT romance that ranges from comedy to suspense to erotic. The latter has scarred her conservative Southern family for life, bless their hearts.

If you'd like to get in touch with her, she's easy to find - just keep an ear out for the Rick Astley ringtone that's dominated her cell phone for years. Or you can reach her at www.BrookeBlaine.com.

Brooke's Links
Brooke's Newsletter
Brooke & Ella's Naughty Umbrella
Book + Main Bites

www.BrookeBlaine.com
brooke@brookeblaine.com

Printed in Great Britain
by Amazon